MW00422718

THE SHAPE

OF

WILDERNESS

THE SHAPE
OF
WILDERNESS

A NOVEL BY SHELLEY BERC

To Judy, Gene, and
amber
Love, Shelley 11/93

COFFEE HOUSE PRESS :: MINNEAPOLIS

Coffee House Press is supported in part by a grant provided by the Minnesota State Arts Board, through an appropriation by the Minnesota State Legislature, and by a grant from the National Endowment for the Arts, a federal agency. Additional support has been provided by the Lila Wallace-Reader's Digest Fund; The McKnight Foundation; Lannan Foundation; Jerome Foundation; Target Stores, Dayton's, and Mervyn's by the Dayton Hudson Foundation; General Mills Foundation; St. Paul Companies; Honeywell Foundation; Star Tribune/Cowles Media Company; Beverly J. And John A. Rollwagen Fund of The Minneapolis Foundation; Prudential Foundation; and The Andrew W. Mellon Foundation.

Coffee House Press books are available to the trade through our primary distributor, Consortium Book Sales & Distribution, 1045 Westgate Drive, Saint Paul, MN 55114. For personal orders, catalogs or other information, write to:
Coffee House Press
27 North Fourth Street, Suite 400, Minneapolis, MN 55401

Library of Congress CIP data

Berc, Shelley.
    The shape of wilderness: a novel / Shelley Berc.
        p.cm.
    ISBN 1-56689-036-5 (pbk. : alk. paper)
        I. Title.
PS3552.E67S48   1995
813'.54—dc20   9-31068
                                                     cip

10   9   8   7   6   5   4   3   2   1

For Alejandro,
who went with me.

And out of the ground made the Lord God to grow every tree that is
pleasant to the sight and good to eat. A tree of life grew in the garden and
also a tree of the knowledge of evil and good. And a river went out of
Eden to water the garden and from thence it was parted and became into
four heads.   Genesis, 2:9-10

To achieve a map you must have a starting point, a refer-
ential beginning from which and to which all points
lead. The maps I had prepared calculated not only the distances between physical things, but how far it is between
good and evil; admiration and jealousy; love and hate . . .
and I asked upon these maps a thousand geographical questions of humanity, such as: How is the distance between
feeling and thing-felt-about calculated—by time of actual
travel or strength of wanting? Does the space separating
desire from fulfillment alter when it is covered by creature
on foot or air, by need or fear; what is the efficacy of dream
when it comes to such traveling; what is the utility of calculating such a distance when it can change as quickly as the
conveyance upon which it is propelled? Which kind of distance, what source of measurement should I then draw
upon the charts of the worlds I am depicting? A book of the
cartographer is an almanac of questioning.

But a map—a map must be a solid thing—a manifestation
of belief in the evidence of discovery. In a map, in its lines
and dots, colors and shading, speculation is transformed
into fact, hearsay and clues are illustrated as absolutes, and
variables are believed to lie only in the painted indications
of the crosscurrents of air and sea. Except when you bind
all the maps of all the worlds together, and then what you
have in your hands is a house of contradictions, an atlas of
bottomless questioning that is the book of the cartographer
that precedes and extends past all mappings.

from *The Book of the Cartographer*, Chapter I

PART ONE: SPRING

Rose and the Raven

THE ANIMAL MOUNDS

You could tell their shapes only from the air. From the air you could see them, as the crow flies. They looked like bear, wolf, giant salmon swimming upstream. You could see them as the crow flies.

Deer, otter, beaver, elk, formed out of the bluffs over the river. The shapes making the frame of the river. You could only see them whole from the sky, the way the crow flies.

Why these forms, and who made them—to be seen only in their wholeness from the far away, the off-the-map, off-the-earth? Invisible to all by virtue of their illimitable size; except for one man who sees them reflected in the constellations he's observing from his place, far away in the Southern Hemisphere. A man who confuses this land he sees with the Northern stars—the bear, Orion, the crab, the scorpion, the deer.

He decides he must go there, Emmanuel, to the land he mistakes for stars, and build his castle in the air on the animal mounds that no one else can see. He decides to go there with his wife and the child in her belly. He wants to go there to build a floating castle in the sky, built on the stars that are these mounds, as transient as the appearance of the stars in their constellations stalking the night sky—the elk, the bison, the beaver—as transient as the shooting stars, as the feet that carry, as the crow that flies.

When he gets there, he finds that what he thought were stars is dirt and he sees, lying down and looking up, that it's the earth that's reeling, not the sky, and what a man needs to keep in step with this is to keep moving.

So he decides to build his castle in the air on the earth of the mounds, and he names it the Hotel.

"A Hotel is a man's house is a man's castle is a man's dream for the people of the new world," he cries, "for the celebration of their transience, their keeping up with the mud."

He leaves his wife there where there is nothing yet and travels north, south, east, and west in honor of the travelers yet to come. He scours the whole world to find the building blocks for his masterpiece. He picks the furniture, picks the fabrics, the tile, the bricks; he builds and builds and builds his transient Hotel: a moveable feast. This he tries to accomplish for many years, before he is gone and our story begins. He will die believing his Hotel must be built on the stars, his castle in the air:

as the crow flies
as the crow flies
as the crow flies.

But he decided to tell his daughters something different.

THE FATHER'S STORY

In the time that was the beginning, this portion of the earth that is now the Hotel was part of a vast ocean. Every living thing that was there swam or drifted or floated. There were no legs, no arms, nor any voices as we know them now. The cities of this ocean were complex coral bodies that came to life only at night. In fact, at one time the whole world was nocturnal. At night, the algae blew phosphorescent tongues and the anemones crawled out of their cones to feed.

These were the islands of life in the vast, chaotic waters where the sea creatures once danced and where the family now lives. And between these reckoning points, there was nothing but wandering. Back and forth, victims of current, the seahorses, the bluefish, the sharks, were born. And this is everything that is for billions of years.

The children of the family who made this place their home were told by their father, whose name was Emmanuel, how the place itself had been made—thrust up by enormous pressure from underneath the sea, pushed away from the origins of itself to become dry land—mountains and canyons, wetlands and flatlands, while what was left of the huge inland ocean dribbled into great lakes and rivers and streams.

But that was where the same story ended and where he chose to divide his offspring in their knowledge.

THE GIRL WHO BREATHED WATER

When she would go walking through the prairies, the elder of the twins, Miranda, would imagine herself walking underwater. And when she would awaken, choking, in the night, she would imagine that she could breathe underwater too. She'd remember what Emmanuel, her father, used to say—that she had to take in less oxygen. Our bodies, he tells her, are the bodies of sea creatures, our lungs are aquatic—they need water to breathe. Our lungs are made of water, he said, if they don't get enough, you feel like you're drowning.

And so Miranda, awake in the night after a bad dream, would imagine herself falling off a great cliff into the ocean. She would be going down and down, smash the surface and drowning, when suddenly, instead of drowning, she is breathing the sea as if it's air, she's walking around under the ocean as if it's a very populous city, she's running with the sea creatures as if they're just a bunch of garrulous people. The fish swim by unperturbed, the crabs lumber around, and the coral reefs open their doors to her like exclusive hotels attending a dear customer. She inhales the saltwater and beams.

In the daytime, in summer, when the light was like a magnifying glass upon the earth, she would hunt the rocks of the parched riverbed and the red canyon for signs of sea life. She would find the fossils of primeval creatures, proof of her dreams of walking beneath the sea. There were nights at the estate that her parents built when she would be so submerged in the aqueous mystery that it seemed the tree limbs were giant crustaceans and the garden snakes were sharks and the fast deer were damselfish, and she herself was a parrot fish chomping away at the eaves of a coral city that was their home, this Hotel.

THE GIRL WHO BREATHED DIRT

But the father had told the younger twin, whose name was Rose, a story of the place's origin that was as different as night and day from what he told her sister.

To this daughter, he said:

"The place where we are living has always been rock mounds and will always be rock mounds. Formed from the eruption of molten stone far below the world's surface, the earth exploded up in the shapes of wild beasts—mountain lion, jackal and boar, bobcat and coyote—distinguished by the rivers that flowed through them, the acrid waters that sweated from the friction of their rock bodies.

"Only from the sky do the mounds take on their true form, the bulls and bears and leopards of stone. Close up they look like any old kind of rock. I have seen them from up there. *Why I came.* You must trust me on this."

We, too, come from rocks. The bones of our bodies are rocks, of course, but so is our skin the pulverized rock that is sand, and our liver and heart and tongue the congealed rock that is molten magma, and our brain the frozen rock that is glacier. All in all man is metamorphic rock, all in all he is always hard, always changing with the pressures exerted from the earth. You must always breathe dust to breathe at all, for you are made of dust, the purest rock of all.

So the two twins, Miranda, the oldest, and Rose, the younger one, lived in different places within the same place and breathed different substances to survive. Miranda believed that at root she was aquatic. Rose believed at the bottom of her heart she was rock.

So the father told the two sisters two different stories and accordingly they grew, while he began to fade away, because he believed that the world's composition was something other than what he told his children; that a body needed something different from dirt or air or water to breathe, that what a man needed to live on was dreams. And this is why, though he loved them, he had to keep on leaving.

THE MORNING OF THEIR FIFTEENTH
BIRTHDAY

"Happy Birthday, child," said her mother, gently shaking the girl awake and leaving behind a large rectangular box as she swept noiselessly out the door. Rose opened her eyes slowly, hoping to merge the world of her dreams with this very promising materiality moored by her pillow. She squinted one eye open, then the other, watching the mystery box grow with the expansion of her vision. The gift had a gold sateen ribbon looped around it, culminating dead center in a luscious bow. She tore the construction apart with less respect than a tiger for its breakfast.

"Oh," she gasped.

It lay on a bed of rainbow-colored tissue paper onto which someone had painstakingly glued hundreds of opalescent star- and moon-shaped sequins. The dress was blush-colored and of nearly grown-up length. It hit a hand's breadth above the ankle, and best of all, it moved. Three layers of fabric made it up: a crinoline topped by taffeta and over that, embossed satin. Rose had struggled halfway in, one leg dangling out like a fisherman's oar; she hopped over to the vanity's three beveled mirrors and stared. The trim. She could not believe the trim! It was lace and silk and grosgrain, with a wide burgundy sash that swept into an enormous ballroom bow at the back. The sleeves came down exactly to the bone at the wrist, where they reared up in curvaceous cuffs of Alsatian lace figured with swans swimming in a pond. The bodice was a bower of flowers made from gathered-in ribbons of a dozen hues of red, and in the center of each, tiny and delicately shriveled, was an absolutely perfect dried rose. The hips were beset with ruby glass beading whose pattern described a Turkish parlor, replete with miniature chandeliers and Persian rugs. The hem was lightly tapestried with a scene of bowmen hunting a deer. By now, Rose had the gown all the way on and was staring around herself like a cat chasing its tail. Buttoning up the final buttons, which went by tiny increments all the way to the nape of her neck, she gazed down tentatively at the neckline. It was cut high but was translucent, a Swiss polka-dot net that reached to the start of her new breasts.

The door cracked open and she heard the laughter of her mother, Cora, and Emerald, their housekeeper. She thought she heard her mother say, "you were right, that pink goes just fine with her red head." And she thought she heard Emerald laugh behind her hands. They must have been spying the whole time, Rose concluded as she stepped away from the mirror. She knew that the small careful stitches that held the confection together, the way a trail holds off the wilderness, were the work of their accomplished hands. How could they not look? she reasoned gleefully.

It was her first best dress.

THE BIRTHDAY FEAST

The glass-paned breakfast room was Rose's favorite place in the house, for it seemed as much outside as in. Cora had decorated it with scores of tropical succulents, making it look more like nature than the land outside the window, which was fastidiously manicured.

When the girl in the party frock galloped in, her eyes bright as leaded goblets, she found the table set with the best silver—a curious set of diaphanous sea nymphs whose scaly bosoms wrapped suggestively around the place where you held the instrument, and their tails wrapped around the place where you put your mouth. Their humanlike faces were very expressive; Rose always fancied that they showed how they felt about every meal. Her mother had also set the table with their finest eggshell Limoges which was painted with wildflowers along the gold-trimmed borders and showed the phases of the moon in the middle of each cup, bowl, and plate.

A large yellow tureen filled with cold cherry soup stood in the middle of the table, and a tall bunch of red poppies bent over it, like a shade tree over a lake. A girl sat alone at the far end of the table, waiting patiently for the rest. Her black curls obscured her long, thin face, and her dark eyes stared vacantly toward the window, from which could be seen an old wooden swing hanging from a willow tree. It was as if the young woman was trying to keep an eye both inside and out, and in attempting to do so had forgotten both.

"Miranda, Miranda, Happy Birthday! Well, aren't you going to wish me something?" demanded Rose of the dreamer. "Don't you remember what day it is?"

The young woman roused herself from her reverie, held out her long arms stiffly and kissed Rose's cheek. "Happy Birthday," she said absent mindedly and went back to her staring.

At first, you would not believe they were twins or even blood sisters; they seemed in body and gesture so unlike. Rose had red hair, the color of a terrible sunburn, and an olive complexion that was a field of pimples. She was underdeveloped for a girl just turned fifteen; her breasts were insignificant nubs and her midriff still rolled with baby fat. Her sister, on the other hand, was a willowy, ripe thing. Her aquiline nose, her pitch-black hair, her waist, her legs were the quintessence of slender and sleek. Her face was luminously transparent. Everything about the girl exuded a see-through quality, and when she walked out at dusk in her dove-gray dress and white challis shawl, people often took her for a ghost. While the younger twin hardly looked twelve, the elder one could easily pass for twenty.

Unlike Rose, who was attempting to maintain a stationary sitting position in the midst of the oceanic ruffles of her very first ever best dress, Miranda never wore anything but. They were all very elegant and unfashionable, as if she had modeled herself after the women's magazines of a bygone era. Her skirts swept the floor, and it seemed as if the many folds of material playing the length of her long, angular body existed solely to cause the wind, the sun, the moonlight, and the rain to pay her homage. While Rose was plain and ungainly, Miranda was known far and wide to be a beauty, but heartless, as heartless as a stone. It was said that she had no human heart at all in her chest, but that of an old gypsy sorceress who had once come begging at the Hotel. Some people even said that Miranda's gypsy heart went flying around at night without her and could be seen pumping its way through the sky or hip-hopping through the farmyards.

Miranda herself never thought much about her heart, perhaps because she seemed to suffer so much in her soul, which she was sure was a different thing entirely. Sometimes, when she caught a glimpse of herself in the hall mirror, she wondered at the vacant stare that came back at her. She knew, though, through her own experience, that the soul is not found in the eyes but lies invisible someplace else in the body, where it moves around like a shy nomad, and you were blessed if you caught sight of it once or twice in your whole life. Most of the time, she reasoned, it puts you to sleep before it wanders off to express itself—making up daydreams or nightmares that only leave you clammy and shivering when you try to remember them. She thought perhaps the surest way to observe the workings of the soul, since you could not see its elusive being, was to watch a person's fingers. Her own were frenetic: always scratching, stabbing, tapping, curling, twisting, flinching. They moved with a beaten expression, one of torture and shame, as she made the beds, milked the cow, fed the chicks, scrubbed the hall; her hands moving so fast, trying not to be seen. She scratched at the skin around the joints and tore back the cuticles hiding the dusty pink half-moons rising on her nails so that her pain became at least a physical sensation rather than an agonizing apparition that walked unpredictably inside her. After all, she had enough of that uncertainty with her alien heart.

She hid her hands, the home of her soul, because she believed that the soul must be concealed or it would hide from its owner forever. Then, too, she had made them so ugly, disfigured them so irrevocably. She held them in embryonic fists, curled until the fingertips practically touched the wrists. Her hands began to resemble not hands at all but those transparent glass balls found shouldering the weight of heavy claw-footed furnishings. She usually wore gloves that, while covering her mutilation, showed off the slender, tapering splendor of her hands. In the winter, when she was not often at chores, she wore cream-colored kid ones with jet buttons at the wrist. In the warmer months she favored open weaves in a feast of colors— lavender, rose, alfalfa green, and larkspur blue. The reddened, rashed skin peeking through looked like a latticed strawberry patch. Her mother saw the work of nails and teeth upon her child's flesh and tried to stop her with bitter creams repugnant to the taste and wax casts that could be neither bitten nor torn off, but Miranda always found a way out of them, pressed hard by the heart and soul that fought inside.

Today, the day of her fifteenth birthday, her hands were sprinkled with lilac water and the essence of lilies. Miranda held them out and drew her sister to her.

"Yes", she said, "Happy Birthday," kissing Rose's ear and showing off the gold ornament around her neck. "This is the gift mother gave me."

They were both looking expectantly toward the swinging kitchen door when it flew open. A pile of silver-domed dishes paraded out, seemingly on their own immense steam; but soon the ambulation was revealed to have feet and stockings. Rose watched her mother's face appear over the steaming platters.

"Happy Birthday, Miranda," she said, and a huge plate of eggs landed beside the girl. "Happy Birthday, Rose," and rashers of bacon piled several inches deep took their place on the table. Then there were the delicacies that Emerald had made: scones, plain and with currants; potted creams and whole-berry jams; fresh churned butter; lime jelly; rose-hip jam; steak and kippers; French toast; maple syrup; hollandaise sauce and capers; several pounds of baby white asparagus. There was orange juice, banana juice, and apricot nectar; fresh coffee, hot chocolate, and English tea; and a birthday cake that was a bright pink replica of their beloved Hotel.

Emerald, who took care of the family, handed each girl a big, badly wrapped package. Inside hers, Rose found some new stuffed animals for her extensive collection. "Hope you're not too big a girl now to like such stuff," ventured the woman who had just made the green velvet anteater and the golden jacquard giraffe.

"Oh no," said Rose, not wishing to offend as she hugged the bright, soft toys to her breast. She began to think about Trapper, the man to whom they rented the old shed in the yard, and was sorry he couldn't be there for her birthday party. Cora had refused to invite him, saying he wouldn't know how to sit at a proper table to eat. The stuffed animals he made were something else altogether, with their real fur and paws and wings and teeth. Compared to them, Emerald's toy creatures seemed so artificial, so embarrassingly babyish.

Looking out the breakfast-room window to the mountains that rimmed their valley, Rose was filled with a sense of great warmth and greater security. Nothing had ever harmed her here and consequently she had never come to know fear. Yet it was hardly a stranger to the other inhabitants of the Hotel; the fear in her family was as familiar to her as their voices. But like a child growing up among lepers, she seemed to have a natural immunity against the disease, and she watched it in others with a scientific sort of curiosity. She wondered at its exoticism and secretly hoped to develop it herself later in life, as one develops breasts and body hair and the ability to reproduce the species. She figured fear was a feature of maturation.

"Blow out the candles, dears," their mother coaxed.

From opposite sides of the table, the sisters faced each other and blew. Rose's cheeks puffed out, her eyes bowed down, she followed the rage of her breath around the burning circle on top of the cake, and in one blow she extinguished them all. Miranda picked up the silver cake knife and began jaggedly cutting.

"Pass the plates, please," said Rose as she picked off the blown candles and all the wax that was dripping down.

IN WHICH MIRANDA MEETS BENJAMIN

She was washing linens by the river when she saw him come up. A small man in a coon's cap and a frock coat, sailing a packet boat with just an old nag on board. The contraption bowed and whistled like it was ready to cave in, but instead it ran ashore. Right up to the rocks, where Miranda beat the white things clean. The bow of the boat right under her eyes, sucking all the water away till she was left with just the cold stones.

She got up off her knees, her hands red and full of soap froth. She flapped her apron like she was shooing blackbirds.

She said, "Hey, Mister, what do you want here? What are you looking for here? You lost or what? The Hotel's up there."

All this time she did not once look up at his face. She was watching her hands to see what they would do. And then he laughed, pure joy tumbling out of him like an avalanche. She had to look up to breathe.

In the future, she could never remember his features, no matter how often she went over them to herself, regardless of detailed scrutiny or time spent obtaining it. No matter how often she counted the ghost scars on his nose or how carefully she measured the angle of cheekbone to the hollow between shoulder and neck. No matter how hard she tried, Miranda came up blind every time. And it started now, at the beginning, when she was just seeing him and forgetting him, from moment to moment, seeing and forgetting, forgetting and seeing, so that every time she saw him it really was for the very first time.

She felt the fire come up into her face and she looked out over it into his eyes: promise and sanctuary.

"Can I give you a hand, Miss?" he asked, bundling her wash under one arm while offering her the other. "Allow me," he said softly.

She stared; instinctively, she shrunk back. Then, like a snake, she struck out and grabbed the arm sharply. Her fingers in his skin were like teeth, but the man didn't seem to notice this or the fact that they did not speak. Together they went up the pine trail to the Hotel, where, in the presence of her family, Miranda offered the stranger lodging.

MY NAME IS BENJAMIN

Miranda lingered at dinner that night. After she served the bisque, brought out the lamb and mint, and even after Rose had passed around the vanilla ice, Miranda stayed, her hands still in her lap, hidden under one of the damask napkins she'd been washing when he came up on the rocks. The hands slept; they had never been so quiet.

The chandelier, a joker object of delicately carved fruits in outrageously dyed colors, swung desultorily, smoothing over the retreating conversation. Everyone was extremely nervous, for other than Trapper, the Hotel had never had a single guest. As for the young man, he was startled to find himself in a refined hotel in the middle of this wilderness. Rose sat on the tall chair with the leopard head carved behind her. It made her mad the way her feet couldn't touch the ground. She had never seen such a beautiful thing as this boy in her life.

Miranda stayed while Rose cleared the plates and silver, while Cora and Emerald offered their guest "another brandy, on the house," while they warmed to the talk, laughing and snorting knowingly about people and places so exotic that Miranda was sure they were storybook concoctions, though in fact they were real.

The colored glass fruits of the chandelier began to twirl merrily—pineapples colliding with Dutch pears, grape clusters shaking like jovial fat men—as Cora drummed the table and Emerald played a tune on the crystal water goblets. The young man began to sing, something about a deserted shore and a heart lost to a mermaid. Rose, who had been gazing dreamily at the stranger for a long time, went to prop her head up with her arm and sent a wine glass flying to the floor.

"You are as clumsy as a pig," hissed Miranda, "and the way you're eating, you're going to be as fat as one too!"

Rose, who was now certain that the young man was the most exquisite creature on earth, was mortified. Benjamin continued his sad song but looked down, embarrassed for the young girl, who, seeing his reaction, burst out of the room in tears.

"I hate you, hate you, hate you all," she cried.

But nobody took much notice as the singer sang on and the mermaid died and her lover went back and became an admiral at sea.

By this time of night, Miranda was usually long gone up the stairs. But tonight she was unable to move. The young man knew this and while every verse he sang was to Cora and Emerald, every note was directed at Miranda's heart. This they both knew, for between lovers, before love comes, there is a chord of silent complicity that is clearer and sharper than any of the impassioned utterances that will follow after it.

Finally, at midnight, they all scraped back their chairs and headed up to bed. In passing, the young man caught Miranda's ear.

"My name is Benjamin," he said. "We'll walk tomorrow."

ROSE RUNS AWAY

She kept running. Down the picture gallery, out the vast double doors, onto the wraparound porch, past the long staring windows where the sharp sound of cutlery kept up its clatter. She threw herself onto the granite walkway, nearly beheading a Greek statue with her flailing arms.

"I hate every last one of you," she cried.

She wanted to hurt them as deeply as possible. Murder wouldn't be enough. She decided to disappear from their world, dead or alive, she wasn't sure which.

At the end of the walkway, where the iron gate stood barely open, sat the pale form of her grandmother peeling a pile of potatoes with a wooden knife.

"Ah, granddaughter," the old woman sighed, "I felt just the same as you when I was little. But what's there to do but grow up and make your own children to torture? Happy Birthday! Those snowshoes over there are my gift to you," she said, and disappeared into the landscape. Rose jumped on the snowshoes and slid through the iron gate and into the forest that guarded the Hotel.

"I must look ridiculous," she thought, picturing the heavy varnished snowshoes and her skimpy frilled party dress. But the first day of spring is such a changeable time, warm and cold, stark and fertile, that in the end she found the apparel of two seasons very comforting.

She didn't mean to go to the river; it was dark and far. But the snowshoes dreamed her on and they took her like a sailing ship gone wild. When she saw the water coming up fast ahead of her, she knew that she would drown.

A tune of her grandmother's came into her head: "The river was river but then it was ice."

Suddenly a white, solid trail appeared before her, and Rose found herself standing in the middle of the river, witless and wordless, on a sharp apex of ice that glared like a lighthouse beacon turned maniacally backward to the shore.

When she realized where she had run, the ice had already started breaking up.

TRAPPER RUNNING

A man is running, running and running. Like Rose, he's running into the river, but he is not at risk of drowning; water has no power over a man like him. He swims it like a dog, his arms paddling paws, his head up out of the water, but wet, very wet from the splashing as he slams back the current. Spluttering and gasping, his mouth afloat with algae and fish, his lungs full of river and silt, he reaches the shore.

The man pulls his heaviness out of the water, shoulders, then arms, and finally the legs dragging behind. Now he's walking, panting, close to the ground, on all fours, weighted down with river and mud, soaked through his animal skins. He spits out enough water to fill a sea, enough dirt to make a country. He has swum across a river that is as long and crooked as the lifeline in his giant's hand. He's swum across it as if it were a time line; the two banks, the water between, the persistent mud without and within are the covers and contents of a history.

He kicks away the vines and sticks that litter the bank. He pulls from their hiding place his wood and steel and leather traps. He tests the setting on each one with a rotting branch.

"From that point to this," the man laughs as the jaws of the trap meet and crush. The debris of smashed sticks go flying.

"From that point," Trapper smiles, as he pulls the jaws apart from their impassioned kiss, "to this."

ROSE OF THE RIVER

"The river was river but then it was ice," she yelled, hoping
that her grandmother's song would turn an increasingly liquid
environment back to something solid again. But the surface
continued to break away until she found herself cringing in a
ball on the tiniest cube of ice.

Rose was freezing. She despaired of her flimsy party dress.
The beautiful snowshoes she threw into the water, for they gave
her no room to stand. She stared as they floated away, like
friends going on a long journey whom you know you'll never see
again. The tears froze in her eyes.

A coyote approached the water's edge, and then another. She
watched as they howled; their teeth tore the sky. Rose covered
her eyes. The wind shredded her skirt to rags.

"The river was river but then . . . oh, who's going to hear
me out here?" she wailed.

Beyond the coyotes and the tree line, she could see the
candles dying out in the dining room and then Miranda's light
go on in the attic and then, one by one, all the other lights in
the house go out, room to room, like a chain of gossip.

"If someone would just look out for one minute before
they went to bed, surely they would see me," whimpered the
girl.

But a freak wind came up from the north, and Rose
watched her hopes tumble as all the velvet draperies in all the
rooms fell closed like sleeping masks over the eyes of elegant
old ladies.

Rose jumped to run, but the ice on which she stood was a
snarling dog and snapped her back. Darkness fumed on all sides
of her. She started to count the stars—a way of calling for
hope—a young girl in a torn pink party dress turning like a bal-
lerina doll on top of a jewelry box. Her ice floe broke down the
middle. She was reduced to pirouetting on one foot, balancing
herself on the white moon that rose full and fat overhead.

Somewhere she heard music, maybe from the honky-tonk across the river, which gave her a feeling of company. But no, it was just the junipers on the river's edge, rubbing their icy limbs together. The frozen fragment that held her up began to groan and separate. Rose pushed out her arms to try to balance herself as she stumbled backward into the liquid black.

BENJAMIN IN THE HOTEL WINDOW

He wanted to get some shut-eye, but his thinking was making him sick. He stripped off his coat and tie, placed his watch on the nightstand, and lay down. The wallpaper was oppressively flowered and he had drunk too much wine.

Two years out and he was still trying to get it complete. He wanted to make it the longest panorama on earth—five miles of canvas painted with life on the river. Exhibition rotundas would be built all over the civilized world to house his giant moving picture of a savage land. As scenes of homesteading and Indian attack scrolled by on the panorama's mighty iron cylinders, he, Benjamin Emerson, would assume the role of fearless explorer, destined to lead his drop-jawed audience on the strange and terrifying journey west.

He loved this place, loved it without compromise, heart and soul. He knew that the reams of canvas he was mercilessly painting would destroy the land they pictured. He knew that when the panorama was displayed in city after city, the people would want to grasp the real thing. At night he dreamed streams of travelers crawling all over its great natural wonders, sawing off and pocketing what they could to place in their solariums or amateur museums. Worse yet, he could see people who did not want travel, who came to stay, heaping their lives and possessions on the land until it was buried and forgotten under a refuse heap. But in the daytime, while he worked, Benjamin had faith in his gift and saw things differently. He believed then that the only way to preserve the land for eternity was by painting it.

His thoughts turned to the girl. "My, she's delicious."

He thought about her with his tongue. He knew he could make her jump. He thought about her with his teeth, his lips, and the roof of his mouth. She was sweet, but he bet she didn't know much. The things he knew bored him. Knew he was a dreamer, a rover, a man whose face was one big searchlight; knew wagons, horses, Indians, long hauls, desert drought;

knew he had a lot of great ideas, knew he wasn't much when it came to realizing those ideas. This last comprehension drove him out of his skin. He tried to find the memory of the girl in his mind, but somehow she had lost him. He got up to look out the window, saturated by moonlight and late frost and for a moment, he thought he heard a lost child moaning.

A man looking out a window in an unfamiliar place can see ghosts sometimes. He sees his family, maybe, back in their warm paneled living room with the cherry furnishings and the ancestors affixed to the walls, the fire poking up through the grate and making all those gathered round (reading, knitting, smoking) look rosy, look happy and serene regardless of what they may or may not be feeling. Maybe, being a dreamer, this young man thinks ghosts are what he's after. He sees shadows everywhere; in fact, shadow begins to overpower materiality in his perception, so that every shadow he sees promises a real image on the other side. Naturally, he follows, running farther and farther away from anything known, anything familiar, but he never seems to see any more clearly, because the shadow's a tease and keeps turning. The young man finds himself in a strange place, all echo and ombré, from which his only vision comes, quite by accident, from some vials of paint. They become his spectacles, magic lanterns that allow him to trans-late the shadows he sees into color and shape.

Looking out the window from this isolated Hotel, it occurred to him that he was living his memory of the old pan-eled room and the reality of the wilderness simultaneously, with-out one informing the other. It was as if his eyes were not a pair at all, but free agents who begrudged one another any informa-tion about their respective journeys.

"Might just as well go back where I came from if that's the way it's going to be," he speculated. "But," he grimaced, "Emersons don't come back empty-handed. They die first."

Benjamin laughed loudly; his mood beginning to lift. He lit a Havana and played its glow against the glass of the window.

His family never wanted him to do either thing—paint or go West. They planned on him being a locksmith, like his father and grandfather before him. The Emersons were a dynasty of men who molded closure with accuracy, strength, and impregnability. They prided themselves on the craft of offering security to the vulnerable, confidence to the insecure.

Benjamin spent his childhood surrounded by locks and keys, blank at first, then molded and matched to a variety of prohibitions. His first boyhood muscle came up pounding the ingots for a leg iron. He was a prodigy with metal. He knew instinctively when to drive the hammer, when to go slow and twist in the grooves. He understood the skeleton key to perfection. When he made a fit, it did not fail.

The Emersons were very proud to have a son naturally bent to the business. They eagerly waited for him to grow up and assume leadership in the trade. But Benjamin, in some perverse turn against his God-given gift, never liked locks or keys. He never closed up anything—front doors, stables, books; he even slept with the covers thrown off. The Emersons whipped him frequently for being a careless varmint, likely to attract highwaymen and worse. Over time, the scars on Benjamin's back came to resemble a transportation system; spidery tributaries, roads, and railway routes were engraved upon his skin like a surveyor's map. After a while, they made him want to travel.

It took the boy two thousand miles by foot, boat, and wagon train to get any relief. He paid his way doing portraits—the leading widow, the only doctor, the prize bull of such-and-such town; he had painted them all.

He was a master of perspective. He believed in the human life measured to the horizon and limited by the vanishing point. His clients wanted no part of this. They wished to see their heads portrayed the size of cabbages and their nether parts miniaturized, to emphasize their sage and lofty difference from the savage land they were inhabiting. They demanded their babies be painted with the faces of the aged so they would comprehend their duty and destiny from the start. Liberty of expression was limited to the eyes and mouths of their domestic animals, who were always expelled to the background, chewing.

His patrons frustrated him, and in the end they didn't want him. Soon he was forced to earn his way doing chores. Meanwhile, he stole the people's images for his panorama: farmers spitting in their fields, tiny as corn seed against the sky; women at the churn with their broad sunbonnets slightly fallen; children playing frog-on-a-stick in the mud outside the school-house. Benjamin opened their faces like a thief picking a lock; they never knew what hit them.

Meanwhile, the panorama grew. And as he hid it from its subjects, he savored it for other eyes, the ones back home and across the sea who would never come to stay, who would dream it giant with their longing, devour it whole with their distant speculation. It was for those people, the ones who would never come West, that Benjamin was driven to vision. The panorama grew as the young man pushed forward. It became but a pretext for another picture turning in his head, bred on stories and lies, until even the place it claimed to represent became just an outline to be filled in by action and invasion. Never had he felt so close to his roots.

The night animals started their howling. Benjamin shuddered at their gray magnification in the moon. He let down the heavy draperies and returned to his cold-sheeted bed.

Dinner had been good but awfully heavy. Probably due to the buffalo fat he detected in the crepes. He loosened his belt. "Butter is too light for a climate like this," "he reasoned, "even if it is the first night of spring. There's no place here for soft things. I should paint rock, timber, tree ridge, ice."

He found his shirt soaked. He thought it was sweat but it was tears.

Suddenly he was glad to be stopped here in this fantastical Hotel that had more in common with a palace than with the sod houses and shacks that lined the river for miles. The Hotel seemed to reflect the young man in its out-of-placeness, in its fastidious attention to beauty, detail, and ambiance. It defied this natural environment, which was single-mindedly attuned to the survival of the roughest. The fact that he and this Hotel had both survived seemed to be a miracle of association, like those lone buildings that stand perfect and untouched when the whole city around them has been demolished.

The girl, Miranda, wasn't that her name? On the inside of his eyelids he could see her floating up, her eyes lowered but sneaking a look. Eyes the color of violets. How he had forgotten about women these last few years as he went after his panorama. Each time he thought he was closer to the end of his work, he found himself somewhere in the middle, a victim of its shadow. At times, it tormented him so much that he'd long for his old home, the dances in the town houses, the pleasures of the hunt, the bolting of the door against the weather. In all the beauty of the river, and regardless of it, life here was basic necessity, which drove him away from his dreams until he found himself washed up on this bank, tired of the phantom that chased him down and mocked him with its hidden face.

"She has eyes that could put you out of your head," he marveled.

Restless again, he got up and unpacked his traveling easel, really just a paint box with collapsible stick legs, stood it in a corner, and stared until she surfaced again with her purple irises glittering at him under lids thick and hooded as serpents. Her hands were beautiful too. He remembered ivory touched with cerulean blue, almost translucent, too light to be human.

He thought she made him dream. Not of the wilderness, nor of the place he came from, nor of the great cities across the sea that he was sure were his destiny, but of a world that he had no sense of whatsoever and therefore could not articulate or quantify. It remained then in a bright, ephemeral state, like some precious stone, and it was this place he called Miranda, and he was sure she was calling him home.

"A girl you met just a few hours ago. A girl you barely spoke to, hardly looked at," he admonished himself. Furrowing his brow, he forced that image on his easel to melt.

Mentally, he flipped through all the diseases of the soul that a frontier land was known to foster: delusive dyspepsia, hysteria of the joints, delirium of the humors. Better any level of mental incompetence than this woman come to claim him with her violet eyes and silence.

"Her hands trembled when I sang."

Benjamin threw the bedclothes across the room and over his easel. He watched a crack of moonlight sneak through the curtains and play in and out of the counterpane. In the interims of space and shadow, her black hair appeared.

"Think of something else, for God's lovely sake," he wept to himself.

"She has eyes the color of violets," a voice marveled inside.

The things that were chasing him had nothing to do with the color of this young woman's eyes, and so, when he saw her or thought of her, these gray pursuers had nowhere to find him. He was shaking so hard trying not to think of her eyes, the only thing that finally let him drift to sleep was to think that he could go there.

ROSE'S TREE

She was falling backward into the water, falling and falling as
if the moment before drowning was endlessly repeating itself,
when a hard, rough thing pushed her up out of the thirsty
river, away from the opaque dark. It seemed to ascend from the
depths of the river into the sky without end.

Out of nowhere it appeared. She was sure it had never
been there before. How could it have been? How could it be
now? Right behind her. As she was falling.

Tree. In the middle of the river. Rooted to the river. Thick
and battered, an enormous old oak tree was growing.

Call it a tree. Its shape and bearing qualified it as such. But
there the common definition of tree ended. A tree like a volcano erupting, but steadfast as a pillar, an alphabet map, a circle of time you could climb, back and forth. Gray hardness and
green pliant. Charts of strange worlds carved all over its bark.
In the middle of the river. Suddenly. Growing up. Animal
horn, petrified flesh, inlaid with dust, moss, roots of stone, of
bone, evergreen reaching up to the heavens like a prayer.

Its sharp protruding branches poked at the girl's ribs while
the last of the ice beneath her feet was dissolving. She looked
up and saw the deep blue clarity of sky around the tree. She
looked down and . . .

"I can do it. I can climb it," she told herself as the last bit of
ice slipped away from her and dissolved into the waters.

She kicked herself up; the thighs wrapped around, the
arms stretched out, hugging the monstrosity. She climbs the
wood—rock—bone—ash—animal thing that only Rose can
touch, that only she can see. She follows it up to see where it
might lead.

CORA

She couldn't sleep at all the night the stranger came. She wondered if maybe his coming was a sign that the tide against them was turning. After all, he was the Hotel's first guest, a miracle after the eternal vacancy. His face was turning in her mind all night; sometimes it was sweet like a cherub, other times it had the look of a famished wolf.

It was hard to say where she had come from, who had birthed her, who had brought her up. She looked as if she had been in this Hotel forever, that the place itself had made her up.

When she was six, she found herself adopted out of obscurity into a wealthy and prominent family that owned one of the country's oldest and finest museums. Her haughty, elegant beauty was balanced by a certain humility of spirit that could have been the result of her sketchy past, but had the effect, in her younger years, of drawing all manner of people to her in an atmosphere of warmth and intimacy. Yet there was something frozen about her, a sound perhaps, a cracking tinny brittleness that could only be heard when she cried out in her sleep, usually as a result of not being able to dream.

Her hair was pure silver, thin ropes of sterling plaited in two heavy bundles rolled like the brim of a hat across the top of her head. When she was gay, she intertwined the braids with red satin ribbons that were always finding their way out of the confines of her coif and went flying around her head, as if they were weather instruments, measuring the strength and direction of the wind.

It is said that when she met her future husband, she fell instantly and madly. Her hair had been the color of corn silk then, and it hung down her back in a torrent. It is said, too, that Emmanuel was her love and her life—that without him, poor woman, she was nothing, lost in a sea of grief that never, through the long years, subsided, though she had in the meantime raised two fine girls and saw to the meticulous management of her husband's property. Cora did nothing to discourage these stories of her hard work and solitude. In fact, she timed her evening vigils on the iron perimeters of the widow's walk to coincide precisely with the setting sun, conscious that the last burning rays would illuminate her magnificently. People from miles around would come out on their stoops or stop for a moment in their fields to watch her, for the widow's walk stood high above the valley and its farms.

She never believed Emmanuel when he told her in the sundown fire of the doorway that he had had enough, was never coming back, that the land was a fool's land, that the railroad had ruined them, that there would never be any Hotel guests and she should leave with him immediately. The girls, at that time, were fast asleep in bed, their servant Emerald was in the dining room clearing the dishes, the hall clock ticked dully away, and Cora looked long and sharp at the man she so had loved, and shook her head "no." For a moment he stared at her, as if he didn't believe her. Then, slowly, resolutely, he turned his hunched shoulders against her and walked out the door. Later, when she dreamed, that is how she would see him for the rest of her life.

She never told anyone the way it really happened. What he had said or what he wanted from her. It's possible she could not even remember how it was, that the specter of his turned back in the blue dark of the doorway had obliterated any recollection she'd ever had of him from before, except for a slight metallic shiver that always came over her when she heard speak of him.

She made it out that he had gone to seek enough people to turn the Hotel into a city, to give it a place of standing on the back of history before it, too, was lost in the wilderness that was always on the verge of reclaiming it. She made it out that he had left her there to be both sentry and queen, to guard and ennoble their domain until he returned someday with hundreds of customers and the deed to a railroad route that would stop right in front of their fabulous Hotel. As in the case of most lies frequently told, Cora came to believe it herself, and her tale became the true story of her husband's disappearance and the prophecy of his eventual return.

As time passed and Emmanuel did not come back, Cora found herself feeling deceived and deserted. She began to hate him bitterly and to pray in earnest that he would never return, thereby concurring with his own wishes in a way she would have found impossible if she had kept to her love of him. After a while, all the love that she used to have for him and that she believed she had for him still, Cora poured into the Hotel, which she made into a shrine to the dreams that he had, by the time of his disappearance, lost himself.

It was perhaps at this stage of her self-deception that she began to have some feelings for Emerald, the woman she and Emmanuel had found, unconscious and dirt-ragged by the washing creek, and whom they had invited to stay on, no questions asked, as their housekeeper when the Hotel was just a series of isolated pillars and partial foundations, resembling some ancient, lost city in the face of excavation.

A year after Emmanuel's disappearance, when Emerald found her mistress hysterical and clawing at the door of her little room by the winter kitchen, she quickly took her in under the covers of her drudgery. From the beginning, their bodies were a surprise and a relief to each other. Warm and supple where embarrassment and resistance were expected, there was no clumsiness in their passion. For Cora, this was a miracle. She had always hated the inevitable awkwardness of bodies in copulation; but with Emerald, the licking, the biting, the sucking, even the force of objects pressing and then entering had only harmony and grace to them. She loved to rock herself up the larger woman's body, stopping to knead and tickle and bite. She divided her lover's body into minute territories, each no larger than what a fingertip or tongue could handle in a single action, and she ignited them into a redness and a beating until what she found beneath her was delirium and upheaval. But what Cora experienced as conquest was only the play surrender of a woman who had, in the past, been so pained and degraded she could never be humbled. As Cora pressed her fingers into the warm, shuddering cavity, she felt her own capitulation. Every time, shocked by this, the frozen thing inside her cried out. Her face went white and her movements stopped and she couldn't hear Emerald calling to her. She could only hear that freezing thing until its rasping, haphazard sound took form, and the form was "Cora, Cora, Cora." The words pushed their way up the rigid column of her body and settled on her lips, which, in later life, would give them that pursed, shrunken appearance as if her own name had all but swallowed them up. When these seizures lifted, Cora would take herself out of her lover's bed and walk woodenly up the stairs to her own, as if nothing at all had happened between them. The more she found happiness with Emerald, the more she told herself that it was Emmanuel, whose soul she cursed every night, it was Emmanuel whom she truly loved.

As love in the person of her servant became for Cora a thing she could depend on, a thing that would not turn its back on her and disappear, she began to set her mind on the problem of the Hotel. Since her husband had left, they'd survived on Cora's pin money and the sale of Emerald's herbs. Perhaps most of all they'd made do: the food carefully put up, salted down, frozen away, to be resurrected in the kitchen, brought back to life in new and exotic forms that would please the most discerning palate. They carefully mended their clothes from year to year, but so utterly transformed the garments that they were unrecognizable from their previous incarnations. But after so many years, materials wear thin, and it was not only clothes that needed replacing but several yards of plumbing and piping; the carpets and floors needed refinishing, the bricks remortaring, the shutters repainting—the whole place needed updating. How were they to do all this with their threadbare savings?

Emerald told her, after they'd gone over and over the huge heavy book that was their ledger, that there was nothing to be done but to sell it—the whole thing—that the list of negatives on the one side had nothing to balance it in the column of positives on the other. Emerald's finger was pointing severely at piles of numerals that Cora could no longer see because she was crying so hard.

"Look," the servant said, "this is the only real home I've ever had, but I'm not about to go and sell myself to keep it."

Cora, who wanted no truck with the merchandising of the self, agreed with her on this, but could not concede to giving the place up, especially now that the handsome young man had come, the first real guest they'd ever had.

"It's an omen, Emerald," she said.

They stared at each other all through the night, the two women emptied and dull, until the room grew blurred in the density of their concentration and the sounds of morning—the brown doves, the sweet grass, and the beetles drew together into a singular thrum that drowned their sorrow out.

ROSE EXPLORES THE TREE

It was the warmth from above that drew her up. The tree, bare as winter at bottom, was emerald green at top. It trembled as she climbed, but in such a steadfast way that she was not afraid to go on.

Clearing trail after trail in the grooves of its trunk to make her way, she rose and rested, rose and rested. She passed from moonlight to sunlight much faster than time could tell. She noticed that she was hungry and suddenly all manner of fruits and nuts and succulents were falling at her feet. She sensed herself thirsty, and swiftly, fresh rainwater dripped branch to branch into her open mouth. The atmosphere changed too. It had an alpine smell, invigorating and haughty, but the sea was apparent, too, and with it, the humbling effect of illimitable space. Best of all, it held the sun, which shrank the black river and cold moon, so recently her sole companions, into a vague nightmare that must have happened long ago and to a person much younger than Rose herself.

Far below her she could see the sprawling Hotel, with its gargoyle rain gutters, mahogany doors, and veiled widow's walk. From her vantage point, the town that had ruined them, gliding along on its shining silver train tracks, seemed too small and harmless to have offered such deadly competition. As she climbed farther, the things below seemed to tidy up into neat parcels. The countryside became a thick swatch of carpeting with trees and hills, rivers and valleys making up an elaborate border. As she went higher, the bare branches gave way to plots of leaves like a feather bed on which to nap or gaze up at the endless canopy of green, filtered with sun. She encountered a river, the color of black and gold marble, in which to cool her face, grown flushed with altitude and light. The river itself was not unlike the one she left below and from which this very tree had grown, and she began to wonder why she had feared the other one so much only moments ago.

As she climbed higher, the smell of mint and bitter chocolate, two of her favorite delicacies, permeated the air so completely that Rose was sure she was eating them in gargantuan
quantities without suffering any of gluttony's unfortunate side
effects. In the end, the smells that made her happy reminded
her of home, so she thought to go there. But she couldn't see
her way back down; it was so dark, while straight above all
stood clear. After a while, she couldn't tell up from down, only
black from light, and it was light she was sure of. It would have
to lead her home.

MIRANDA'S HANDS

Her hands were like damaged ivory, cracked and bruised in the carving. She found the cold months most favorable to her craftsmanship of mutilation for then the skin dried, broke, crusted, and bled of its own accord, the way laid open by nature for her own mortifications. This work of penance was her daily preoccupation.

But at nightfall, she changed.

She would excuse herself early from the dinner table and climb the flight of stairs to the attic. She'd take a gold-colored key from her apron pocket and turn the lock of the door. The last light of dusk would collect in blinding shafts through the casements, as it always did at this moment of the day, when she opened the door to this, her room, her worship place. The poor stricken hands would help her into a white linen smock, with lace at the cuffs, where swallows danced in the curve of a willow tree. Here, in this holy uniform, on a high wooden stool by a narrow window, she would sit expectantly.

Prayer was what she called it. Prayer, for Miranda, was a fervently active thing, and in her it concentrated in the gesticulations of those harmed hands. Rising over the attic air in supplication, they seemed to possess the senses of sight, hearing, and smell as much as touch. She had a real bedroom on the second floor, mint green and white lace, but she didn't like it. The attic was her personal cathedral, her sacred receptacle of light, with its high, vaulted ceiling and its gigantic wooden arches effortlessly supporting the whole house, which draped below it like a sorcerer's magic cape.

Tonight, as Miranda unlocked the door so late that it opened out into darkness, her mind was on the future.

"I want tomorrow to be here now. His name is Benjamin. He smells like ocean, he sings."

Gleefully she rearranged her white pinafore and examined her job of ironing.

"He smells like apples, like cinnamon, like wine . . ."

She adjusted the figured cuffs so that her battered hands might roam free. She played piano in the air. She tossed her thick black hair around and lay on the floor, legs up and feet wiggling like an overturned insect.

"He smells like horses, like rainstorm."

On the shadows of the floor, she imagined his face: the nose straight, long, swooping down into the curve of his nostrils, which flared in and out as he spoke. His hair was thick, chestnut, and wavy, and she was sure it would capture the sun like a prism. She wanted to nuzzle against it as if it were the muzzle of a mare. Sleepless, she paced up and down the raw boards that made up the fantasy of his face.

"He smells like me."

The thought hit her hard and suddenly, draining her of all her recent pleasure. The image of him on the floor began to look sinisterly familiar, like a person known and possibly feared in the past who has come back, at first unrecognizable.

"He smells like me," she repeated to herself.

Her mind dredged up every human being she had ever encountered in reality or dream, but she could not find him anywhere, though she felt and now heard him everywhere she went, in real time or fantasy. Her heart began to pound in the old, familiar way she dreaded, and she knew that soon it would drown out every sound, every thought, every shape that bound her to the world. The excitement she was experiencing only made it more horrifying, for she knew the minutiae of the torture she was about to feel. Like a person without air, she dragged herself to the window, saw the moon in full and the willow tree of her birth shivering against it. In her pain, the image of the young man shrank to a stain in the black passage of the attic. Unable to stand where she was, she took herself out.

ROSE AND THE ROSES

"The beauty of climbing," thought Rose, "is its effortless reversal of space." As the girl went up, the pink and white canopy above became a bed of roses below, upon which she now sank. For the first time in her life and everywhere she turned, Rose saw the image of her name. Everywhere was Rose, on the ground in the sky. It was as if the cheeks of china dolls had somehow been transmuted into these flowers. And by association, by name and admiration, Rose, saw herself as the most beautiful creature on earth, full of endless folds and manifold mysteries. She had never thought of mystery as a part of her. No, it had always seemed to have something to do with the animals in the forest or her sister's perfume. Now, surrounded by these objects that shared her name, she knew herself as enigma and felt, for the first time intimate with herself in a singular unknowing.

It was in this giant place of closure, this tree the size of a forest, guarded by a thousand blooming flowers that Rose felt, also for the first time in her life, exquisite in spirit and form. She bent over to touch the petals with her lips as if to drink a mutual life in. She brushed her cheeks against the outer rim and worked her way through to the innermost cup of the flower before she opened her eyes. A small pool of rain water had settled there; it rocked slowly back and forth, perfectly clear and colorless, an inverted telescope of reflection.

But what she saw inside it was very, very strange.

If it had been any bigger, it might have scared her, but as it was, tiny and contained in the bud of a rose, it only aroused repulsion and curiosity. What was it doing there, this ugly thing with its sharp broken beak and molting body, so buried in rose that it didn't notice the girl, though it appeared to be staring right through her?

Rose decided not to waste her wonderful time on a mangy apparition and to be on her way. "Wherever that is!" she yawned and stretched, "I'm the one to find it."

It was a fantastic day, a day nothing could ruin, for this was the first day in Rose's life that she felt beautiful and, hence, to her mind, absolutely indestructible as she climbed and climbed and climbed. She was, however, thirsty. She remembered the pond and went back to drink from it. The sun was already at noon, and the air was hot and so dry she could barely taste her tongue.

"Oh this is good" she sighed, and drank deeply. As she raised her head from the water, her hair hung wet and tangled on all sides. She went to arrange it in braids, but as she wove, the hair started cracking. Rose looked in the pond to see what she was doing and her reflection she could not find, neither on the smooth surface or in the recesses below which she beat frantically with her fists trying to uncover it. Where was her face? That beautiful face that deserved the name Rose?

But the only thing she could see looking back at her in the water was that stupid little scavenger bird with its beady eyes and its sopping wet wings.

MIRANDA'S NIGHT

When the girls had been quite young, an old gypsy came by the Hotel. Knock knock knock on the door: "Ma'am can I stay the night?"

She had a gold tooth and she pointed to the ground.

Emerald was terrified. "She'll make your kids into freaks," she cried and started pushing the old crone away.

But Miranda, who was just learning to talk, went up to the woman and said "be our guest."

That night it snowed and the gypsy tent was crowned in white. Cora, wishing to propitiate the gods of hospitality, went out at sunrise to bring the woman some coffee, but there was no one there, not a trace there had ever been anyone there . . . except for an old, dirty handkerchief and upon it, sparkling in the fresh snow and sun, a gold tooth and around it three drops of blood, glistening like rubies on the ground. "For Miranda, God bless her heart," a red scrawled note said.

Now when Cora had first seen the gold tooth in the old gypsy's mouth, she hadn't noticed how beautiful it was. But lying there, in the snow she saw it was the color of a hearth fire and the shape of a heart, with a diamond buried inside, like a star in the sky. She wrapped it up in the handkerchief, placed it in the twins' hope chest, and vowed that when Miranda turned fifteen, the age of womanhood in her husband's family, it would go upon a golden chain around her neck. Emerald, having watched the proceedings from a discreet distance, spit three times on the ground and lit a roomful of votive candles daily for the duration of the month, though she knew it was probably too late to do any good.

So it was that Miranda grew a gypsy's heart. When the only deep desire within her was to stay put, this gypsy heart would beat and stab, pound and flutter until Miranda would find herself suddenly days away from home, not knowing how in the world she got there. She became a silent girl, some thought dumb, who had nothing to say to the foreign environments she frequently found herself in. Home, a smell and a sound she loved beyond all measure, became the casualty of her vagabond heart. It was a common occurrence at the Hotel to receive a message from some way off place saying that a young dumb gal with your address pinned to her collar and no money at all was lost in their town. Cora would send a ticket and Miranda would come sheepishly back. For days after, she'd run around the Hotel in a tactile fit. She could be seen tracing the filigree work on the serving pieces in the china closet, embracing the food stocks in the pantry, rolling around frenetically on the Persian rugs. She begged her mother to build a high iron gate around the Hotel and promise never to give her the key. Miranda became a stay-at-home, recluse, shut-in, hermit. She stopped sleeping in her pretty sea green and lace bedroom with the canopy bed and took to catnapping on the attic floor where the nails came up and cut into her body.

Miranda would stand for hours at a time in the south window of the attic looking out over the enormous backyard willow tree. In the place where the gypsy had set up camp so many years ago, and where she had left the three drops of blood, there had grown this tree. It was three stories high by the time Miranda turned fifteen. It was gold and lanky, full of grace and full of strength. Everybody called it Miranda's tree, for it had come up as she did, sapling to sapling.

But there was more to it than that, though nobody much liked talking about it. This willow tree was her tree, utterly and entirely. No other child dared climb it or swing from it, no grown-up, no matter how tired or hot, would seek its shade. It was Miranda's tree and the two came to resemble each other deeply. Miranda with her long sinuous limbs, the willow tree with its silky tress-like branches. They adopted each other's natures, too—animal became vegetable, and vegetable—almost human. Miranda came to comprehend the world through the perception of the tree—seasonally metamorphic,

photosynthetically transformative. For the girl, growing up in
the wilderness with a heart that despised her and a family that
treated her like a beautiful but odd curiosity, the willow tree
was the only real friend she had. During the day, she hugged
its side or swung over the world from the rope swing she tied
to its branches. At night it was her window into the galaxies.

But even the weeping willow tree could not save her from
her own heart. As time wore on, it grew heavier and heavier.
She tried to ignore it, but while she scrubbed the floors, dried
the dishes, milked the cow, it gnawed at her and hunted for a
way out. As Miranda grew to womanhood, the gypsy heart
grew to hate her, plotting its revenge against all the years she
dismissed its beating for the washboard, the pig sty, the
kitchen, her mother's voice calling from upstairs.

She tried to convince herself that the iron bands tightening
around her chest and the cold sweats percolating her forehead
were just the stray results of the mid-summer heat or lack of
sleep or the cicadas' incessant droning. But the heart grew a knife
and it chopped through her breast. Miranda thought that inside,
she was slowly bleeding to death. Each night, as she washed up
for dinner, she would check the progress of deterioration on her
lips. Pressing them against the washroom mirror, she'd sigh:

"Bluer and bluer, thinner and thinner . . . till there's not
one drop left."

She estimated that by winter, she'd be dead.

Then after the meal, for which she'd have no appetite, she
would trudge up to the attic, open one of the rusty casements
and peer out over the head of her beloved willow. Her eyes on
the tree were a swing to the stars. Every night she'd choose a
different one to concentrate on—blue or green, yellow, red
depending on the quality of her anguish and she would pray:

"Please take this awful thing inside of me away. It wants to
leave but I want, for all the world, to stay."

In her mind's eye, she pictured it going, this joyous gypsy
heart, bursting through the galaxy, trailing her body's blood

behind it like the tail of a comet. How she loved this heart of her outside herself, the way one can love a person, long abandoned who because of love had caused you great pain.

But the heart did not leave, it nestled inside her like a claw. It chewed at the lungs, clutched at the throat. Every breath she breathed took everything and still she felt she was getting no air. She called on the stars nightly, her fingers knit together in supplication. She would have given her youth and her beauty, nay, her life to be able to clean a cabinet, arrange a bouquet, prepare a meal without gasping, without needing to be vigilant over the automatic functioning of the breath.

She thought about the young man and the way he made her feel and how hopeless it was for her to try and meet that feeling. She fell on her knees, begged, wept, howled, demanded but the attic was far and no one heard the terrified girl. The agony of breathing began to feel much worse than the fear of dying.

It was midnight to the minute when she made her move. The moon was riding a single cloud in an otherwise vacant sky. She put on her shawl and headed out to the backyard. There, in all its sway and majesty, stood Miranda's tree. Even in the dark, it shone; as if everything that was hope and love and promise, emanated from that tree. It was perfect in color, size, and symmetry and this perfection was the place that Miranda ran to from the chaos of her battered body; this weeping willow that was so delicate and light but able to survive the most brutal tempests; it would bend but never give ground.

She had never wanted to hurt it, never wanted to see it maimed. It had been so perfect. Even in winter it retained its full mane. Never had it shed a single twig. She slipped the small, double edged hatchet out from under her pinafore. Turning her back on the tree, she tested the blade against her parched lips. The white day lilies trembled in the garden. Her face was a sheet of tears. She pressed her bloody lips to the trunk of the tree.

"Forgive me," she said and brought the ax down.

❦

She only chopped off a single branch. But to Miranda's mind, she might have as well committed murder. Over it, she closed her raw, bleeding fist and ran towards the Hotel. Some sap dripped a sickly green over her pale night dress. Her heart was pounding out of her chest. Up the backstairs, two-three at a time, she hurled herself on the attic door, slamming it open, shut, and locked up in one move.

Once in the room, everything she is goes slow motion. She sleepwalks to the window looking over the yard. The willow tree stood strangely still in the windy night, its silhouette like a stiletto stabbed into the attic floor. She positions herself with care, so that her heart rests directly under the moon, as though it were a surgeon's lamp. She wants to think, but thinking is impossible. Her fingers undo the tight small buttons, mother of pearl, releasing the neck, then the shoulder yoke, down to the chest. Carefully, as if it were covering a terrible wound, she folds back the cloth of her dress. Her breast exposed is a vacant field.

"X marks the spot," she says.

With the willow branch she traces the outline of a heart around her heart, very lightly but it still draws blood. She lifts up the branch, its severed end oozing and dripping.

"X marks the spot," she laughs "with a dot dot dot." Then she makes a series of punctures upon the heart around her heart. At the tip of the aorta, she thrusts the tip of the willow limb in. A well of liquid spurts out, half blood, half some other strange substance that looks to her to be made of stars. "This is heaven" she exclaims.

At this point, her vision goes. The dark sky and her mind become the same thing. For the first time in a long time, maybe since the time of her beginning, the terror inside dissolves. She thinks she hears the willow branch drop to the floor and she thinks she feels the floor, soft and vegetative, heaving up around her. She breathes deeply between spasms of pain. As the pain grows deeper, she is not breathing at all. The air is impenetrably still, as if awaiting a storm. The sky is glazed in golden florescence.

"Bon Voyage," she managed to say.

Hours later, morning set its sights on the attic room. All the sunlight running through its narrow windows seemed to escape down the stairs to the bedrooms and, finally, the big bay window in the kitchen, leaving the attic in a dreary half light. The moon, now a cold impotence, still weighed in the sky. The girl Miranda lay in a motionless lump under the eaves, the willow stick, black and scarlet by her side. Thick, dark colors emanated from her body as if someone had dripped candle wax over her and across the wide planked floors.

At first she thought she had succeeded; that she had cut the gypsy heart out of her chest and it had left her for its own adventures. But the heaviness inside her told her she was wrong. She was inhabited by it still and the flood of red across the floor had changed nothing, finally. The smell of blood and urine on her person humiliated her. Her hair was caked with grime and dead leaves; the taste of salt rimmed her lips. Her head spun and her hands lay cold and useless.

She stares around the room and it looks completely wrong. That's when she realizes that she's lying on the floor, her body twisted up like an octopus digesting a reluctant dinner guest.

"What am I doing alive?"

She was out of her mind with fury. It was then that she saw the garish thing, staring up at her from the attic floor.

It was a kind of painting, seemingly made from oil crayon and oil paint though where they came from and who did it and when she had no inkling. It had happened to her before, the pictures on the floor of the attic when she woke up there, morning after morning, roused by the acrid smell of turpentine and paints. They seemed to have come from her own body—these translucent pigments that had no like in nature or art. The blood, the humors, the fluid of the spine the bile of the pancreas the gold of the teeth—she could find the corollary in her flesh for every color and texture on that painted floor.

She has to stand up, though it makes her dizzy. She lowers her head, straightens the knees, and backs away. She touches herself, absolutely everywhere. She looks and she sees. Perfect everywhere. No wounds, no cuts, no scars. And the willow branch of blood and sap? Green green green and complete, as if it never had been pulled from any tree, but always existed as its own separate entity.

A shock of sun suddenly hit the room and the floorboards splintered with color. Miranda gasped at what she could see under her feet. The painting . . .

It had a huge tree to it; straight trunk and curvaceous limbs like the willow she loved swinging in. But instead of weeping willow leaves, this tree was hung with plump, beautiful babies, the size and color of silver dollars, dangling down like ripe fruit. The trunk was etched in charcoal and had a sinister sheen. The roots of the tree were visible, and spread throughout the attic, like rapacious vines, tangling up all the sparse and broken down pieces of furniture that had found their way up there.

The rest of the mural seemed almost silly, painted in primary blues, reds and greens as if designed by a child's hand. There was a cozy forest cluster of alpines, a little rose garden, and a big black bird with the face of a girl. Far away and in a corner, there was a beautiful young man sailing on a patch of sea who, if you looked closely, had no face in his head. But still, Miranda felt she knew him from somewhere, though she couldn't put her finger on it.

ROSE AND THE RAVEN

A girl who sees herself as a girl, and a pretty one at that, for the first time in her life, only to find her new identity just as suddenly changed to that of an ugly, raucous, clumsy bird—such a girl feels so much loss, such grief and frustration, that she can no more be called a child. So thought Rose, now become a raven.

She tried to keep climbing but found herself flying. The great tree's sky of branches became a jungle gym of perches and swings. The clouds, now level with her position in the tree, promised home—for that was what flight was to Rose-now-become-Raven. The ancient oak, so indomitable to her girl-mind, was but a way station and feeding ground to the raven. So, too, her sense of yearning changed. The steady pillar of its trunk now left her cold. She wanted only to ride the air.

She shut her eyes, as the girl in her was afraid of heights, and flew to the highest branch to see what lay beyond it. Opening her eyes cautiously at the summit, she looked out and made note:

> *neither day nor night*
> *neither cloud nor clear*
> *neither hot nor cold*
> *neither shape nor no-shape*

It made her want to go immediately someplace else, for what she sensed and saw seemed to call her own materiality into question. She prepared to take off in flight.

"Naturally I can do it," thought Rose. Her bird-feet crept to the brink and her wings drew in tight to her body and then suddenly spread up and wide like holy terror.

A whistle sound. Watered down. Remnants of sound carried to her by the wind. She tried to fly up but the sound pulled her down.

Whistling a song she knew.

Little bird, little bird,
Where will you go with that worm?
Why don't you eat it up right now
Before the eagle snatches you away-o?

A song she knew. The one her grandmother sang when she
was darning. There was a space in the refrain for when she
had to hold the needle in her teeth. Tears welled up in Rose's
eyes. Everything about her that was flight froze inside.
Hundreds of feet up in a tree that just minutes ago did not
exist, a girl who is a girl but also a black scraggly bird is listening to her dead grandmother sing. Now instead of wings,
she owned a pair of scraped-up knees. Before she knew it,
Rose found herself halfway down the tree and completely
homesick.

"What on earth are you doing in the middle of the river?
You'll catch your death."

It was her grandmother yelling at her with her red nose-
blower waving in the breeze.

"I'm not in the river," Rose called down. "I'm on this big
old tree. Grandmother, can't you see?"

"What I see, little one, is that you are skating on thin ice!"
snapped her grandmother, and turning her huge back to the
river, she muttered her way back up to the Hotel. That was
when Rose realized that even ghosts cannot see everything. It
made her unhappy to think that the vanished old woman
could not see the enormous tree her granddaughter was climbing or how she became a rose and then a raven.

At the start of her fifteenth year, Rose slid down from the
tree growing in the river and swam through the muck to shore.
When she got to the pine trail and looked behind her, the tree

had already disappeared. But she knew that although it was invisible, it was as close and present as the fragment of whistle come up to get her from a dead woman's spittle.

MIRANDA AND BENJAMIN GO A-WALKING

Light-headed and full of questions, Miranda took herself over to the window. There stood the willow tree with its one stolen branch breaking the symmetry. And here, in her fist, dripping red, she held its missing limb. The sun was rising in the east like a basket of oranges. She was alive and whole of heart. The only real changes in her world were the mutilation of her beloved tree and the grotesque visions on the attic floor— which she knew she'd have to clean up.

Angrily she wondered who could have done this to her and why she hadn't heard them, even when they had painted her body like a warrior chief's, with splotches of brown, red, and green, on the night she meant to die? She wiped her forehead against her wrist; it, too, was sticky with paint. Her scabbed and scarred-up hands she hid behind her in a fist.

> *Go dig up that red rosy bush*
> *grows under the willow tree*
> *and it will tell the wide world round*
> *that she's forsaken me.*

She heard it spill in from the backyard in a high and low call that could only be coming from the rope swing off the willow. Heard it, tenor clear, over and over, washing over the prisoner heart and its warden alike.

> *Go dig up that red rosy bush*
> *grows under the willow tree*
> *and it will tell . . .*

She was nauseous, with a thick salt taste in her mouth like somebody else's tongue. Her head reeled and she lowered it to keep from fainting.

"Monsters and devils using me the whole night long," she muttered and fumbled for her handkerchief.

> *. . . and it will tell the wide world round*
> *what she has done to me.*

Up it came again through the panes. Now she was sure it was the voice of the young man she had found by the river, whom she had forgotten in the destruction that had stranded her between night and morning. It was the voice of Benjamin, who smelled like ocean, like apples, like forest, like rain.

Miranda steadied herself and searched for the root of the sound. Outside, the crows were ranging for food; earthworms and June bugs squirmed in their beaks. The willow tree swing was empty, but it was twitching back and forth as if someone had just jumped off it from a great height. Empty. Empty of him, both earth and sky.

Her eyes squinted past the thicket where Trapper lured the quail that was her mother's secret weakness, down past the pines where she played hiding games with her sister. She found Benjamin in a narrow clearing at the foot of the ridge that led to the canyon. He was setting up his wares, a paint box and easel. There he was, singing that fool song that woke her up. He had a forward, strained look on his face, like a jockey out to win a race.

Miranda liked spying, liked it a lot, in fact. Secret viewing, to Miranda's way of thinking, was the true vision of life. The clandestine nature of seeing had become for her, out of habit, the only faithful representation of sight. She bit her lip hard so as not to cry out.

She watched as the young man laid his colors out in careful rows. He took off his jacket, then his vest, for the sun was reaching on high. His shirt, too, he unbuttoned, and his chest sailed out, as he sang the same song over and over and over in sad, pleading cadences, though his face looked happy in its

patina of sunburn and sweat. Suddenly, in a casual way, he
turned to the house and waved up at her.

Miranda went white, her hands started trembling, and the
willow branch clattered to the floor. No one had ever caught
her spying before. No one had ever forced her to acknowledge
what she saw by staring back. She sank back into the recesses
of the eaves. Benjamin kept waving and smiling. And then he
was walking right at her, gesturing to her to come down. He
was singing:

> Go dig up that red rosy bush
> grows under the willow tree . . .

What would Cora think if she heard, if she saw him now, out
like this at dawn calling her daughter down? In a response derived
half from pleasure, half from shame, Miranda went to him, running down the stairs and out the back door, covered all over with
paint. There he stood, grinning, in his shirtsleeves, on the other
side of the screen door.

"Come with me," he said gently." It's a fine day for two to
go walking."

She wanted to run back into the house, but her body
refused her mind's offering.

"Do you know this country?" she asked him, hopelessly
stumbling for something to say, to fill the space that demanded
motion.

He stared at her as if her body was the sea. He said nothing.

"Do you know this country?" she repeated, desperately,
placed out of herself, foreign of self and alien of place in this
encounter. The green of the backyard seemed to grow right out
of his limbs.

"What is this country?" she wondered in panic as he
opened the screen door that hung between them.

He took her by the hand. He led her out.

CORA'S MARK

Alone, they ate their dinner in silence, the night after the stranger came. The silver platters and porcelain pots pushed noiselessly back and forth on their green felted feet like listless turtles, even though the women hardly ate a thing. Neither of them seemed to miss the girls at the table or to question where they might be. Customarily, Cora was rigid about the family eating the evening meal together, but there were times like today when a paralyzing melancholia overcame her. These times were more often than not associated with the monthly closing of the books. Today Cora had been forced to face the fact that the Hotel, beyond all help or doubt, was bankrupt.

"Did you like the cutlets?" Emerald inquired, hoping to deflect the storm she saw brewing on her mistress's face.

"Yes," answered Cora.

"Not too much rosemary, do you think?" Emerald despaired.

"No."

There was a long silence. "Maybe an overabundance of tarragon?" Emerald ventured.

"No."

"A smidgen too much curry?"

"No."

"How about the quantity of ginger?"

"No, not at all!" Cora snapped, immediately remanding her concentration to the gold and flowered borders of her plate.

She felt a twinge of guilt for her abruptness. But her mind was on such desperate things that she had no energy left for politeness. How was she going to save the Hotel, her husband's Hotel? What would she tell him when he returned home and found his dream boarded up, or worse yet, open and flourishing under another owner? Although she had not seen nor heard word of him in over ten years, she had a morbid feeling that as soon as the Hotel slipped out of her hands, he would come back and claim from her his due. She remembered his temper and she feared it. Furthermore, Cora had grown to love the Hotel. It was her hope, her pride, and her industry celebrated in brick, marble, and gilt. To lose it was to be banished. She was nearly forty now, not that to her mind forty was old, but time was changing the face of her and she began to feel the proximity of impasse, to which she responded with a reckless craving for the immortal. Her yearnings were now not for the arms of a lover, but for something that could outlive the uncertainties of time, nature, and man. She loved her grand and solid home, situated on the precipice of all that was unknown and savage.

Every night after dinner, Cora went to the counting room to settle the day's bills and speak to her husband. His handsome figure sat in a mahogony frame over the mantelpiece that looked down over the massive counting table. His small, hooded eyes seemed to covet every article in the room.

Cora looked up at his portrait and said, "Emmanuel, see how much money I saved you today?" She held out the palms of her hands. They were empty.

In the first years of his disappearance, her hands would be piled so high with gold that all the pieces would topple over and clatter to the floor before she could venture a word to her husband's portrait. "Look, Emmanuel, how much money I saved you today," she would say, playing girlishly with a few strands of her honey-colored hair. But as the years passed and he did not come back and her hair grew less gold and more gray than perhaps it should have at her age, the money, too, thinned out to a sparse collection of copper pennies. She was no longer bold in her pronouncements of money saved, but whimpered of inflation and bill collectors. Indeed, as she stood this day before the portrait of her husband, there were no coins at all in her tiny palms. She filled them, instead, with her own weeping, miserable head.

"I've lost it, Emmanuel, everything you ever wanted or believed in or loved."

She was really inconsolable, thought Emerald, who took up sentry duty outside the counting-room door. She pressed her eye to the keyhole. There was Cora, her head bowed on the heavy oak desk. Suddenly she straightened up and began to speak to her husband's portrait.

"I'm going to keep this house," she said. "I'm going to keep this house till I rot. And do you know how I'm going to save it? I'm going to turn it into an auction house! That's right. People may find it inconvenient to sleep and eat here, but they'll travel any length to buy and sell."

Emerald fell into the room on her knees.

"You are out of your mind!" she screamed. "Haven't we suffered enough buying and selling? I had enough of that "turn around, turn around girlie, show your teeth, raise your ass, hold up those tits. Going once, going twice.'"

Cora took Emerald's head in her hands and kissed her lips, her forehead, her cheeks. "I'm not selling people, silly. I'm going to auction off things. All those fine, foreign, heavy things left behind on the trail year after year by pioneers who could not afford the weight. Now, listen! The whole idea is to move the items for sale quickly. Make them liquid, a river of merchandise, a boundless golden stream. There are all these people around dying to buy, and all these other people that are dying to sell, but they have no way of meeting. That's where we come in—kind of like matchmaking. And for our payment we'll take a nice, fat percentage of the sales. We can use the third-floor ballroom for the auction room, it's ideal." She laughed. "We're going from pioneers to auctioneers. We're going to save this Hotel!"

Emerald looked around the dark-paneled room and shook her head with a defeated smile.

"Sold, sold, sold," Cora cried, "sold, Emerald, sold. This is a home away from home, for the people. An American Hotel. What a good thing it will be to spread beauty around by buying and selling. When Emmanuel built this place, he insisted that it be furnished with the most splendid things. He believed that a new country must be piled high with beauty if it is to start aright with history.

"We'll use this auction business," Cora continued, "not only to make money, but to educate the tastes of the people. We'll hang red velvet curtains, we'll place the French provincial side chairs in spectator rows, we'll hand out programs with technical descriptions and personal histories of each object on the block. We'll have concerts and dramatic readings between all the selling. From week to week, the people, the prices, the merchandise will change. Nothing settled, nothing sterile, nothing ever the same."

She was spinning herself around on top of the counting desk. Joy filled in all the wrinkles on her face.

"But Cora," Emerald braved, "why do you suppose if nobody wants to sleep here, they'd want to come out and shop here? We're not exactly close to town." She pointed her long skinny finger due west, to where that hateful place and railway lay.

Cora abruptly stopped her acrobatics; her face was sharp, her expression severe. "Because," she said, "people may want to sleep in a crowded town conveniently adjacent to a dirty, noisy railroad. But shopping, Emerald, shopping is a different thing altogether. Shopping is an adventure and people will go most anywhere for that. Why, for civilized people, shopping is the same as hunting—and what's the challenge of hunting in a predictable place like a town? An auction house has that special element of chance, of natural selection and fate inextricably linked."

"But Cora . . ."

"Listen, Emerald, I know these people. When I was a girl, folks would travel for weeks to get hold of that first Chinese silk, that French porcelain, that Indian spice. Up and down the seaboard they ran to be the only one in their town, in their county, in their state to have that particular thing. Why, to own rarities transforms a person into a creature of respect, his home into a living museum."

"Well, I'd best be getting back to my baking," Emerald said to her friend, who was now slumped over on the floor in a post-excitement heap. "But I think it's a gamble. Because even if, as you say, folks love to buy, who's to say we'll find any-one hankering to sell?" She shut the door sharply.

"No, dear," Cora said to the woman who was no longer there, "we're not counting on them bringing us anything to sell." She glanced around the room, catching every vase, paint-ing, and item of furniture with her eyes, as if they were fish-hooks. "No, dear," she said wistfully, "in the realm of having something to sell, I don't approve of gambling."

DO YOU KNOW THIS COUNTRY?

They had come by way of the two hundred steps that led from the Hotel to the gardens. The gardens were still bare but for a few crocuses half-frozen in the soil. Benjamin and Miranda passed through the topiary garden where, as a child, and even now, she often played. The trees and bushes were sculpted to represent a fantastic bestiary; animals real and imaginary reared their stupendous heads high into the clouds. Panthers, llamas, hyenas, gazelle, sea serpents, and the lushest brontosauri marauded through the animal forest. The topiary succeeded in keeping away unwelcome guests, the scavengers and vagrants of the trail, who came to fear the Hotel by reason of its sinister botanical sentinels.

She took him where he led. Showed him the birch and the juniper, the plane tree and the palm, the eucalyptus and the mimosa; where the healing herbs grew, the cornfield, the alfalfa, and the soy; beneath which rock lay the scorpion, under what cliff the sleeping hare; where the sea came up from the desert. The land that her father Emmanuel had claimed was immense, bigger than life nearly, and even though he was gone and no one tended it, still it bloomed and grew as if some careful farmer was laboring at it daily.

As they walked on, she ventured to speak to him. "We have a special wind in these parts," she whispered. "Gives voice to what a body can't speak."

"I can speak for myself," replied the man, touching his lips with his fingertips.

"Benjamin," she said, as if the name was choking her inside and must come out.

"Miranda, there's no wind in the world that can speak for what a person thinks but won't speak."

"This one can."

"Then it's lying, girl. It's just plain lying."

"Well, sir, then I've got to ask: Who is doing that lying, the wind that moves or the man who speaks?"

Benjamin laughed softly. She had wisdom to her, the girl, and it pleased him. They continued walking, the tree creatures falling into their own green shadows.

They walked past the brown river where his boat harbored and his nag grazed, down a thin, weedy path that looked like it went nowhere, then suddenly fanned out into a great field of wildflowers that came up to his waist and covered her breasts—daisies, honeysuckle, sweet william, Queen Anne's lace.

The ceaseless sound of insects made their conversation sleepy. They spoke in half phrases, finishing each other's sentences.

"Over there, can you?"

" Yes . . . sassafras, maybe mint."

"We could . . ."

"And inside there . . ."

"You saw it, too?"

A lynx and her cubs were slowly crossing the valley.

"In these parts, Miranda, there's a special voice that makes a body feel things."

"You're wrong!" she said, as if to bury her face by averting her eyes.

"Can you guess where it comes from? Who it belongs to?" he asked her quietly.

Silence.

He looked at her with pity, snapped off a piece of sweet grass, and plugged it between his teeth. His breath sent it whistling.

"No, Miranda?" he asked, taking her face firmly in his hands. "I can tell you one thing: that voice doesn't come from the wind."

It began to rain urgently. The vegetation around them had grown up into a jungle, and they huddled under a huge rubber tree until the sun came back out. Slowly they headed north and the land divided itself up into neat little portions—golden tobacco fields, fields of green and yellow squash, of peas, of melon, of string beans. Two white church spires stood in the distance, like gates to nowhere.

Then they headed west, and west was all scrub and treetop. Vultures with red eyes and bald heads flew overhead and screeched as they circled the empty holes of red canyons. Benjamin and Miranda followed them with eye and foot, over broken and eroded peaks that crumbled into an utterly flat land, a bone dust bowl that quickly caved into desert.

Miranda slipped out her tiny pearl penknife and carved up one of the hundreds of cacti that punctured the land. They drank its clear green liquid and poured it over their heat-aching heads and laughed as the sticky drops held fast to their eyelashes and chins.

Shoeless and stripped to a minimum of clothes, they sifted through the sand to the clicking sounds and guttural calls of the invisible wildlife. The sun began to hiss softly as they came up to an ice-blue desert, and Benjamin tried to tell Miranda about this natural oddity; but before he could speak, she said, "It's not what you think."

"What I think?" he wondered, his head spinning from the bright heat. "What I think?"

He found his feet wet and cold as ice, because the desert he thought was blue was really a sea they'd walked into.

"Water is the best thing to breathe, you know. Our lungs still think we live in the sea," she said, diving under.

The salt on his face was no longer the sweat of his body but the mineral life of this body, this aqueous eternity that Miranda, pulling on his hand, kept walking through, for it

looked so much like the sky that it was natural to confuse the
two. Later, he would marvel at how he had trusted her, how
the thought of drowning never occurred to him as they
descended into a marine world where algae grew as tall as trees
and fishes of all sizes, colors, and dispositions carried on their
commerce. Her face was blue under the sea, but her black hair
obscured it as the underwater waves hurried them through the
scuffled trails of octopi, the swimming lanes of whales, and the
cavernous coral mansions. Later in his life, while crossing the
sea to the Old World, he would wonder how it had grown
there, that huge desert of ocean in the landlocked midriff of a
great country. But now there was nothing on his mind as they
traveled.

The water gradually grew shallow until it drained away,
and they walked through the earth comfortable as worms as
they made passageways through the stone, ash, and mud that
made up its crust. They learned to tell time by the rock layers,
but only in eons, and they wanted to know the exact hour
because that would give them some sense of their own time
and what was left of it. So they trudged up the walls of inner
earth until they came out on top of the land. From where they
stood, they could see the edge of the planet, and the white day-
moon surrounded in cloud seemed gigantic and close enough
to touch. But when they put their hands out, it shrank away
like the backward flight of a frightened squid.

They walked the curve of the earth that day, and the earth
fit them like a glove. He wanted to take her hand, but he
couldn't bring himself to do it. Instead, he cultivated intimacy
by gesture, guiding his arm around her shoulder in an arch that
did not touch her. He thought he heard her suck in her breath
and he figured she must be cold. He was surprised at how shy he
felt. Looking at the girl, who had her face to the cliffs, he had
the suspicion that he wanted something from her. He wanted to

open her up like a tin, cutting through the smooth, clear expression that seemed devoid of need or desire. When, in his efforts to bring her out, he asked her specific questions, the answers seemed to have no connection to his own way of thinking or feeling. Yet in their natural silences and half-phrases they were practically one breath. Bitterly he wished they spoke disparate tongues so that the comprehension of their common language would not deceive them so.

He had to find her out, unhinge her remoteness so that she would not be his danger—his enemy in closure. So the questions of family, of geography, of local history continued, as did her careful answers that told him nothing of what he wanted. What he wanted was that she not be a locked house against him, throwing him out onto the heaps of his exile in a land that went on without end.

"It's time to go back," he proclaimed, aware of the fact that she had without asking begun to lead him to the Hotel.

"As you wish," she replied, hoping that her acquiescence would please him.

Benjamin spit in the dirt in a yellow stream of rage.

"What I wish?" he said, "what I wish?" deriding the words and mimicking her expression.

"What do you wish, Miranda? You tell me."

"I don't wish anything," the girl stammered and walked quickly ahead of him.

He ran after her, yelling until he caught up.

"Everybody wishes for something, every human body."

He had her by the shoulder.

"I don't wish anything," she repeated.

The Hotel was in sight now. She'd be home after the next hill.

"All right, Miranda, then if you don't wish while you're awake like us normal mortals, then all that wishing turns in on itself at night. At night it turns into dreaming. What do you dream, girl?" he pleaded.

It was a question she could not shrug off. Although she could not remember her dreams, she believed the desecrations she woke up to every morning on the attic floor were evidence of their horrific visitations. She knew with regret that she would tell him about them, that she couldn't stop herself from telling him about them. But how could she tell him, in answer to his real question, that he was wrong; that the dreams of the night and the wishes of the soul had nothing in common; that it was the dreams that were destroying her soul, paralyzing her aspirations, making a mockery of her wishes.

"Let go of me!" she screamed, unable to move away from him.

"I'm not doing anything," the young man smiled.

"We should hurry," she said.

The sun was a luminous line lying flat on the horizon, and the portion of daylight it left behind gave the gold and green fields an incandescent light while the sparse shadows of mountains and trees crept in and began to turn the world black.

As they crossed the river and went up the pine path to the Hotel, he kept looking back. The sea, the desert, the timber, the canyon, the valley seemed to occupy a singular space, as if all the geographies of the world had come together at this one point, in one simple claim of land, and on it lived a woman Benjamin felt he could follow like a river. He wanted her vision, he realized, watching her race down the hill in the last light, that special vision of the unseen. How he envied her. She could make herself invisible and so nothing in nature or man was hidden from where or when she chose to look, because it was as if she wasn't there to see it or to stop it. He realized this as he chased her down the final rise before they reached the veranda and the trip they had taken this day would be hidden away from them by the iron gates, the topiary zoo, the formal gardens of the Hotel.

PART TWO: SUMMER

Of Legend and Of Scale

The North of love is hate, which is just a form of love left thirsty; and its southernmost reach is sanctity, wherein the object of love is held in utmost care. Both are spheres of great warmth and devotion: protection from the empty eternal from which one can draw the lines of reason, trembling from dot to dot.

Cartography was not originally meant to define physical space, but to ascertain the whereabouts of otherworldly realms, such as the Garden of Eden, Rivers of Babylon, Heaven and Hell. The purpose of a map was to navigate its owner's way out of the physical world into an immaterial one. When the first explorers from Europe came into the New World, their mandate was to confirm the geography of the liturgical. When they returned home, their journeys were regarded as a disappointment and a disgrace by many because they had discovered only wilderness and ways to make money, when they were sent to locate God and the devil. Thus cynicism, which is the crossroads of desire for the physical and its scorn, was born with the age of discovery and its heralding of a new world.

There is no such thing as a neutral map.

from *The Book of the Cartographer*, Chapter II

THE HOTEL

It was a house, like a city.
A dream and a fortress.
Thin air and substance.
You'd get lost in its variety.
From room to room,
you'd forget who you are.

It was a house (like a city)
Built for the multitudes,
For all their thought, all their feeling.
The expression of the people.
Fantasy willed into fact.
House like a city. For the people.
An American Hotel.

The rooms ranged like prairies.
Faucets running like great rivers,
Flushing into basins,
Copper pipes joining everything,
A bloodstream, really.
So no one ever had to be thirsty,
Never had to go dirty.

The public rooms—God! Variety!
Greek fountains, Egyptian terrace,
Medieval Dining Tapestry Piano Room, Louis
XIV ballroom,
And the New England in the Chapel and the
Rockies in the Saloon,
Grand Prairies of the veranda, Tahiti solarium,
Hallways promising the Great Divide.

House like a City, a metropolis of promise
Where each man, woman and child could feel
themselves Owner
And no such thing like servant, like guest, like
interloper.
No! An American Hotel was home for the people
For whom home was forever on the move.

A house like a city of ages,
Excavated through time and living in all times.
Even the future time,
Even the nonexistent one.
Ready to disappear in a moment.
House like a Palace—for the people—
An American Hotel.

FAMILY TREE

Emmanuel:

Where I was a child, they stole me like a piece of day-old bread, a little tough and used, but soft enough to squeeze more out of, and cheap, cheap as day-old bread. But the mountain was so beautiful. Gold, my dears, gold. And the voices there . . . .

Cora:

Maybe it wasn't that he didn't have a heart; maybe he had too much, and so it became divided until he did not know what side he was on. Love of family, love of country, love of possessions, of beauty, of progress; all in all they sliced him up too thin, until the loves warred against each other and none got enough attention to thrive. . . . until it was as if he loved nothing or no one.

Emmanuel:

I had worshipped beauty the way some men worship power. I believed that if I could capture enough of it, I could transform the planet. I could make people aware that their love of gold is really love for the sun; their love of diamonds really love of the sparkling clear air; their love of money, the love of the fertile, green earth. But time passed and no one remembered that what they thought they loved, they did not really love. And I had to admit that beauty failed.

Cora:

My husband was the kind of man who fell into things, and when there was no more to fall into, he left.

They were a family in which the four corners of globe came together. A father from the South, mother from the North, children to the East and the West.

His name was Emmanuel. He was strong and handsome and he was fierce, but his mouth belonged to the angels. The man hated the South, from where he came. The South was the wrong house for the man, so he moved out of it and took a wife out of it, called Cora, a woman from the North.

He was a believer in the impact of beauty. He was sure that a beautiful Hotel in the middle of wilderness would bring people from everywhere. But as the years passed, and the rooms went unrented, he had to admit that beauty had failed. He began to leave his family alone for long periods to go traveling. To towns clear across the continent, he went to hawk his vacant Hotel and its hypothetical city. He would stand on street corners, at lunch counters, in bars, libraries, and parks, declaring his newfound land and the Hotel of wonders he had built upon it.

He'd search the crowds gathered around him like a bird of prey desperate to feed its brood. He needed but ten men to mark a roadway, twenty to build a municipal hall, fifty to put up a school, two hundred to incorporate. But he was sure there was only one thing that would make his dream of a city a reality. That thing was a railroad to run right by the Hotel. With a railroad would come thousands, maybe millions of people; the steady line of tracks would bring them to him, across the lands and oceans of the world. So he looked for a railroad to come, but the officials of each said they wanted to own their own hotel and asked him to sell them his. And time after time, Emmanuel said "No, I will not give you my Hotel, the work of my life, the fruit of my labor. I will find another railroad to come and build tracks and let me keep what I have made." But no railroad would build upon Emmanuel's land because he would not sell his hotel to them.

North, east, south, west he wandered, while back home, his wife oversaw the construction of the hundreds of rooms. She built as fast as she could with what labor she could get: immigrants, native sons, slaves who'd come up the river to free-dom. All put in a few hours more of servitude for what was supposed to be freedom and turned into debt, the freeman's slavery. It was the gold-mine mountains all over again, Cora thought, as she looked out from her new widow's walk, as yet unpainted, watching for him to come home. She'd think and she'd let the thinking pass; for she loved him, a man who could dream past anything.

Emmanuel, father of cities: This he would be. He felt it in his hard worker's hands, this mission. It was his joy and his demon. He did everything, went everywhere to satisfy its longing. And everywhere he went, its unquenchable thirst grew. So he kept traveling, kept preaching. On his travels he kept collecting: piles of exquisite furnishings, bought or repossessed. Wherever possible, he scavenged and he stole.

"That's the way of the country, any new country," he wrote his wife. "That's how its conquerors procured it, that's how they kept it, and that's how new blood like ours shall make it grow."

Emmanuel continued the tradition of stealing, which was to him a form of patriotism. "Manifest Destiny," he declared. He did it all in the name of the Hotel and the city he would build upon it for the multitudes coming West, for the country that was inventing itself out of the dreams of dreamers like himself.

THE GRANDMOTHER AND THE
INVASION OF THE JUANITAS

*Truly, she was forgetting some things and remembering clear as day
others. It all had to do with her sense of smell. Her life was divided as
if by an equatorial zone between the time in the South, when she could
still smell every grain of the continent, and her latter life, after she had
crossed North and her olfactory senses deserted her. After a while, she
could only remember clearly the things she could remember smelling.
This was how Rose's grandmother came to live as a ghost long after her
death. In the South-time, the time of smelling.*

She lived alone with her toothless father in Talampaya, a
miraculously flat slab of land in the middle of the world's
highest mountains. Some people said that it was the place
where God dragged his fingernail. But the Indians knew it
was holy.

It was in the time of the invasion of the juanita bugs that
the woman who would one day be Rose's grandmother made
her crucial decision. She was at her wooden cookpot when a
swarm of them, attracted by the smell, infiltrated the hut. In
love with her sweat, which had a taste both sweet and bitter,
they settled on her arm and peed there with fervor. The waste
of a thousand crusty-shelled insects burned like acid into her
skin before she could shake them off into the boiling pot, con-
signing them to a hellish death but ruining her dinner.

"Owww," she moaned and raced outside to the well to pour
water over the welts that were already rising up all over her
stricken limb. Holding the arm up to the sun to dry, she saw that
the juanita piss had burned the word Emmanuel into her skin.
A thousand more juanitas were lazily buzzing in the nearby tree,
as if awaiting her response. She figured it was a sign. She said
good-bye to her father, packed her very few things, and for the
first time in her life left the village to search for her long-lost son.

She came down from the mountain on foot. It was dry-hot and the sky was red with clay kicked up by the storms. She could see lightning in the distance. She turned back just once to look at the cloud-ringed mountains where generations of her family had lived and died, where the mixture of her blood was first engendered, generations back, between the Indians and the conquering whites.

She whistled for her son as she headed down the red mountains. The boy she had not seen since he disappeared many years ago at the age of thirteen, the day she had taken a rope to him for teasing the hens. The next thing she knew, he was gone. Why not? He was handsome and pigheaded and strong—too much of all three to stay and rot in that hole of a village. Then there were the stories that he didn't run away at all but was kidnapped and enslaved in the mines. Yet it never had occurred to her to look for him. Not until the juanitas came.

She was halfway down the mountain now; it had taken five, maybe six days. She kept track by counting the number of meals she had missed: fifteen, was it, or eighteen? She couldn't remember. The sky was closing down for the day and a few stars competed with the sun for the brightest light. Vultures were circling, casting about for some dinner. It was getting cold. She raised the arch of her hands into a house of prayer. Her voice found her thoughts and dragged them up: "Please give me back my son."

The next day, when she awoke, the sun was already up. The light was cold but the heat was unremitting. She remembered, as she finished the last of her water, that she had dreamed of him, for the first time since his disappearance.

CORA AND EMMANUEL: THE BEGINNING

She came from the North. Her father, that is the one who adopted her, owned a great museum of curiosities there. A place full of dried mermaid tails, shrunken human heads, asteroid chunks. He spent years teaching her how to evaluate the authenticity of marvels and how to make related discoveries. When she was eighteen, he sent her away on a long sea voyage. To collect for him.

She was a lady who had come six thousand miles in search of wonders for her father's museum. He was the sweep boy in an antiquities shop in the Capital. She was beautiful then, and Emmanuel would always remember the moment he opened the door.

He stood speechless at the sight of her. Well-practiced in servility, he kept his head of dark curls down in her presence. Which is how he came to stare at her exquisite feet. They were wrapped in smooth white kid, with abalone buttons up past her ankles, which were as delicate as the bones of a whitefish. He fell in love with her the moment he saw her feet.

Her father had forced her into this vagabond life; at first with him, later alone. By the time Cora had reached the door of this industrious young sweeper, she had traveled hundreds of thousands of miles in search of freaks and curiosities.

He was looking at the floor. She was looking at the floor. They found each other looking at her well-traveled feet.

She was wearing a long string of cheap garnets she'd bought from a hawker on the street. She had been crying all day and her tears made the rock crystals sparkle. She was in an agony of missing—her father, her home, everything familiar. Her eyes were on the floor because they were so full of tears that she feared if she looked up, they would break apart and crumble. She hated him, her father, for making her go away over and over again like an unlearned lesson. And she was always seasick, always frail, and the sailors jeered at her, and sometimes they assailed her for traveling so, such a young pretty girl, all alone. Whenever she could, when it was at all safe—which meant on dry land, where there was space to run away if discovered—she wept bitterly.

He fell in love with the waterfall of tears hitting the ground before her feet while his broom swept them up automatically. *Jewels*, he thought, as he gathered them up.

She puts her hands out to study her surroundings. So many tears she can't see. With her hands she can feel where she is and, she thinks, maybe by feeling where I am I can get back to where I want to be; *I want to be home,* she weeps. But his hands have swept around her now and they are lying on the floor in a pile of dirt and tears.

She forgot about her home, her father. There was no returning. The seas wouldn't carry her back there now, and neither could her memory nor her mission. Hot with skin and dim with pleasure, she perceived in the dust flung around her head a route through the wilderness. Feet would do it and the hooves of horses, the wheels of a wagon; immovable conviction. There would be no more floating on the surface while the true needs drowned. She would walk on her own now and home would be what they whispered as they fucked each other clean.

"Love," she heard him say in the silent new language that was the breath of their bodies. "I will never push you out, never push you away from me. You are my home. My country."

She could see a hearth in her head; fabulous flames in his black hair, acrackle in his black eyes, a tumult and rage, the two of them tearing at each other. Two young wolves curled into each other.

"What is your name?" she pleaded as they lay on the old broken urns they had overturned as they thrashed on the floor. "What is your name?" she begged as their flesh bled afresh from the cuts of the shattered pots.

"Tell me your name," she said, grabbing at his hair.

But there was no answer. He just burrowed deeper, a tick under her skin, until she stopped questioning him and was only screaming. With no words in her mouth, no words at all in her mouth.

She had never heard herself scream before; it was a frightening sound, but mesmerizing. It was the way she felt on seasick days, staring out on the too-bright water. Everywhere she turned with no land in sight, her stomach sick, her head thick and dizzy.

She feels him come in her. Warmth and water. She is floating on her own insides, rocking in their fluids, surrounded like an island by the blood of their cuts and bites and scratches.

The shock of their melding broke the forward motion of time, stopped it so that their bodies lost their boundaries and their separateness suddenly dissolved like salt in the sea. He tied a place in her body, a beautiful snake he twisted in the womb of her body. She thinks his name is home.

Much later, she discovered herself alone on the floor, looking up. The shop was cavernously long and dark. Smokey lanterns swung from the high tin ceiling, leaving the impression of twilight on the dirt floor, which was lined along the sides with ancient carved stone dolmens. They seemed to be moving, up and down, like debris on the sea; and she wouldn't believe it, later, when he pointed to show her that it was she who was writhing back and forth on the floor, and not those rock effigies.

He was sitting at a rough little table, drinking some foul-smelling tea through a metal straw from a silver gourd. He looked over at her and said casually that his master was gone for several weeks, on a buying trip, and that made it a good time to leave.

He took her by the hand and pulled her to her feet. He said, "We are leaving."

"But wait," she said indignantly, "I'm not going anywhere until I get what I came for. I'm here to buy some curiosities."

"Eldorado," he said.

"What?"

"Eldorado," he repeated, his tongue making the word echo in her mouth. "We'll steal what we can from here, but that's where we are going. You and me."

They gathered up what they could in their arms and hurried out into the night. He did not bother to lock the door behind him.

HOW THE GRANDMOTHER
FOUND HER WAY NORTH

No one could ever understand how an Indian got such a color hair. But all the women of that mountain had hair like hers. It just happened to them living in the midst of the tamale sun and those ferrous clay buttes—hair the color of calf's blood and oven-fired pottery. It was said that the mountain gods dyed the women's hair red to match the color of the mountain and to brand them always as belonging to the mountain no matter where on earth they went. The older they got, the redder the hair, the more beautiful they became. And so the elderly ones were considered far more desirable than the young. But in the land below the mountains, people said her hair was really her blood, that she was the devil's own daughter with the circulatory system on the outside so you could always watch her evil vital signs. She tried to change it, but it was in the dust, in the air of the mountains where she was born, this color. And once it got in the hair, no pails of water nor grains of soap could ever wash it out.

She walked until her feet were a bed of sores, her mouth as dry as a cave. The old trail was deserted; she met no one on her way but black scavenger birds that traced circles in the air not far from her head. She was thankful for them; otherwise she would have believed the rocks themselves were speaking, so hungry was she for company, especially since the water had run out.

She dreamed of him again that night.

He is so tall he has to double over to address her. "Mama," he says, "you've grown so thin." He has a fat moustache, the ends of which curl up like a pair of dueling pistols. His eyes are the only thing in his beat-up face that seem to have any peace, as if they had no idea of their body's hardships. She does not know him.

When she awoke she was surprised her son was not there, so real was the dream. Instead she saw the lights of a city, and she followed them.

Eyes, full of hunger, grow as luminous as precious stones. This is what attracted the man to her as she held out her hand in the city, a new beggar by the steps of the church. He put a few coins in her palm and pressed it deeply. He came again and again over the next week. He said, "I want you for my wife." She did not understand. The next time he brought an interpreter. "Marry me," he said. She thought she understood. He loves the idea, this European, of having this Indian with her one long braid to decorate his salon. He regarded her as connoisseur does an antiquity just dug out of the dirt, as one who can see beyond to the object's restoration to glory.

He was a diplomat who, having made some excellent mercantile treaties (of which he retained a substantial share), was returning to a more civilized appointment in his native land, thank God. He told her, again through the interpreter (for even lies need translation), that he would make her a lady and they would live in the city where he had seen her son once on a festival day. She thought he was taking her to her son. She was hungry to believe; she said yes. He ordered her cleaned up and put in the hold.

"Where am I?"

She didn't know what a boat was.

"Is my son here . . . Is this the insides of a city?"

She couldn't understand the size of water.

"Is this what it means the word wife?"

She suffered terrible seasickness, and when the seas were calm the man raped her.

"Is this what it means the word marry?"

He thought her eyes more precious the more frightened and starved they became, so to enhance her natural beauty, he beat her and withheld food from her.

After a while she was thankful to be seasick, for when she was well the man hurt her. When she was sick, he stayed away; his stomach grew queasy at her smell of vomit. When she looked out the cracks in the hold, all she could see was water, this

mountain woman who had only known little streams and well
water, liquid that soothed and quenched and cleaned. Now there
was a world of water, bitter to the tongue, stinging to the eye,
noxious to the stomach; it rocked and roared, turning distance,
time, the seasons upside down. How could she find her way, she
wondered, in all this sameness of water? It consumed her understanding; made her a fool who remembered nothing, not even
the son she had gone in search of. The proportion of things had
so rearranged themselves that she could believe in nothing anymore, least of all her eyes or memory. Who in her village would
ever believe water could come to this?

When they landed, the man took her into his home. She
lived in an unheated closet in back of the kitchen.

"How do you like being my wife?" he would ask her when
he came to sleep on her. "How do you like it?" he laughed.

He said she had to earn her keep, pay for the privilege of
their relationship and the cost of the trip. She was put to doing
housework for his family—his real wife and the six young children. She started at sunup with the cooking and she went to
bed at midnight after cleaning up their frequent parties. She
had no identity card, no passport, no money; she could neither
read nor write this language she landed in.

The first words she learned were barking sounds: *scrub,
sweep, give, turn over, bend over, this way, do it again.*

She grew nearsighted from her labors; after a while there
were only vague mountains everywhere she looked, but they were
made of people, mountains that rocked like tidal waves, that
made her sick, unable to breathe except when she was crying.

One night, she dreamed of her son again, remembered she
had a son. That he was here. That he did not know she was his
mother. That he harmed her as only someone who does not
believe another individual is his mother could.

She was better as soon as she understood money. She
learned to steal it without getting caught, a few coins forgotten in the lady's dirty pockets or slid onto the floor during a

vigorous session with the master. When, in his ardor, he asked her what she wanted, she said she wanted all her rotting teeth replaced with gold ones. An investment, she suggested, which he paid for as one cares for the welfare of a good horse or cow, until in her excitement she had exchanged even her good teeth for false gold ones.

She learned from his children that she came from a place they called the Americas: That was her savage home, and wasn't she lucky not to be there anymore. She learned to her horror that the only way to get back there involved water and a boat.

One day when she was supposed to be buying groceries, she sneaked off to the docks. She booked passage with all of her stolen savings and a few of her new gold teeth. To find her son, she was going home. To America. How could she know that there were two—the South and the North one? She took a ship to the North when she meant to go to the South. But how far could the distance between them be, she reasoned, these two Americas with the same last name, aligned as they were by the same violent sea?

EMMANUEL IN THE MINE

*What does he want with her, North-girl, sea-girl? What does he want
with her tight mouth, her yellow hair, her string of a body? He doesn't
know what he wants, he only knows that between their lips there's a
tunnel of dreams, and these are the dreams through which to breathe a
new land to life.*

When he saw it, sunken like a jewel in the pit of the mountain,
he dropped her hand and began to weep.

"Give me your money," he demanded of Cora. "Give me
what you've got lined in your cape, tucked in your breast, hidden
in your shoe."

He was prying off her clothes, piece by piece. She watched
them slide down the miles they'd climbed.

"Why not," she said inside herself. "Why not?"

She withdrew a pouch from the rim of her sun hat and
threw it at him like a bone.

"Here," she yelled, looking at the mountain, "now go buy
the goddamn thing."

Her gold in his hand, he ran up ahead, as if incline and
altitude had no effect. She trailed after in her long underskirt,
heels digging into the crumbling rock. She was waving at him,
but he wasn't looking. He was buying his mountain, taking
over the derelict mine that would make him a laughingstock
for miles around.

"My money, his money," worried the girl, trying lucklessly
to scrape the mud from her boots. She thought of her distant
father and the bag of gold he had given her to acquire artifacts,
and here she was, using it up to buy a hole? But his body
moved in her womb; she could feel him coiled up inside her all
day long as they climbed the summit. "So why not," she said,
"why not?"

He knew things about the mine that others did not. He knew that beneath the ashes of those who had died of work lay a mother lode. No one but he dared explore down there; the owners disdained its stink and the workers feared encountering the ghosts of their predecessors. But Emmanuel had no choice. They sent him down alone once, as a punishment, to dispose of a dead body. He was just a boy; they never told him what wrong he had done. He had no choice. He dragged, hefted, lugged the corpse they gave him, but he slipped on a stone and fell beneath the weight into the pit with the dead man. Drowning in the mud of decomposed bodies, he drew his breath through a hollow femur bone he found as he fell. He kept sinking, down, down through this never-ending pile of bodies murdered by labor and lain one atop the other in a heap in a hole in the mountain.

Finally, he hit hard rock again and a narrow isthmus of air. He followed it out of the mouth of suffocation; it led him into another cave. He stood up like a man again, as there was now space to stand. The rocks around him were shining, as if they stood in broad daylight instead of hundreds of feet underground. He put his face to them and could see his reflection, jaundiced and crusty in the distortion. His lips that had been sucking through the marrowless bones of the dead now kissed the bright, shining surface of rock. He knew what he tasted in the metallic cold could be only one thing and one thing only. He knew it was gold.

He was gone so long they already thought him dead, so it was easy to escape. By the time he came up in their camp, they were all sleeping, slaves and overseers alike. The acid of the corpses had eaten off his chains, and for the first time since he had been brought here, he moved freely. He felt his feet like skates on the uneven, solid earth. He descended from the mines to the city.

Now, some ten years later, there were two small figures standing on the summit of a tired, eroded mountain: the one with a heap of flapping green bills, the other with his stiff white documents. They ceremoniously traded their piles, shook hands, and one of them leaped in the air with joy while the other one trudged back down, absorbed in counting his easy money. What of the woman standing a bit off to the side, the woman with her now-impoverished pockets and her once-careful wits. Why had she done this, she wondered? What on earth for?

WORKING THE MINE

Underneath the rocks and boulders, between them and atop the subter-
ranean mountain range that sank a hundred million years ago; in this
space of the all-beneath and the mountaintop below, between the
unburied bodies of his people and the veins of gold, he felt safe.

Day after day, he worked the mine with the vitality of a man who
is no longer a slave, a man who proudly owns the portion of land
upon which he labors, no matter how many laugh at him.

It took him more than a year to get rid of all the bodies;
generations of murdered flesh that had been preserved in the
cavern's inexhaustible mud. He alone did this work, with Cora
sometimes helping. A year and more of digging and lugging,
nothing else morning to night but the shovel, the pick, the
earth, and its corpses heaved up into the light of day. Finally
the bodies were cleared and their remains reburied in reverence
to those who had expired in the bondage of the mines. Now he
made Cora stay outside. "The work to come is hard, too hard
down there for you," he said. But really, he couldn't bear to
share the sight of the gold he remembered there— it must be
his vision alone. He sent up the ore in sealed boxes she must
never open. There was so much gold here; probably more than
the whole world, north, south, east, west, had ever mined.
Sometimes it seemed to him that the dead bodies of the slaves
had been drawn there, to the pit, century after century, to hide
and protect the mother lode. But Emmanuel had found it.

For nights and days, he stayed underground. Digging. He
neither slept nor ate, drank only water from the subterranean
stream to keep himself alive and no more, as he hacked away at
the shining yellow earth. He finally fell asleep in his digging. In
a tiny crawl space of air he was hard at work dreaming, held
afloat in his narrow sky. He dreamed hoards of people from
everywhere on earth converging upon him, in some unfamiliar

country. He was stretched across the land like a tightrope while the people walked over him, built cabins and farms on top of him, planted him in alfalfa, wheat, grass seed. He had never known such happiness in his life.

Other times, he dreamed he was holding a torch in the middle of an enormous city. But it was not like the city he had just come from, full of dirt and greed. This city was a song of delight on everyone's lips. Everyone who came there became a brilliant light in the sky of the world until people could see this city for thousands of miles around and were drawn to it, guided to it by these buoyant human flames.

Once he found himself in a dream so vivid that he fancied it couldn't be a dream at all. Before him, he saw the entrance to the very mine shaft he was working, but it was so brightly illuminated that it looked as if a glittering palace stood in its depths. He walked toward it slowly, a little fearfully, because he knew, in general, that places that looked like this were not palaces at all but enchanted morasses swarming with evil. But the sparkle mesmerized him, so he kept on walking until he came to a huge front door, a door as wide as twenty men and near as tall as fifty. A door of solid blinding gold.

Emmanuel knocked the golden knocker—once, twice, thrice—but no one answered. He tried the door; it pushed open with ease as if it had been waiting for him. In the entryway stood an opal staircase; its translucent blue seemed to be on fire underneath, and when Emmanuel, who in his curiosity had to see what was inside this place, walked these stairs, his feet were burning. Just when he felt he could stand it no more, he reached the top, and when he looked down to see the damage to his body, there was not a mark upon on it, neither burn, blister, nor scar.

At the top of the burning stairs he saw two long corridors, one leading left, one right. Each hallway was lined with hundreds of rooms to which all the doors were slightly opened. As Emmanuel went down the hallways, he peeked inside the rooms, and each was more beautiful than the one that came before it. Each was authentically furnished in the style of a different period of history: ancient Greece, Rome, the Ottoman Empire, French Regency, Imperial Russia. He had only seen such wonders in picture books. Getting from room to room was a challenge, because the hallway that connected them kept changing. Emmanuel would turn around and he was no longer crossing an Oriental rug but a rugged mountain, no longer passing a lighted lamp but forging through the heart of a volcano, no longer walking a slippery parquet floor but traversing a clear-as-glass-stream. He wandered from room to room wanting to stop and rest, but he could not stop, could not rest until he finally woke up from exhaustion.

He started to tire of digging. He was only content when he was dreaming the magnificent palace. He barely ever came up from the mines now. One day as he was walking through the spectacle of rooms, bathing in one, dancing in another, feasting in a third, he suddenly approached a room that was not splendid at all, but dark and gloomy. He tried to pass it by, but found he couldn't. Its walls were covered with a yellowish fungus, lit kerosene blue by a miner's lamp, from which faces peered out, indistinguishable in the grime. There he stood staring, nauseated by memory, the waste of his childhood chained underground. He stared at the room for days, until it seemed to him for the first time in his life that he belonged somewhere, that the whole glorious palace, now that it contained this room, really belonged to him.

How he wanted to share this astonishing feeling: that a man like him, once a poor slave, an illiterate, a no one, that this man could possess such a place and all that lay therein. He wanted to show those who came after him that they, too, as they passed from room to room, could enter their own room, the room that could belong to no other person in the world, the dirty, shaming place that would give them ownership over the entire magnificent edifice.

When he awoke, he would feel such emptiness, so much loss, that nothing, not even the riches of his mine, could comfort him. Then, in desperation, he would hunt the miles and miles of connected caves for this palace that seemed so real it could not be a dream. But it only appeared when he was sleeping.

One day it occurred to him that if he could not find this palace in life then he must build it; that it would be both a home for him and a beacon for men like him. There was no question in his mind that he would create this place, a refuge to the transient ones coming up out of the mud: a Hotel, a palace for the people, for whom home is forever on the move. He thought no more of gold, but of what it could build him.

Cora, at the top of the mountain, was sleeping and dreaming, too. She dreamed herself in a golden cave next to a dirt-blackened miner who was sleeping and dreaming of a palace he would build. There he was, her husband, and the riches he was hiding in the mines. She wasn't angry that he kept them from her. She understood distrust, but she could never stand waste, and all this hiding and dreaming was wasting time. She climbed down into the mines, woke him roughly, and together they tore up the golden walls that would buy them out of this wilderness.

FOLLOWING THEIR DREAMS

Soon they believed they had enough gold to build the Hotel of their dreams. But where it should be, they did not know. They decided to keep dreaming and follow what they saw there like a map. They took turns; when one was awake, the other slept arduously. In sleep, the dreamer would describe what appeared and the waking one would strive to find it. The dreamer would mumble things like "go north two miles, pick up the path by the stream, take a quick left by yew tree, and then right to the fork by the feeding deer." From day to day, minute to minute, they did not know where they were going next, as they awaited the directives of sleep.

They ignored all route signs unless the signs agreed with what they had dreamed. If a famine was going on and the dream said go through there, they went into the land of the famine. If a war was taking place in the region the dream demanded, they went through the war zone, because any other kind of following—of roads or waterways, of good sense or fear—would be lying, they reasoned, and instead of escaping bad fortune, they would never get anywhere. The few times they tried the sensible way of traveling—the way of compasses, maps, and road signs—they found themselves all the way back where they started in the mines, no matter how far or how long they had traveled.

It seemed they traveled for years, but perhaps it was only months. It was difficult to say because it was the quality of dreamtime that led them. The only sure thing was that they kept dreaming and moving. The land was hot, the land was cold, parched, soaked, flat; was mountainous, was by the water, by the desert; was crowded, was without a soul. As they traveled, they learned each language of the people until they knew all the languages of all the land's people. They both fell in love with the land and its peoples and wanted to stay with them, but still their home was nowhere, still their dream pushed them on.

As they strived to match the places they saw in sleep with the miles they were covering, Cora grew heavier and heavier, but the child remained inside. One night they reached a valley. Looking up at the constellations, it was as if they were floating in a giant's enormous wine cup, with only its mountainous brim protecting them from drifting away into the night sky. They cooked a meal over the fire, some flour-wrapped beans they had brought from the south and sweet potatoes they dug from the ground they were camped on. As Emmanuel slept, Cora trudged down to the water, a small stirred-up creek in the deepest part of the valley. Happy, she looked back on the figure of her husband. She knew that he was dreaming the next leg of their journey. Buoyed by her weight, she stepped into the cool black water. Up to her breasts in water where, in a silent stretched moment, she gave birth to the girl inside. Out of her womb of water and into the creek, the howling child of water, Miranda, was born. Crawling back onto the land, Cora and her babe fell fast asleep. Hours later, still night, the new mother woke up feeling sick, as if the birth had provided no relief to her swollen body. Slowly, she got up off the bank and placed the newborn infant asleep in her sleeping father's arms.

Slow and stiff, she stumbled toward the water, but she could not walk that far. Suddenly the water was miles away and the sickened woman was alone, crawling in a desert. Then she heard a gruff voice say: "Come inside my rock cave where you shall be cool and safe."

The woman crept into the red cave that was within hand's reach. She clung to the sharp cold rocks and was held in turn by the soothing spiral voice with the rough cracked skin that had summoned her there. Her contractions grew until she could not breathe and the world turned dark and distant. Suddenly, she felt such relief that she exploded into a singing she could not stop. As she sang, she saw by her feet a mound of soft, glowing volcano rock that seemed to be twitching, as if possessed, and singing too, a kind of deep sweet wailing. Then the woman saw that it was not a rock; that here in this cave, she had heaved up from the bottom of her being another living child. The voice in the cave said: "This is your other daughter, the one born out of the bowels of the earth."

Cora laid this child next to her twin. She named her Rose, because she had been born at the point where the sun rises up out of the night. When Emmanuel awoke, he saw neither his wife nor his two new-as-day children. He only saw that the spot he rested on was the very place in his dream where he was to build his Hotel and bring forth his city. That was the family's true beginning.

A PALACE FOR THE PEOPLE

It had started from love to begin with. The man loved the land; the ways in which it rose and set like a lunar field, the ways in which it bore fruit and begged for harvest. It was out of this love that he wanted to bring people to live on the land; to tend it, nurture it, reap its fecundity, recount its legends, and in doing all this, to announce its existence to the world outside its boundaries. Emmanuel worried about the people he hoped to bring. He knew that upon first seeing this new world, they would have no past correlatives to which to compare it and thus, it would seem to them without beauty or abundance or comfort because all those qualities needed an aspect of the familiar to strike home. So he devised a plan to encourage people to stay until the strange became the familiar. He would create for them a travelers' haven, here in the wilderness, until they too took to the land and desired to stay on it, dedicate their lives to it, make it their home. He wanted to spoil them, so they might believe that the land was spoiling them, with all its richness and plenty, rather than inflicting torment with its heat and frigidity, its famine and drought. So husband and wife had gone to their labors.

He began to be absent for long periods at a time, collecting the marvels that would furnish the people's Hotel. He traveled far and wide while Cora stayed home to oversee the construction. Each time he returned, he brought more treasures. They acquired hoards of Greek and Roman statues, Renaissance paintings, Spanish thrones, piles of porcelains, a library full of books, platinum serving pieces, gold-leafed dishes, carnelian-and-jade encrusted sideboards, a ship's worth of nautical instruments. There was a clock in which the flight of a devil told the time, his horn on the hour, his tail on the minute; there was a chandelier with a jester's head in the middle with colored lights that blinked off and on like chuckling; there were series after series of tapestries in which Hannibal crossed the Alps with his

mystified elephants, in which Columbus discovered the jungles
of the New World, in which unicorns drank the draught of death
from the cups of beautiful maidens. Through all of them, in the
background, were the fabulously wrought supernumeraries: ele-
gantly aloof hunting dogs, hooded falcons, shy monkeys, farmers
crushing wine grapes in tall oaken buckets, guildsmen hammer-
ing out doorknobs in the shapes of ladies' hands.

Cora loved the native arts of her husband's country, the cere-
monial cups, the clay idols, the geometric cloth weaves, in which
value was based equally on aesthetics and utility. But in his new
domain, Emmanuel banned all objects from his former home, for
no matter how beautiful they were, to him they could not be
beautiful. While Cora yearned after objects that were useful as well
as pleasing, Emmanuel wanted no part of what was practical, or
folksy, or even slightly primitive; such things reminded him of his
poverty in the South and the abuse in the mines that blighted his
boyhood. He despised practical things, he said, because they were
civilization's chief excuse for condoning slavery. It was a riotous
melting pot of Western art that he was after, a chaos of classical
beauty. So he hung the Gobelin tapestries in places where they
would create no warmth, he nailed the Wedgwood dinner plates
to the walls so they could never be eaten from, the Regency sofas
and chairs he stuffed upside down and sideways in corners and
crevices so it was impossible to sit on them.

The Hotel rose up like a miracle from the land, a gigantic
genie twirled from the dust. Five hundred rooms; after that
they lost count as they built on and on, without thought of
order or respite. Room swallowed room like a voracious food
chain; each one grander than the next.

The day he left for good, he ran from room to room until
there was no room left. He cried: "My God, I have been a
slave, a miner, a builder, a thief, and none of it is enough!" He
stood in the doorway of the entrance for a moment, looking
out, waiting just one more time. And still no one came. His
wife did not follow him.

GETTING TO THE WRONG NEW WORLD

She wondered how to get back home. She was so turned around, having been accustomed to the America of the South, that being here in the North, she kept turning, as if by instinct, in the wrong direction. The people she stopped in the road to ask which way to go acted as if she were crazy. When she begged them to tell her where America was, they'd throw things at her head and yell.

It was true that after so many months without a bath and no money to buy another set of clothes, she looked and smelled like dirt; one of those gypsy types who would just as soon steal your child or rob you blind. To be on the safe side, the people of the North chased her away. They chased her to the place they chased everything they didn't like, couldn't trust, didn't know what to think of but might need or want someday; they pushed her West.

She wandered year after year like a refugee, with no papers, no money, her house upon her back. One by one she yanked them out, her precious gold teeth, traded them for food and lodging, in search of her son, trying to return to the South, where she believed he must be. But something kept drawing her west, sucking her in like the eye of a twister to the middle of the North until in the middle of winter, starving and sick, she arrived at the door of an enormous house. And she knew, the moment she saw it, that it was his house. In her fever, the façade had his face, the widow's walk his thatch of coalish curls, the long sad front windows his hang-dog eyes, the veranda and its awnings his thick moustachioed lips. She knocked on the door and a young, pale woman answered. "Yes?" she said. "Can I help you?" and she knows this must be his wife, the woman that lured him North.

She looks as cold as the North, thought Emmanuel's mother, *as sharp and as brittle.*

Two small girls clung to Cora's knees, peeking out and hiding.

"May I sleep on your grass?" asked the older woman weakly. "I have my own tent," she said, and pointed to her ragged shawl.

"Yes," said one of the little girls before her mother could speak, "yes, be our guest."

What a night it was for Emmanuel's mother, the last night of her life. The sleet broke through the patchwork of her tent and she found herself lying in a bed of diamonds freezing to death. Then the snow came down in thick, twisted strands. *Like a rope to heaven*, marveled the woman inside her holey tent. And as the crystals fell and buried her, she offered no resistance. She realized then that she had always wanted this to happen; she wanted to be a ghost, for in her life she had always been treated like one, but without a ghost's power to appear or disappear at will. No, her appearance had always been in the power of her father, her husband, her son, the man who had kidnapped and raped her. But a ghost can choose its moments of visibility and its range of vision; past, present, future are all simultaneously available to the black-hole eyes of a true ghost. She realized that she hadn't come all this way to find her son at all, but to become a ghost—a creature like herself, but with power.

Happily, she watched her life slip under the fragile white; the dissolution of her olive skin, her fire-pit hair into the invisible air. Here she would stay, on this land, a specter between living and dead, watching out for his girls, watching for him to return from his wandering. At dawn, she was still breathing, but her hearing and vision had begun to fail. Vaguely she sensed the coyotes calling and the ravens who came to clean up after their feasts. The dirt bats were flying to their caves for sleep, the candles were just being lit in the windows of town, while the Hotel slept on and on, like the court of Sleeping Beauty enthralled to the witch. The mother of Emmanuel faded into the blizzard, evaporated into nothing, awhirl in the storm that was white as a ghost.

ROSE GOES TO THE TRAPPER

"It's amazing," thinks the man as he handles the dead animal, searching for its seams, "that I can feel anything anymore, considering how hard my hands have become." Yet he does; he feels the cool softness of its fur, the slippery heat of its blood. He thanks God he still has some feeling, for without it, he would not know where on earth to cut.

On the day she came down from the tree in the river, the day after her fifteenth birthday, Rose entered the Hotel, climbing up the barren rose trellis to her bedroom window. The house was extremely still, a corpse in the dawn of the day. Investigating the emptiness, she found her sister's room deserted and her mother and Emerald, head to head, asleep and snoring across the great desk in the counting room. She wasn't tired herself, although she had not slept. In her bedroom, by her pillow, she discovered some of her old stuffed toys, a chewed-up teddy bear and a horsehair leopard. She wondered how they had gotten there (she had burned them ages ago) and hurled them across the room. She wandered back outside; the air was warm, but the remains of the night's frost sugared the grass and conifers. She stared across at Trapper's shed.

Trapper's shack was a fungal green, with a rotting-wood, glass-paned door and a heavy rusted padlock. Rose never could figure out how he could lock it from the outside and be on the inside at the same time, as was often the case. He had taught her not to believe in barriers, so she became expert at digging her way into a place or twisting and climbing through some vulnerable window. He taught her how to use the most basic tools—paint scrapers, saws, jackknives, screwdrivers, wedges of paper—to make her forced entries. He taught her that he loved her and that the passing on of knowledge was an expression of that love because, in Trapper's words, the highest aim of love is the beloved's survival. She believed what he explained to her, because in her life, he was the only one who ever explained anything to her. And so, when she came down off the tree that grew in the river, she had to see him.

She didn't want to make any noise and wake her mother, so she didn't knock on his door. She took a bobby pin from one of her braids, ran around to a small side window, jimmied it open, and climbed in. She lowered herself into the tiny hide-drying room, which appeared to be empty but for a few faded skins and the head of a longhorn cow left to cure too long. From where she stood, she could see into the two rooms of the shed that Trapper had made into his home and taxidermy workshop.

Rose loved taxidermy; it was what she had wanted to do with her life for as long as she could remember. She remembered the first animal they ever did together. How powerful she felt and how deeply he had approved of her. He admired her fine stitches and clapped her on the back, saying that one day she'd be a great taxidermist too. *She, Rose.*

When no one called her to dinner, he always took her in. He fed her bear meat, onion, newly dug potatoes. And he gave her bitter coffee, in tin cups, full of grounds. She had never had coffee at home, never been allowed. She would hold the cup up close to her face, anointing one cheek then the other with its heat, drifting in its steam, her two small hands wrapped around its body.

He told her stories, most of them about the wilderness, where it was common practice for men to turn into beasts to obtain some prohibited thing, and then, after gaining it, to be unable to turn human again. The tales usually involved a long journey and several harrowing tests, and sometimes the men would die, or they would have to spend the rest of their lives as centaurs or gilded monkeys, staring out at the prizes they had captured but had absolutely no use for in their present condition. The stories—and they went on and on past nightfall— were deeply ingrained in the girl; they reminded her of when she was little. Back then, Trapper would hold her for hours on end, while she pretended he was family and sometimes, when she was loneliest, that he was love. The two fantasies grew sharp and intermingled until they penetrated her blood and he truly became a part of her. She began to dream of him frequently.

Trapper encouraged these dreams, nourished them in the girl, night after night as she stood in the doorway of the Hotel, her eyes red and tense, waiting for him to come and kiss her good night. But sometimes, when she acted too eager, too familiar with him, he would withdraw from her, because he never wanted her too secure in their love. He wanted the pliancy that comes from a nurtured insecurity, but he never succeeded in making her easy to handle. She had an innate self-confidence that put her out of reach of most manipulations. The only way he found to possess her was by discovering that she couldn't bear to watch wild animals die brutally, which is the way of nature, by predator or starvation. With this knowledge, Trapper drew her into submission, where want of love or family never could.

Once, when she was very young, he had found her wailing in the meadow over the body of a freshly shot fawn. He took her in, under his jacket, and told her how animals could live forever if you killed and stuffed them right. This was why he became a trapper, he said. After doing the job for a while, he realized he couldn't save every last animal and that's when he got into the habit of killing some to sell their hides.

"After you been at it a while," he told her, "you see that some of them don't deserve to be stuffed."

She asked him why, if the animals he stuffed were really alive, they didn't move or even breathe.

"Animals, when they're living," he told her, "move because if they don't, they'll end up as some other animal's dinner. But when we stuff them, they don't have to worry their heads about predators because they have forever-life fluid running in their veins. And I put it there. I'm the only one who knows how to put it there. Maybe someday, Rose, I'll teach you."

He pointed proudly to all the specimens perched on the granite mantel and the ones scattered and falling over on his bedroom bureau amid his traps and guns, and the ones hovering on the walls, casting their shadows where the sun should have come. To Rose, these animals looked glorious, heroic in their frozen animation. There was a haggard owl emerging from a swoop, a mother brown bear with her head lowered and claws out, a beaver chewing timber, a bobcat poised to lunge. They did not seem at all scared or threatened, the way the live ones she'd seen in the forest or on the river were. So she continued to believe in this conviction of Trapper's, even when the other stories he told her—stories of sky fires that belched devils, and cows whose manure made a fool man wise—even when she outgrew these tales, she believed in the story of taxidermy and she wanted its secrets for herself.

THE LESSON

It was his knowledge and expertise that the man held over her like a weight and a temptation. She remembered the first time he taught her. He had just come down off the mountain—she had been about nine—he had a few pelts slung across his shoulders. In his arms he gently carried a bear cub.

"Hold this," he said. "I'm going in to see your ma. I hear she's doing poorly."

He laid the cub inside the cradle she made of her arms. It was very soft, very warm. Delighted, she kissed the space between its eyes and behind its ears. That was when she saw the blood. A hole the size of an apple seed ran straight through the neck, barely big enough for the blood to drip out. But soon her hands were soaking.

Trapper looked back. "That's what you call a clean kill," he laughed. "If you don't have a clean kill you don't have anything worth stuffing."

He headed toward Cora's room, but Emerald barred the door. "You know you're not allowed inside of here," she yelled. Her figure ate up the whole doorway. "Trapper, you go on." She held up her rifle.

Trapper just showed his teeth, dropped his shotgun on the ground between the girl and the woman, and kept walking forward. Rose could hear her mother upstairs groaning with fever and she saw Emerald cock the trigger. Suddenly, Trapper turned his back on her, as if she weren't there. He faced the little girl and started coming toward her, slow and steady, his teeth flashing in a wide smile.

"Now, little lady," he said, bending down to meet her eye, "I guess that loosens up my time. So, I'm going teach you what you've been wanting to learn. I'll pay my respects to your ma some other time." And he put his arm protectively around the child and walked away with her.

The cub was hot and wet and it made Rose's fingers red and sticky. She wanted to run inside to her mother, but Emerald had locked her out. With the bear cub in her arms and Trapper's arm around her shoulder, she went with him to his shed.

They entered a close, musty room, its ceiling hanging with animals deflated of their guts and its floor cluttered with sulfurous vats. Two clean, varnished wooden worktables arranged in the shape of an L provided the only refuge of order in the chaos. It took awhile before her eyes adjusted to the lack of light. She couldn't tell if what she was seeing were real things or mirages from the interplay of dimness and dust. Meanwhile, he had taken the slain cub from her and had begun to work it.

When he made the tiny notches, lifting up the fur from the silky flesh, she wanted to run, but she couldn't. From his rawhide pouch, the man pulled out a long, thin, spun-glass straw.

"This is what the moon uses every night to drink up the sun," he said to her, holding it nearly in her eye. "Now, watch close." He moved slowly, with great deliberation. "See . . . one end to my lips, the other end to the specimen."

The straw made a glowing line in the dark air above the animal. The cub rested in a curled ball in Trapper's pink fleshy palm. The man held it so close, so tight, that Rose figured he was trying to bring its little heart to life.

Then he said, without looking up, "You take a deep breath like you're going dive to the bottom of the river and then you suck the innards out."

He thrust the straw between her lips and pressed her diaphragm into her back. The girl sucked in and vomited, sucked in and vomited until she brought up blood. The body of the cub grew skinnier and flatter, until it looked like a miniature bearskin rug.

"Little lady, little lady, control yourself!" Trapper was calling to her from what she felt was a long way off.

"Taxidermy is an art that can't wait." he growled, his hand on her calf; but where was that, Rose wondered, the whole world of her body flying upside and down. He stared at her, disgusted.

"This cub's going stink to the sky if we don't hurry and finish up."

He grabbed the straw from her dripping mouth and spit out what was left and stamped it into the dirt, crushing it underfoot, like it was nothing, never had been anything, ever; it was gone.

Then he took from his pocket a tiny scalpel, placed it in the girl's trembling hand, and put his hand tightly over hers, until it felt like he was crushing her fingers, but really he was just guiding her along. The two of them held the little knife steady and cut a deep, imperceptible hole into the cub's chest. He held her hand there, above the blood's warmth; he would not let go.

"No matter how sick, how scared you are, girl, when you come this far, you don't run," he said.

He took out a large syringe filled with a honey-colored liquid that smelled like bleach and burned the eyes. With his hand over her hand, like a father teaching a child to write, he pressed the syringe through the open cavity. Rose felt her fingers go numb as the cub's body turned glacial. The liquid flowed through the holes where the liver, the heart, the kidneys, the cerebellum used to be. The man and the girl filled the creature until there was nothing left inside, neither bone nor flesh nor blood, only the golden cool embalming solution.

As the girl kept her fingers pressed on the glass and steel syringe, revulsion slowly emptied out of her. It occurred to her that there was beauty in this thing; the small, still bear flushed with apparent life, but without the need to animate that life. Rose felt her face grow hot with envy. She held the animal out to the man.

"Keep it" he said. "You did a real good job, Rose. You're a big girl now." He put down his tools and walked out.

She caressed the motionless creature in her arms, felt its fur between her fingertips, kissed its flank, its belly, and each of its paws.

"Mine!" she cried. "Mine."

She took it to her room and set it among the stuffed animals on her bed, the ones made by Emerald from old party dresses, bits of leather, velvet, poplin, and cotton batting. She gazed critically at the toys. They seemed so false in comparison to Trapper's cub. That night, she gathered them up and took them down to the pit where in summer they made campfires and roasted pig. She raked up last year's coals, poured a can of kerosene, and struck several matches. The flames came up in a fast rage. She threw all her old toys in.

She went to Trapper's more and more frequently after that, and little by little he taught her the art of taxidermy. But he withheld things in his tutelage, vital things she needed to know to execute the process on her own. He would not divulge the names of the chemicals, the powders, the draughts brought to bear upon the rigid bodies, which gave them back the suppleness of life. Early on, he forced her to realize that without knowledge of these, all the technique in the world—and he had made her a prodigy of technique—would not make these dead animals live again. So, in the gaps of her knowledge, she stumbled like a cripple. In the six years that had passed since he gave her the first lesson, when she should have been experiencing a growing self-confidence in her powers, she felt only limitation, frustration, and helplessness.

This one dark place choked her. She must have these secrets—the formulas, their names, quantities, properties, conditions. Trapper knew that as she grew up and needed him less for family or love, she would need him more for this knowledge.

☙

On the day she came down from the tree in the river, the day after her fifteenth birthday, she went to Trapper's shed and entered through the window. She could see him through the doorway, a man like a hole, far back through another doorway and reflected in a mirror that showed more silver than glass. There he was sitting hunched over in a rapture of concentration, spectacles sliding down his vein-broken nose, which he wore for fine work, such as the insertion of eyeballs and the reattachment of claws. Her tattered birthday dress blew around her in a tangle and its satin sash caught her, holding her back. Struggling out of its frills, she hung it on the hook for the pots and pans. She pulled off her patent-leather heels, the first ever in her life, so as to enter soundlessly, holding them high in one hand.

He was calling the names: *hennebelle, tribulus terrestris, cuscuta.*

The sounds were like candy in her mouth. She rolled over in the mind of her delight. He looked up, sensing her presence in her joy. She thought she heard him growl. She knelt and placed her shoes by the hearth. Standing barefoot and in her petticoat, her raw red hair in ruined braids, she folded her arms in a façade of patience and said, "I've come for my birthday gift, Trapper."

Nobody called her to breakfast that morning or dinner that night, or to sleep, so she stayed. The wind shrilled through the chimney, blowing a draft of ice through the shed, but by the fire where they stood facing each other, there was a blistering heat. She was not a girl who knew fear, but when he built up the fire, she felt her stomach drop. His small, merry eyes teared up in the smoke that pressed in on the room. He penetrated her immediately, standing up, his teeth clenched, bearing into her with a desperation, a loathing that confused the girl, who was in too much pain to speak. Later, she would remember the time chiefly by the image of him struggling up, naked, to hurl more wood on the fire, over and over heaping the logs, as if he wished to bury the flame as much as make it stronger. He made her lie down with him until the world out-side was very dark. He whispered long names into her ear: *sub-carbonate of potash, camphor gum, arsenical solution.*

And he pressed against her with all his might until she could not remember the very words she would have of him. She tried to fix them in her mind by repeating their syllables to herself, but his thrusts made her lose her concentration and the words were the longest ones she'd ever heard. As he threw her dress to her and she quickly put it on, she begged him, "Please give me just one, tell me just one I can remember."

She felt a sharp burning pain like a cut from a razor blade between her thighs, and the stinging smell of ammonia com-ing up from the fur-poisoning vats made her reel back. But this did no good, she discovered; the smell seemed to be coming from inside her.

He muttered something, then changed his mind and wrote it down. She had never seen his handwriting before, and it astonished her: an elegant, spidery calligraphy that was nearly impossible to read. She wondered where in the world he had learned it.

"Take this," he said, not looking at her as he thrust a paper into her hands and moved quickly to the coffeepot. "It's just the beginning. Happy Birthday, Rose, Happy Birthday to you," he snarled, pouring the brew.

She held the thin, worn scrap of paper he pushed at her, out-stretched in her hand, and did not move. He had a whole body of knowledge that she wanted, considered her survival and her due. The paper he gave her held just one small fragment of this.

Conostegia xalapensis, it read. But it did not say what it did.

"It's a powder that must be administered at once to the freshly killed specimen," he said, as if reading her thoughts. "Without it, the embalming process won't work. Come back tomorrow and I'll show you how and when to use it." He turned his back on her, his body more geological than human as it rested against the stone hearth before the orange embers.

She didn't move. Somehow she had put on her clothes but she hadn't moved from her spot on the floor. A light pink stain trickled down her legs, and she feared that the dye was bleeding out of her dress. It seemed curious to her that her legs could not carry her forward; she, Rose, a girl who was never scared, who loved to run, and jump, and climb to the very tops of trees. Many times after this night she would wake from midsleep, rigid and voiceless, but desperate to run, to scream.

"Come back tomorrow, Rose," he said, shoving her into motion. "Knowledge to be knowledge comes slow . . . just like how a young body grows."

He turned to her abruptly, and it seemed to the girl that an immensity of love welled up in his eyes as he stared past her. At first it looked as if he were appealing to the heavens, but she followed his gaze and saw that it led to the upper stories of the Hotel, where a light had come on in her mother's window.

"Get out!" he bellowed at the girl. "Get out before I kill you."

She found herself hours later in her own room, crouching half-dressed on top of the bedspread. Unable to sleep in the cage of her bed, she yearned to return to the taxidermy shed, to the promise of life that was there. But he had locked her out.

That night, in her ragged dreams, a raven kept flying at her face until it pulled out her eyes and stuck in its own. She was a girl with raven eyes that saw everything in terms of prey and flight; and then in the sky she saw the raven with her own stolen green eyes in its head, and it was flying into the branches of a huge tree that grew up out of the middle of the river. Up, up, up into a future it could not see. But it seemed to Rose, in her dream, that she could see it, even with the heavy body of a human child who couldn't get out of her bed. She watched, paralyzed, while the wild, shrieking creature with her eyes swooped and plummeted, rose and glided through space.

Without the sense of the sight it had stolen, the raven kept getting further and further lost in the mountain of tree in which
it was flying, until she saw it starving to death on some high
bare branch. Helplessly, she watched it die with its own black
darting eyes burrowing in her head.

THE PICTURES ON THE FLOOR

"Follow me," Miranda said with a tight smile, her hands grabbing each other ferociously behind her back. "I want to show you something."

Up the windy back stairs they went, flight after flight. How many flights had they passed—five, six maybe? Benjamin started whistling to set his mind at ease. Each stairway grew narrower and darker, until they were squeezing through on their bellies and knees.

"Follow me," she said, "I have to show you something."

They reached the thin blue door at the top of the stairs, and she felt in her pocket for the key. The door unlocked easily, and they found themselves in a huge, cavernous place that might have been the dank belly of some leviathan.

From the outside, the attic appeared small and brooding. But inside, it was amplified space. If an echo could be made visual, it would have been this attic that went on and on, forever repeating itself. Benjamin, for the life of him, could not figure out how the Hotel held this attic up, like some enormous, billowing basket balanced on a woman's head. The towering ceiling was crossed with thick i-beams and the walls were pitched at extreme angles. A series of leaded casement windows sat squarely at floor level; like misers portioning out their hoards of gold, they rationed the sun so closely that the floors and walls of Miranda's attic were a checkerboard of famished light.

Bang bang, he heard and jumped automatically. Benjamin was ashamed to discover that it was just the unhinged shutters slamming against the windowpanes in the breeze. He told himself he had better calm down. What could possibly scare him in an empty old attic with a beautiful young girl?

Miranda lit a rancid oil lamp and held it shakily over the floor. The attic was suddenly changed into a world both shadowy and bright, as if it had preserved a primordial light, filtered through an atmosphere that no longer existed on the planet. It was a light comprised of the secretions of giant ferns, the upheaval of ice-age glaciers, the eruption of the first volcanoes, the breath of the last dinosaurs. Miranda's attic was a chamber diffused with the glow of extinction.

Her fingers pointed to some huge, deep recesses Benjamin hadn't noticed before. It took him a while to see that the floor was painted, like a fresco, divided into panels, held together by marble and jeweled frames, which turned out to be fabulously executed trompe l'oeil. In each frame-bordered cavern were colors that one only experiences in dreams: blues that were the essence of flight and of drowning; blacks that were absolute obscurity; reds that seemed to be ground from living blood; earth tones that flowed like rich, smooth milk; thin, sweet yellows that tied the functions of the body to those of the sun; and grays that were a coagulation of pure thought and human dust. Benjamin had never seen colors like these before. He probed his mind to deduce their chemical makeup, but he could find no explanation. They were unearthly hues, he thought, and he remembered news reports of giant meteors crashing to earth, creating lakes and canyons, and he wondered if they had secretly created new colors too.

The girl stood cowering in shadow, her face pressed against her embittered hands.

Benjamin saw that she was weeping and was moved to comfort her, but his impulse faltered in the swell of color and shape before his feet. He found himself experiencing design and geometry through touch, falling into the territories of painted shapes as if they were real.

"This one I call 'Ham's Fork'," she said.

"And this one," she said, stepping into the light, "this is 'The Mounds,' and over here's 'The Willow Tree Weeps Babies.' There's 'The Burning Bush,' 'The Fish Devour the Lamb,' 'The Green Vale,' 'The Red Butte's,' 'The Tortoise Lady,' 'The Alluvial Bottoms,' 'The Demon's Delight in the Blind Man's Sight . . .'"

He stopped her with his hand on the air in an abrupt gesture that scared her. His vision was leaping now, leaving the
rest of him behind. If she hadn't pointed them out, he never
would have seen they were pictures, he was so stunned by their
color, shape, and light.

"Did you do this?" he asked.

"No sir, I did not," she said. "I dream such things and
worse, and when I wake up, someone's painted them on here
for real, someone, I don't know who, to torture me. Then I
clean them up." She gestured to a bucket of white paint. "But
the next morning, the pictures are back again. Different ones,
new ones, but just as horrible."

She was afraid of him now. She had never told anyone
about this, and nobody had ever entered her attic before. She
wanted to tell him everything that happened to her in this
room. She was sure that to tell him would be to lose him, but
like the returning presence of the pictures on the floor, it was
a thing she could not help. She looked at him as if he were
already gone, which gave her the courage to take his hand and
lead him through the paintings.

"Maybe you'd like to see the rest," she asked, "before I
paint them over again?"

It seemed to him like one giant illumination divided into
several individual and highly detailed fragments. Each was so
different from the next in style and content that they could
hardly have been painted by the same hand, in the same
country and century.

As he walked from image to image, he saw a trio of Indians
paddling a long boat through a swamp of white-steepled
churches; a group of upstanding ladies and gentlemen swathed
in the skins of wild animals that seemed to leap from their
backs; he saw the river with a city growing underwater, rushing vehicles and careening faces pressed to a surface they could
not penetrate. The river itself seemed to be drowning. He saw
portraits of caves within caves with faded paintings on the

crystalline walls depicting the hunt of bull buffalo and woolly mammoth, as well as several abstract signs and symbols that looked familiar but that he could not translate. There were pictures of hunters with muskets shooting at birds; there were pictures of palm trees and polar caps thriving together on a bed of roses. There was a picture of a man with an ax, standing next to a tree that seemed to bleed, although it had not yet been cut. From the blade of the ax grew an enormous eroded mountain that was Benjamin's face, but grown old, very old.

The pictures went on and on, places he immediately recognized and then realized he'd never seen before. Images of the river whipped up and cut through him until he found himself fundamentally confused, without bearing. His imagination could not improve upon the girl's reality, or whatever it was on the floor of this attic that shook him so profoundly that he felt himself a distant tributary of his self, wholly out of contact with what he had assumed himself to be.

He threw himself from foot to foot, progressing forward sideways by the smallest increments. He stared at the images, he did not blink, he hardly moved at all but for that swaying motion, like a horse asleep on its feet with the vague awareness of insects overhead.

The girl watched him closely. To her he looked like a man in pain; but she knew enough not to touch him, to let the pictures have their way until they spit him out. She looked nervously to the floor for an answer, but it remained the same inscrutable series of pictures that she dreamed every night and woke up to each day. She turned quickly back to the man's face, like a warden traveling with a prisoner through an unfamiliar territory. She was afraid that through her incompetence to follow, he would escape her into a free land, a wilderness from which he would never return.

The paintings set up house in his eyes. The fish devouring the lamb, the tree weeping babies, the room with the serpent walls, the men with the bears' heads, the women with the parrot claws. Every picture she had ever seen glowering up at her from that infernal floor was passing right now into his eyes. She shuddered. Seeing them so miniaturized should have made them look harmless, but it didn't; they grew sharper, more ominous. Inhabited by these creatures, his pupils emptied of sight and began to burn.

She tried to get him to speak, hoping that might release him. "What are you seeing?" she asked in a whisper.

He didn't answer, though his lips worked themselves in a horrifying way.

"What is it?" she cried, shaking him. "Where are you? Where are you?" He knew that getting back to her would be a feat. His mind turned over, a feverish, lumbering thing in its fascination. He drew himself by force out of the sphere of one picture, only to find himself falling headlong into the influence of the next. Nor was it, as he would write many decades later in his *Autobiography of an Artist-Explorer*, a predominantly visual experience. "The pictures were such that," he stated in his opening chapter, "as they absorbed your attention, you lived them, lived them, in fact, as if each one were your whole and only life."

So he found himself that day a wolf on the edge of a forest, a missionary in a tropical swamp, a drowning child, a single rose, a willow tree, an earthquake, the color green, the shape round. From picture to picture he plunged, a drifter with no gravity but imagery, with no rope but his mind or maybe not his mind at all, but his soul, something he wasn't sure he believed in, or maybe it was the voice of Miranda that was his trail of crumbs leading him back to the Hotel attic. When finally they had finished with him, he emerged from the paintings like a man who has been picked up and hurled out by a maelstrom. His eyes clouded, his limbs infant-weak, he crawled to her on his hands and knees. She let him stay there.

THE TRAPS

He cast the traps into the river, making sure to set them deep enough so that when the beaver hit bait, it would drown before it had time to chew off its captured leg.

Trapper spit into the iridescent sunrise water and stretched his body with a yawn. He stifled his pleasure at once, realizing that it might frighten off his prey. He decided to retreat to the bushes, where he could watch. He had laid a tiny pouch soaked in castor within the jaws of the trap. It had a sex smell the creatures couldn't resist. The trick was to leave as little human scent as possible near the traps, for as much as castor provoked the beaver to ardor, the smell of danger superseded that.

The man loved to watch his traps from the brush, unseen and unknown, concealed by the smell of the pines. He loved the waiting inherent in his profession. It gave him time to think without seeming to be wasting his time. He took a hunk of dried pemmican from his satchel. He liked the way it made his teeth work.

It was really too soon in the season to be at the foot of the mountains. Avalanches were common in early spring. Everything melting did not always melt in an orderly fashion but left the ice hanging in precarious cliffs. Trapper had known several fools, eager to get to the high ground after a winter of civilized incarceration, who ended up buried under a hundred feet of fallen ice. Trapper usually waited judiciously until May to get up to his stake, but he was fidgety since the girl and needed some clean thinking air. He eyed the water; the best part about drowning animals was you didn't have any bullet-holes marring the pelts. He thought of the girl and what she might trade for the bits and pieces of his know-how. He wondered how much it was worth to her and if she had gotten that far in the comparative notions of things. What would she trade for a supply of that precious scent that drove the clever creatures straight to their deaths?

He had a certain knack with beavers; he knew how to sniff them out and bring them to him. But he excelled with other animals too. He knew the marmoset, the antelope, the wolverine and the grizzly, the porcupine, the mountain lion, the red fox; they had all graced his walls with their heads and his body with their pelts. He was a lover of animals in the wild, a devotee. Perhaps his feelings for Rose were akin to that, though she was something opposite to the hunt, contrary to animal. She thought too much, yet had no concept of fear, and even in flight of pursuit she did not seem aware of being prey. She was too absorbed in what she wanted, it seemed to him, and suddenly he was proud of the part he had played in bringing her up to be such a uniquely human thing, obsessed as she was with abstract need and immortality. What she won't do to learn the secrets of taxidermy! He let out a belly laugh and turned to the sky.

He prided himself on his honesty. He knew himself for what he was: a man who is afraid of everything. This is not to say he was a coward. He would confront any danger; in fact, he put himself in the way of danger almost habitually. But whether he was crossing a quiet stream or facing a killer, he felt the same terror. He believed that his fear was the most democratic and unprejudiced thing about him, and as such it made him proud. There was no difference for him between danger and comfort; they both compelled him to attack or run away. Trapper honed his fear diligently, the way a laborer might scrub his nails each night to clean away the dirt. At the same time, because he was afraid, he hid his fear from everyone, like an immigrant concealing his foreignness to make sure he isn't sent back from where he came. Trapper was in this wilderness to stay. He was sure that his salvation was here, in the blood of his trapped beasts. He took to hiding and watching them die, as if by observing he might pick up some crucial understanding that would someday kill his unspeakable fear.

His taking of the girl was something new, or perhaps so old he could not remember. His work was mostly with the animals—

the last beasts of the wild, vanishing under the hordes of travelers and settlers heading west and trampling over everything. To his mind it was better to preserve something dead than not to preserve it at all. He rubbed himself absently upon the image of her childish breasts beneath him and the confusion on her face when his semen settled and sealed inside her. He wanted to transform her into the animals he hunted; then to preserve that hunted victim of prey, not this forever girl who was the opposite of animal, who knew no instinctive hunger or fear, whose only hunger was to learn, whose only fear was to remain ignorant. He had known her so long . . .

Ever since she was the littlest thing, full of kicking, screaming immediacy, he had helped to educate her. While her mother's energy was absorbed in keeping the precarious Hotel afloat, he taught her geography so that she might find her way in the world, and mathematics so she might know the distance between herself and all other things. Trapper taught the girl everything he had gone into the wilderness to forget, as if she were his secret diary.

But now he wanted to change her back.

He heard a snap in the direction of the river and a struggling sound dulled somewhat by its occurrence underwater. He did not need to look to know he'd got one drowning. His heart heaved with an innocent joy. He could time the moments to the animal's death in his mind; it would be over before he even arrived. Ten steps down to the river and the creature would be a trophy.

He wondered what the girl thought of the deal she had made for herself and if she were old enough to understand what she had done or, he surmised, she would continue to do with him for a very long time, until she finished getting what she wanted or until he tired of her wants. He smiled as he considered how fine she might become both at the arts of taxidermy and the arts of love, for she was a girl who sought perfection in everything she endeavored. He wondered why he wanted her at all, for even in passion she left him cold and he found himself completely alone in the shuddering time of his coming, as he pulled away and lay on his side, suffering his body's indifference to her. Maybe, he thought to himself, it was an attraction forced upon him by his mind, which took the girl for revenge more than for love or prey. No matter what he did, the fact that Cora would not have him left him in unassuageable pain. He thought of taking her child again and again as he watched the abandoned wife crying on the widow's walk night after night for the husband who would never return. The mother might not take him seriously, but the daughter would, he vowed. He looked to her and through her, like a person convinced an empty flask holds a drop left to drink. He would make love to the child for as long as it would take to educate her on how animals sacrifice themselves to nurture human life. He would have her as long and as often as it would take to kill in her all division between human thought and animal life.

The water had stopped trembling and no noise remained from either current or beast. Trapper came out of hiding with a blustering gaiety. He plunged into the freezing water and, hand over hand, he pulled in his traps.

It was a fat, full-grown beaver. The man marveled at the allegiance to instinct even when instinct means death, for he was certain that if the beaver had not been so excited by the scent of castor, it would have detected that other smell—the human killer concealed in the evergreens—just as he believed that if the girl were not so hungry for a knowledge that she believed meant eternal life, she would detect the misery and deception she was building in her own young spirit by her liaison with a man who wanted her to suffer. He yanked the sack of castor off the trap, and wrapped it in several giant wet lily leaves he'd pulled up to keep it free from the scent of his hands and clothing. He held the corpse of the beaver up and at a little distance, as if he were observing a painting.

"This one's a beaut," he sighed.

He had his hunting knife out in a second and slit the thing from throat to gut. Carefully he reached in and pulled out its castor sac. He took a whiff and was elated. The animal was mature, and its sex smell would draw many beavers when its glands were affixed to his traps. Worth more than a hundred hides, he figured to himself by the size and the stink of it. A windfall for a man with his mind far from his work. A gift from heaven; a sign, he suspected, that he was doing right. Trapper felt a deep peace settle over him as he stood with the castor gland in his open hand.

Coming to his senses, to the duties and responsibilities of his trade, he placed his treasure in his shirt pocket and quickly skinned the beaver, now drained of blood. He turned it inside out, stretched it as tight as possible on a makeshift splint of willow branches to dry, and hung it over his mountainous shoulders.

It was only then, the animal heavy on his back, that he remembered what he had promised the girl as he filled himself inside her. He had promised her a fine, grown beaver that he'd instruct her how to stuff.

THE STICK

Miranda, Miranda. He wrote her name over and over again with a stick in the sand.

His eyes couldn't take the sun when he crawled from the attic. Her leading him out the same way she'd brought him in. When they got to the backyard, she vanished and he was left alone to find his own way in the too-bright morning. He had stumbled down to the river, a man in peril of losing his sight. He took to drinking the water there and pouring it over to cool his burning face. The surface was stirred up, to sight impenetrable. He poured over himself more water than he needed, and when he got up, his whole back was dripping wet and he had to shake himself off like a dog that had gone swimming. He stumbled over a fallen tree branch, unable to see ahead with all the river water streaming down his face. He took the branch up and figured to use it for ciphering, an old habit he had when he was feeling muddled, to see what kinds of codes he might come up with from the unmediated motion of his hand and the stick. But the letters all came out in the order of her name M-I-R-A-N-D-A.

And *Miranda, Miranda,* he wrote over and over again. Blind, with the stick in the sand.

Before, he had pursued her, close as a tack. Now, he wanted to run away, but his eyes hurt so much he had to sit down and close them. The pictures on the attic floor had impaled themselves on his lids. He opened his eyes to hide from them, but there the images were again, made enormous in the sky as if the sun itself were projecting them. Like a wounded dog, he yelped in pain as the pictures inside his eyes and the pictures in the sky conspired to suck him in.

He marveled how his absorption in the girl and his absorption in the attic floor had become so crossed; one conjured the image of the other. He was seeing the pictures and he was seeing the girl, simultaneously; though the girl, he ascertained by her stance and size, was not in the pictures, but rather removed from them, a baffled observer. He was in each picture, though, and each picture was the stretch of a full identity and lifetime that became his identity, his lifetime. He had no idea if he was rejoicing in art or love, for the image of the one brought up the image of the other. He only knew something troubling—like water held in the palm of a hand—that there was nothing transportable in the girl or the work. He had believed all his life in the portability of beauty, the transferability of pleasure, but it was impossible in this forsaken place. How could he take what was seizing him? he wondered.

"How do I take this?" It worried Benjamin deeply. Very deeply.

THE GIRL WHO . . .

When Rose awoke, alone in her bed, she wanted to run. She rubbed her eyes until they hurt, so thankful was she after what she'd dreamed that they were really her own and not those of some thieving, screeching, carrion-eating bird. Her body ached, as if it had been gutted inside, the carcass left standing as a memorial.

She wanted to get back to Trapper's shed. Never had she wanted anything so much as to preserve these poor hunted creatures of the wild. She believed he could help her and would, if she were only worthy enough. What does it mean, the girl wondered, to be worthy. . . to be worth . . . What must she do, how must she be in order to make the man trust her with the secrets of taxidermy? He had given her the first words, hadn't he? That must prove something. Bit by bit, he would parcel them out to her, and one day, all the secrets would fit together like a giant jigsaw puzzle. Then she would know how to do it without his help.

She walked slowly to Trapper's shed. This time she knocked, but no one was there to answer. She went over to the front window and peered in. The stuffed trophies stood and sat and lay everywhere in beatific poses. Not one of these animals was killing another one, not one was harming another one, not one looked fearful or trapped, as they so often did when she had come across them in the wild.

She wanted to travel inside their quieted skins, like Trapper did. He told her that as soon as he put his hands in their skulls, their thoughts and feelings came to him and he could under-stand exactly what it was like to walk around in their bodies. For this, she needed the man badly. So she waited.

She sat all day, in the dirt, in the backyard, by Trapper's shack, waiting for him, but he did not come. He hurt her so much the day before, but in one degree or another he had always hurt her and cared for her, so the girl could not part hurt from love. And she was so hungry to learn, to learn and dream.

He didn't come and he didn't come. It was nearly night and still he didn't come. She started to be afraid that he had gone for good; left her so starving, so half-full of knowing that she could not survive, as if a surgeon had cut her open to heal her but had forgotten to sew her back up.

"Trapper! Trapper!" she screamed.

The silence drove her wild. She battered her head against the earth. Smash, again, smash. She could enter his room, open all the bottles, pour out all the chemicals, take out all the saws, but what good would it do when she knew so little, so pitifully little?

She hit her head against the earth, over and over, side and front, like her head was a pick and an ax, until it had dredged a hole in the ground just wide enough for her body to squeeze into. She lowered herself down, head first, without hesitation, into the brown warm bed. She lay there, stretched out under the earth, thinking of the animals, her finger on the trigger taking them down, her hands in the cavities of their bodies, up to her elbows in their blood. She imagined herself packing dirt into their emptied skulls.

"Dirt," she cried, "is the secret breath of immortal life. And Trapper and all his skills and potions can go to hell."

It started to rain, lightly at first, like little kisses, and then very hard, turning the earth to mud that flooded her hole.

She breathed in the mud until mud filled her up. She felt cold, and she wrapped her thin strawberry arms around her childish belly to keep warm. The mud dripped down in rich volcanic streams, coating her body. She pressed it in her mouth, her ears, her eyes, closing up every orifice of her body until she was a full-fledged being of mud. She believed that a body needed earth to breathe, without earth a man could not survive, and she inhaled until she was so full of mud that she was choking and coughing up mud from her lungs into the mud that was raining down from the sky.

She hears a loud, thunderous cawing in the distance, a cawing and a beating of wings, as if the two sounds were resonating off each other somewhere far away but tied to her very insides. The sound sets her moving; she can't stop moving. As paralyzed as she was before, lying in the earth like a dead thing, now she's a lightning streak of action. In seconds she's down the pine trail to the river. And she's there, yearning out over the water's edge. Her eyes are caked with earth, so everything she sees is through a film of earth. Her ears are so stuffed with mud that everything she hears is full of mud.

What she hears and sees are ravens.

There are black birds hanging in the sky over the river, perched in midair. The sky is thick with a thousand screaming birds. The girl hears herself screaming. Screaming and scream- ing. Just like the sky. She can't stand the sound. So she runs into the river. She dives under the water that she hates, under and under until she's struck the sludge bottom. Here she can breathe again, she believes, here she will be safe from the terri- ble water, the monstrous sky. She breathes in and out method- ically, digging with her hands until she is under the floor of the river, burrowing through the mud that makes it up. Everyone and everything on earth doesn't matter anymore. She isn't homesick, doesn't want anything anymore, just to keep swim- ming in this dirt. She hears the roaring of water above and those enraged wings. She thinks she's going down and down, but really she's rising, up through the core of a tree. The tree that had appeared in the river and saved her from drowning comes back again, to rescue her again. She's back in the tree- top. She perches upon a fat, green branch, with nothing below or above but air.

She's no more a girl of dirt, she's a black motion of wings. A raven on the verge of flying.

WHITE SAILS

Benjamin couldn't remember if he left her or if she had vanished behind one of the several heavy doors on the second floor, where he now found himself alone in his chamber. Nor could he remember shaving in the mirror set up for him by the sunniest window while he was gone.

He only remembered seeing himself reflected in the sober river, choked between swamp grass and fallen rock, his face apparently smooth but for the tide's slight agitation. He recognized himself there; a young man trapped in his face, and he yearned for another one that could take him through what he had begun to surmise was life, the way this one with its cool, empty chart, this one could not. A face can be like a whirlpool, he thought, void at bottom but so turbulent all around that no one, not even its possessor, can guess at its emptiness. He stared off at his boat, looking for something and then not.

Mentally he latched onto the sight of his canvases, rolled up on the peeling deck like neat cigars, one on top of the other. He had made a good deal for them.

"Not bad," Benjamin whistled to himself, "not bad," showing his teeth in the mirror of the room, which quickly disappeared into the memory of the river from which he had just come, where he had poured water over his face until his body was drenched and he was blind. Backward in thought, he rowed the river until he entered a great inland sea, where he had once met a captain of sorts, one with the title but no vessel.

They had encountered each other on the docks, both of them engaged in the transient work of loading freighters. The old salt hired Benjamin on the spot to paint a clipper ship at full sail, with himself at the helm, steel-whiskered and squinty-eyed on an indigo carpet of perpetual sea.

"I'm sure," said the captain, "that painting me on a clipper will make a real ship come to me."

He talked of nothing else for days and Benjamin finished his commission quickly to be rid of him. When the painting was done, the old man set it up atop a tall wooden ladder looking out over the moored boats to the open seas. Deep into the night, Benjamin, who had little money and slept tied to the docks with a mangy length of hemp so he wouldn't fall off, could hear the old man praying feverishly in front of the painting.

As time went by, the captain's hope of materializing a real seagoing vessel from the painted one began to deteriorate; but as it did, his belief in Benjamin grew even stronger. In the old man's mind, the transformative powers of the painting were transferred to the painter. He began to commit talismanic acts, taking Benjamin for some kind of magus who could secure for him his heart's desire. The captain's attentiveness grew fanatical and Benjamin began to find small sacrificial offerings by his head when he awoke in the morning. The first ones were simple: a plug of tobacco, a slab of cheese, a fine flint.

"I know what you want," the old salt would say to the boy when he was sleeping. "I'll get you what you want," and he'd limp away determinedly .

Then one morning, Benjamin woke up and found himself surrounded by towering rolls of canvas sheeting. Over the distant top, as he strained his stunned body, he could see the old man staring down at him. He was smiling widely—something Benjamin had never seen him do before—his red, empty gums leading back into a black tunnel of mouth that smelled of fish and garlic.

"How you like it?" he asked with an eager confidence.

"What the hell is it?" snarled Benjamin, who clumsily tried to climb up and over the heavy bolts of cloth.

"This," answered the captain reverentially, "is your full and total paid-for fee, which is what I reckon you been after all along as is your justifiable right and my ignoramus wrong." He kissed the ragged edges of the sheeting.

"Old man," said Benjamin with a desperate thrust of his crowded elbows, "you already paid me for my painting."

It was as if the old captain hadn't heard a word he said. He continued: "If I give you these here fine sails, you could make that boat you painted for me tear out of its frame, and take me for its mate."

The old man paused a moment, as if to give the thought some time to digest; then, after some preparatory coughing, he went on to tell his story: "In my day, lad, I had many a ship under my sway. I sailed for whales, for salt, for silk, for tangerines. I commanded great ships, powerful and fair: The Fruitful, The Nights of Heaven, The Grace of God, The Clare Marie. I spent my life rocking back and forth with just a few feet of deck between me and the watery deep. I have seen the Orient near and the Orient far, the pashas of the Ottoman, the kings of Ethiope, the sheiks of Araby. Why, after all I've done and seen, there's no man, fish, or fowl that could be surprising me."

Benjamin yawned loudly in an attempt to cut off the captain's catalogue of feats and geography, but his elder rose over his sighs in a declamatory crescendo: "Fierce and foul, foreign and familiar, all have been my friends and, better yet, have traded wares with me. Why, in my last voyage—we were docked at a Persian port—the potentate there took a real liking to my slaves and wanted to trade me something for them."

The old man laughed hard here, so hard he couldn't speak, and, forgetting himself for a moment, he slapped Benjamin, who had fallen back asleep. Then he remembered his mission and raised the startled youth by both shoulders and kissed him hard on each cheek.

"Well," he continued, "I looked over all his vast storerooms, calculated what would be too much to ask without seeming to insult the man and risk myself getting chopped to pieces. Then I saw them: In the corner of his warehouse, behind the piles of copper trays and clay urns, standing fifteen hands high if I'm a day under seventy-five, the most beauteous rolls of canvas I had ever seen in my whole life, on or off ship rigging. There was enough to make seven great sails, enough to sail a ship straight round the world and back a thousand times, and fast, faster than God's own lightning."

"I asked the potentate if my slaves might meet the price he wished for that pile of rags. He nodded and smiled with his teeth snapped shut, a sure sign he believed he'd made the far better end of the deal."

Benjamin found himself fingering the canvas while the old man spoke, as if his hands might discover Persia itself in the grain. Fixed on the sensation of the cloth against his skin, he could hear the sea captain talking, but at such a distance it seemed to have little to do with his own growing appreciation of the canvases.

"I wept to see them," (and indeed the old man wept anew), "to feel them, smell them lying there on my own decks. I spent my days at sea, cutting, trimming, rigging my beauties—for that is what I call them—until there were seven; seven sails to take me traveling everywhere there is water. And with them I set out to sea.

"The first day was fine—why, finer than fine. The second and the third, the same, clear sea. We were halfway round the globe by the time the seventh day arrived. The sun was our constant companion, fish swam at our sides, the wind licked our heels, the waves were no bigger than a bathtub's; we flew.

"Then came the fifteenth day, and with it a gray-black sky and a still blacker wind. It came up out of the north as we were turning the Horn. The sky went to ash and rained down upon us like knives. My white sails, my poor sails! The wind whirled up and cut them down. Then the hull cracked and the mighty ship and its crew went under. Something struck me on the head and I, too, went down into the vortex.

"When I came to my senses, the day was bright and uncommonly still. I was floating, alone, somewhere in the middle of the sea. How did I survive? What held me up, saved my life? I looked below me and found I was floating on the rolls of white canvas sheeting. I had lost everything—ship, crew, cargo, dreams, everything—but the white sails."

The old man stopped speaking again and looked so desirously at the stacked canvases that surrounded Benjamin that they seemed to take on the very life of sailing masts on a clipper ship. But Benjamin turned his eye from the captain's dream; it filled him with inexplicable envy.

"For the last forty years, since the day they saved my life, I have dragged these white sails around with me. Forty years of them at my side and on my back and three hundred and twenty beautiful pounds at that. I swore to set them like jewels on their own proud ship and let them sail wheresoever they pleased. For forty years I've been trying to honor this vow, traveling from one longshoreman's hall to another—on sea, on river, on lake, on stream. But I never got another ship and now that I'm old, sailors throw their fish bones at me."

The old captain bowed his head. He was weeping. As Benjamin watched the drops stream down the cracked and wrinkled face before him, he began to feel some sorrow. He wanted to give the old man hope, and at the same time, he had fallen under the spell of the white sails of his story, so much so that they no longer resembled a colorless stretch of material to him, but a smooth perfect space on which an entire map of the life and history of the continent could be told. At that moment, Benjamin had a revelation in which a new image of himself appeared. No longer was he a hapless traveler searching and adrift; he had found his subject and the fabric upon which to depict it.

There was a river not so far away that had its mouth in this inland sea. It fed on the sea and ran away from it into the gullies and canyons, the straits and trails of a land that was more immense than imagination could fathom. Benjamin, encircled in the arms of his white white sails, believed that this was the river he must paint and these sails the canvas he must paint it on.

His desire led him on. Before he knew it, he told the old man that, indeed, yes, he could turn the painting he had made into a real sailing ship and make it his, that he was right to offer in sacrifice the rolls of pretty sail sheeting. The old captain smiled at the young man. Slowly he picked up the rolls of cloth, gathered them in his arms like a beloved, and, kissing them lightly, handed them over to Benjamin, who staggered under the weight and breadth of them. But Benjamin's limbs quickly grew warm and supple with the bundle. The innermost side of the material felt like a woman's hair. He was excited, and he was embarrassed. He focused on the old man, who was now small and shriveled before him, sobbing desperately at what he had given up.

Benjamin rose to his full stature and cleared his throat. The canvas fell over his arms and skimmed the ground. Assuming a deep, solemn voice that he believed fitting for prophecy, he said to the old man: "I am going with the white sails to a faraway land and in their wake, you will find in the harbor a beautiful clipper ship waiting for you. Now this will take some six days time. Until then you must stay here staring at the portrait I painted of you. You must not move an inch from this spot, or your ship will never come and you will die the slowest, most agonizing death."

With that, Benjamin turned his back and trudged off with his precious bundle to a rickety packet boat, leaving the old sailor and his portrait staring at each other on the shore.

"Six days," the young man considered, "that will give me plenty of time to disappear in a country where everyday things are lost or discarded or so deeply changed as to be rendered unrecognizable."

He poled his boat out of the inland sea into the strait of the river. Days passed before he dared rest. Starving and nearly mad with thirst, he did not touch his provisions, but rather took to unrolling and rolling the reams of delicious canvas. He felt dizzy when he first saw them spread out on the rotting deck, their fragile whiteness swimming in the sun and shadows of the junipers that lined the river. Instantly he understood that they were the finest of the fine, canvas made for the brush and not for the sail. How had their real use been so tragically mistaken?

wondered the young man. The old fool had been so in love that he failed to remember that in sailing, such fineness has no end but destruction.

Benjamin, furling up his shoulders in his room at the Hotel, wondered what had become of the old man he had deceived. He pictured him, weak with hopelessness, dragging himself over the huge exhausting country in search of his ship and his sails, with the full weight of the lost canvases behind him, a heavy ghost upon his back. Like the sea captain before him, Benjamin never seemed to be able to use them all up. It was as if the rolls redoubled themselves every time he cut them. And every time he did, he wondered when the images of the river would stop and he would finally be free to sew all the pictures together and be finished with the panorama. Meanwhile, the white sails went everywhere with him, just as they had gone everywhere with the old captain. They were as the shirt off his back. Now, he wanted to use them to cover the dirty floor of an odd girl's attic.

He recalled himself, down by the river, coming from Miranda's floor, stumbling blind to his boat, feeling for the canvases with his hands, kicking them gently open with his feet. He prepared them with salves to help them hold the paint. He scissored them up as evenly as he could, but his head was reeling with the images of the attic floor. They made him sick, but he had to have them. He tightened his grip around the canvas bundles. He would lay them out like traps in her attic. They would capture the girl's pictures in transportable form. Then he could carry them far, far away like beautiful princesses he was born to rescue.

He cooled his face in the basin by the razor strop and, still holding the towel in his hand, he walked over to the door of his room and slowly opened it. Looking down the long, empty corridor, he saw nothing to arrest his vision. Then, suddenly, his eyes stopped at the stairway landing. How did they get there; when did it happen? There in the hall lay his rolls of pure white canvas, at the foot of the stairs to Miranda's attic.

MAKING PAINT

She is safe here, alone in the attic, the narrow blue door locked and bolted. In the swollen belly of the whale. She is in front of the row of windows, her back to the windows, with the willow stick like a whip in her hand. She is determined she won't do it today. But her ardor is unspeakable. The shadows are everywhere; it's getting darker and darker until she can't see anything, until she can't remember ever seeing anything, and she believes she's always been blind. She faints, she wakes up, mute and blind. She faints, wakes up; faints, wakes up; all night long like this.

Oh the willow stick is sharp,
And the willow stick she's mean, she sings.

Standing up, she steadies herself from foot to foot until she finds her grounding. She holds the willow stick up to her face. Everything in her stomach rising up, bursting to the surface in proclamation of the not-she.

"People call it waste," Miranda, shaking her head, thinks to herself, "but really it's the body reaching out, trying to find the communicative link between what keeps it alive and the elements in which it must live to survive. This is the only true paint; all the others are fake."

She eats flowers and vomits up flowers. The petals of daisies, of lady's slippers, of wisteria chewed and crushed in the mortar that is her body. This is what she paints with, what makes her hungry to eat at all.

And dictates what she will eat that day. Some days, to paint flowers she devours flowers. Some days it's a day to paint river, so she drinks from the river. Sometimes it is the texture of a thing she is after, not itself. There are the paintings in which a man's face must have the roughness of a tree trunk, so that is what she eats, for the sake of the face of the man. She does not understand her food cravings and she can't help them, but afterwards, when she sees the metamorphosis of her body, she understands. She doesn't want to keep doing it, but she starts to understand.

Last week it was a taste for snakes that hounded her mouth.

She goes out, turns over the rocks in the desert to find snakes. She eats and throws up snakes, eats and throws up snakes for days until the mound of regurgitation provides her with a store of colors and consistencies for the work of her willow stick. She never paints a snake after eating one, but everything else about the painting says snake—the curvatures of the imagery, the reptilian texture of the landscape. The color of the sun is a serpent's tongue, the foothills and mountains follow the slithering shape of a snake's journey, while the clouds in her skies move like its just-birthed progeny and the river is the color of its venom and the planted fields its diamond back and the emptiness in the distance its missing feet, and "This is everything that is for billions of years," she cries as the snake comes alive in the painting in which it does not appear.

This is everything that is.

She doesn't think of her body as the maker of her materials, but as a kind of conductor that lets them pass through; the catalytic link between one world and another while her own sense of self is momentarily lost in the transmission. What is her body, she wonders, that it can collect, transform, dispel such beauty from waste? She picks up the stale cake lying on the floor and shoves it in her mouth.

There are things to do that must be done: the washing, wiping, cooking, cleaning, straightening, sweeping, but this is not why she eats; for this a morsel would never pass her lips, for this she would do nothing to keep herself in the daylight world of the living; but it is not for this, it's for the night she fears that she eats, for she knows that when she is starving, the paintings are eating her, feeding off her, skin and bone, as she cleans the pantry, sets the table, tends the garden, eating her alive but always leaving her alive, in agony and yet unable to end her life. And so, night after night, year after year, a hand on the mouth, a finger down the throat, making the paint of her painting. Tonight, the whole night is like this. Now all her nights are like this.

TRAPPER AT HOME WITH ROSE

The room was grimy, the dust and the dirt laced together like necklaces from which the dead insects hung.

He wouldn't let her on the bed, that was for him only.

"You are my dog," he said. "Dog daughter! Make me dinner. Dog daughter! Lick my cock."

She broke inside. She grew up broken inside, one part smashed glass, the other part savage beast. They fucked and she was glass, perfect glass; but inside she was the last animal they slaughtered together.

Meanwhile, she learned from him the secrets of his trade. He taught her how to create a sense of flight in a dead pheasant, a feeling of wily freedom in the jackal, of tenacious industry in the beaver.

As his belly slammed into her back over and over again like a fist, she imagined herself a wild animal, foraging far away from the predator's rib. Each time he raped her she became another animal—one that had already been mounted and stuffed. Until there was no animal that she had not killed left to become.

ROSE AND THE RAVENS

She can fly, she discovers in the paralyzed place. She flies and flies in the dirt floor, pinned under the man's body until she can't remember anymore, until the bird brain is spilling over. Then she comes up for air.

Their feet with claws extended glide motionless under a cape of wing. Ravens. Three thousand of them, shearing through the clouds.

Sound came down from the black swooping sky as she hovered in the farthest reach of the giant oak tree. She knew they were looking for her, her only, as they hit the trunk like jags of lightning. She covered her ears, she buried her head, her toes she dug hard into the bark. The wind was up and blew at a steady fury. She saw the pine trees by the river rise up on their haggard roots like a church choir in unison, then crumble and crash down into the river. Trembling, off balance on the last bit of branch in the fractured air, she heard: "Rose and the Ravens. Rose and the Ravens. Rose and the Ravens. The Ravens."

"Come with us," she thought she heard them cry, and she thought she felt them pecking at her toes and flying at her eyes. But when she dared to look, she saw nothing, no birds, only the invisible sky.

She did not know if she wanted to be a bird at all. She did not know what she would do without feet to walk, arms to sweep, hands to stuff, without a human tongue.

"Dear God," she cried from the treetop. "I walked in the river, nearly died in the river. I climbed the tree in the river, hand over foot to the top, and now must I jump off into this nothing?"

The sky is black and beating with three thousand pairs of wings. The only sound on heaven and earth is the emptiness pushed back and forth by these wings.

"You're not supposed to be afraid," they screeched. "You're a girl who knows no fear."

"Fearless girl, courageous girl, nothing-can-scare-me girl, nothing can scare me . . ."

"But it is not a day for a human child to be out running, and I am a human child," wept Rose the Raven, pushing the feathers away from her bulging eyes. "I'm a human child!" she shakes her fist and screams until the world around her is all screams and the ravens are cawing, cawing, beating their wings against the green oak leaves and pushing the girl to the brink with their sharp, rough beaks.

Is the girl screaming, or is she calling like a raven to its flock when it finds carrion to eat? Is the human child screaming or cawing as she holds on for her life to the fragile twig beneath her claw feet?

Then the ceiling of sky lowers itself on top of her like a cool sheet of steel. She feels her skull cracking open as the flight of bird fights against the pull of earth. She doesn't notice the growth of her own black wing-span or the iridescent feathers sprouting on the crown of her head; now she doesn't know anything at all but flying. Down there means nothing. The earth is obscured by cloud; it is as if it didn't exist at all, ever at all. Never.

THE ATTIC AND THE WHITE SAILS

I'll take up your floor the way you take up your skirts when crossing a stream and there will be nothing but emptiness below you. And you can start all over again, anew.

—Benjamin

He had knocked first, but he knew she wouldn't be there. He picked the lock and found himself again in Miranda's attic. With his body lurched forward and the cumbersome rolls of canvas tucked under his arms, he looked like a second-rate aerial act from a traveling circus. The room was still, but his footsteps creaked loudly on the floorboards and to hush them, he tiptoed through the huge, hollow space.

He knew she had come back here after leading him down, for all fifteen windows stood open and in front of each was a white vase of paperwhite narcissus and a small mound of blood-orange peels, through which the wind flipped and whirled so turbulently that Benjamin thought himself in a blossoming orchard rather than the dust-blown attic that had nearly suffocated him the night before.

"Miranda, Miranda," he called her name softly, as if he were calling a wild animal that he did not want to frighten off.

He meant to be invisible, but he could not help himself; he wanted her to be there, to correct his idealistic memory, to wound the aura of the presence she had left behind.

"Miranda, are you here?" he whispered, seeking to sound her out from the dark cavities of rafters. Even in her absence, she seemed to fill this dim, inconclusive place with other places; every time he turned to the windows, the flowers, and the fruit, he discovered himself someplace pleasurable else.

He shut his eyes, hoping to limit his distractions. Displacing the floral shrines, he put down a roll of canvas, laying it flat against the wall of windows. All he had left to do was kick the canvas over the length of it, let it flood the attic floor.

His foot poised, he panicked when he saw that the paintings there had vanished. Now it was just wood, dirt brown, scratched and slivered. Either the pictures had disappeared into thin air or they had never existed at all. He refused to consider that. They had been there. He was sure he was no visionary.

He kept unfurling the white sails. They made a slight harp sound against the brittle floorboards. He found some old chimney bricks and laid them over the corners of the fabric until the canvas was rolled out smoothly, stretched securely over the entire floor. The wind hit up through the windows, throwing a shaft of air underneath each one, setting the canvas billowing like a bedsheet. Benjamin could picture the paintings stirring under there, the way children laugh and squirm under covers while a parent struggles to tuck them in, their feet kicking up the quilt and letting it float down and down. He could see the paintings rising up beneath, the very ones from the night before that had disappeared into the splintered old floor. Floating up through the canvas sheeting like the faces of the drowned.

Benjamin straightened the bricks and smoothed the white canvas. He smiled with satisfaction. He had figured it out, neat as cracking the combination of a safe: how to trap them here, in their own place, these visions. He had found a way to carry them away on his sea of white, white sails.

ROSE AND THE RAVENS

She sees his hands in her mind, moving back and forth, mechanical crea-
tures redundant and slowed with age. Oh, how many revolutions? Her
wings go up then down in such quick motion that there is no perceptible
movement at all and he is farther and farther away until she can't
remember the tangle of his fingers, the fumble fumble of his hands in her.

This time she made the transition from girl to bird with ease.
When she arrived at the edge of the last branch she did not
hesitate, she swooped.

It was as if she had always been living a parallel life, and
had never known it. That old oak might have been her home
in the air all the while the Hotel was her home on the earth,
though neither existence could recollect the other. Were the
two lives destined to meet someday? And if so, would a scrappy
blackbird with her girl-hands and girl-eyes sit down to dinner
with her family and expect to be served bird food? And what
would the family who raised and loved the girl do with this
strange half-breed she had become? Would they throw her out
into the field for compost? Banish her to a dark, curtained cage
on the veranda like the parrot?

She had to stop speculating and concentrate on navigating
the thick fog cover. Her heart beat fast and hard, her eyes
blinked, and a second filmy eyelid edged its way down over her
field of vision, giving her sight an ultraviolet light that guided
her through the opaque gray. The sun was lifting through the
clouds and she could see behind it a cluster of heavy forms. It
looked like a city hanging in the air, a cacophony of sharp geometric shapes.

"What on earth," she thought, "is a city doing here?"

The raven tried remembering herself as Rose in the hope
that she might be able to solve her confusion with some element of human logic or riddle of reason. But calling to her

girl-self here, in the midst of flight, did not provide the help she had hoped. It only made her homesick and caused her to start falling.

The moment she mistook glass for air, she smashed through the window and was knocked out. Coming to her senses, she is a girl again, lying alone and bloody in a house made of windows; even the floor beneath her is a window. She gets up and walks around in the pleasure of her human feet. She goes over to the one piece of furniture in the room, an old oak rocker. Back and forth she rocks herself, pumping hard as if she were on a swing. Outside, the ranges of clouds are adrift at eye level, and below her the tree in the river is a dense forest. She is at home here, neither trapped on earth nor locked in flight. She thinks: I can live here always, a girl inside a glass house forever looking out.

MIRANDA RECEIVES A GIFT

She opens the narrow blue door and steps in miserably, expect-
ing the familiar darkness and dust.

She can't believe what her eyes see. A carpet of light over
the attic floor. A floor that is now as white as a sheet of paper;
a floor that, every morning, she can roll up and throw away.
Softly she runs her hands over the canvas and slowly she lies
down on it, rocking back and forth until rocking turns to
rolling and she rubs herself around the white surface like a dog
in a meadow. She loves the way it smells, this linen, like the air
between winter and spring, the scent of complete possibility.

And the colors he left her! (For it must have been him,
who else?) At least a hundred tubes and cans and vials of paint.
Pigments of every imaginable shade and ones she'd never
dreamed of. Earthy reds that were dusted with the blue of a
summer sky and the greens of a northern sea; fertile yellows
that were composed of dandelion and the finest strands of a
silkworm's journey. The paints Benjamin brought belonged to
the world of the manmade as hers belonged solely to the body.
And the body has its limits, it occurs to her, as she rifles
through the new tubes of paints and the variety of brushes he's
left her by the south window in clear, neat rows of six. She
holds the brushes up to her face and tickles her nostrils with
the bristles. She tries to use them, but they make no sense to
her hands. She leaves them where she found them, by the open
windows, with the orange peels and narcissus rejects them for
the bent, broken willow stick. But she cleaves to his wonderful
paints. She picks up her willow stick and its strokes fall forward
and down on the gift of Benjamin's paints.

She watches as the colors disappear into the floor, gulped
down by the white, the canvas. After a while, as she stares, the
colors reappear on the surface, seeping through like a spread-
ing bloodstain. She answers with another sweep of the stick.
The pigments shimmer in the dark, tiny phosphorescent fish

in a white night sea. For the first time she is content in this room. For the first time, she feels a harmony here in the chaos of color and shape.

Though it is dark, the space gleams, either by way of moonlight reflected through the windowpanes or by the floor's own interior light. It pales and glows as the wind comes in and blows the canvas, each contraction of air bringing forth a new image on the floor from behind, from underneath the blank surface. Miranda, lying down, moves her willow wand across the floor of a room that is suddenly bleached white by the stretch of her staring. A staring that leads to the gift of paints he's left her. She loves these paints he's left her, loves them body and soul. But she knows they are not enough. She sticks a finger down her throat. And keeps on staring.

ROSE IN THE GLASS HOUSE

Tears swam in the eyes of the girl who wondered if she could ever get back to either sky or earth, where at least she was either bird or girl instead of this mongrel, mixed up thing rocking back and forth in a house of windows.

She sits and she rocks. Back and forth in the glass house, the walls of windows fanning out like petals all around her. She is surprised how at home she feels in the girl's body she thought she left behind for good in Trapper's shed, a gutted thing hungry to be filled in with a substitute of human flesh.

She rocked and she watched out the window. For hours she watched, maybe for days as the city of shapes took form outside her. Sometimes the images she saw from the glass house were so sharp, so striking that they made the windowpanes appear to fall away, leaving her unprotected, a creature without a skin.

A Gothic cathedral pushed up against the windowpanes and hid the heavens. Its savage gutters spit in her eye. The saints' faces on the tympanum were leprously worn off by dirt and rain, the stones that composed them a sickly yellow, as if the rocks themselves had been drained of life. The artistry that had made this building a weightless container of divine light escaped Rose, for at such close proximity the rotting rock carvings looked clumsy and crude. The gigantic edifice wavered back and forth as if it might start falling. Indeed, a dagger of spire broke off and spun through the air, threatening to crash through the glass into Rose's face, a cavern in which a thousand voices of a thousand centuries could huddle for warmth and prayer. Shrinking back, she squeezed her eyes shut.

When she opened them again and straightened out the frozen tangle of her limbs, the church had vanished. In its place she saw a dreary plain rising. Tall gray tomb-shaped rocks from some primitive age jutted out at intervals all over the landscape; miles of them, positioned with a careening hysteria that seemed to follow its own convoluted logic. She looked in vain through the window for something to climb out on that would lead her to this place, for to go there seemed less treacherous than to look at it. But there was nothing, and she wondered what would happen to her if she just walked out the glass door of the glass house into the air. Would she be falling, or would the tree that grew in the river return to catch her? She thought about this tree that she had climbed. It seemed she was the only one who could see it, and it appeared to come and go at its own pleasure. Where was it now? If it was gone, her escape was gone, and she would be a prisoner of this transparent house for the rest of her life, looking out.

The landscape exploded as if from within, and a granite pyramid, half-robbed of its facing, crested in front of her. Small bits of grass, moss, and fungus edged up between its ancient stones. The structure impressed her as hollow inside, almost like a brass cornet, and like a cornet she wanted to blow on it until the echo of her lips upon its emptiness became a sound between them. She absorbed the events of times past through the monuments that swelled up beyond reach outside the glass house. It was as if the told and untold history of humanity was a single song sung into a bird-girl who had run away from home and climbed a tree, and when she reached the top had learned to fly by falling. A girl who had landed in a place where she had no name but absorption, no need but inundation, no words but *tell me tell me everything and about everyone who ever was*. Monument after monument whirled by her like devastating cyclones in the sky's flatlands.

"Tell me," she prayed to the monuments, "the stories of the unknown, the forgotten; the slaves, the masons, the carriers of rock, the artisans of stone, all the stories of the invisible, the mute, the anonymous locked inside these cornerstones."

Face to face they confronted her: flesh to granite, to marble, to cement, to steel; the pantheons, forums, temples, granaries, railway stations, abbeys built up and thrown down by nature, time, and mankind. The buildings, the landscapes, the voices of past and of future raged against the walls of Rose's glass house.

ROSE IN CONVERSATION
WITH THE STUFFED BEASTS

It has been said of the earth: when man sought to know how he should live, he went into the wilderness and cried until in vision an animal brought wisdom to him.

She keeps going back to Trapper's shack so that the animals will share their secrets with her. They tell her: how the man-made of the land chops into the nature-made, how the two cleave to each other, how long ago it all started, why it goes on and for how long it might continue, this desperate corridor of communication that is invasion, that seems to be the journey of life after life.

They tell her where the sun comes from, where the moon goes, how a river carries its sorrow, what happens to a memory you can't recall, how to make hate; what a particle is, whether particles joined together make up a feeling, and whether particles can thus make hate, and turn to murder; why there is no smell to justice, how the sound of a bullet hurts the night.

When Rose asked the beasts one of her questions, and there were many, for she was unquenchably curious, the answers often took days, even months to complete, as they were formulated from so many different perspectives—the philosophical, the metaphysical, the scientific. Each answer was like an apple pared and cut into slices of what we do know, what we don't know, what we'll someday know, and what we'll never know. Each answer led to ten new questions until the girl and the beasts had run out of answers and talked to each other in a syncopated series of questions:

—Why are there bad people?
—Why are there good?
—How many years did it take for man to learn to
    make fire?

—How many years did it take to want to eat cooked things?
—Why does it rain?
—How deep is the ocean?
—How high is space?

They would go back and forth like this for hours, the girl and the animals alone in Trapper's shack. She was sure that once she had stuffed one specimen of every animal on God's green earth, she would know everything she needed to answer all her pressing questions—questions so bare and simple that had she asked them of adults, they would have laughed at her for being silly or just young or given her some clear-cut answer that ultimately left everything of importance out.

But the animals in Trapper's shed would sit by her for hours on end, for as long as she could keep her eyes open, for as long as her mind might work, and together they would consider the things of heaven and earth. Yet for all they gave her, they did not know the process by which they were stuffed and thus preserved. They expressed a deluded belief that they had always been such frozen perfection; that growing pains and death were things experienced by lesser beings. They seemed so happy and secure in this knowledge that it was hard to remember that they were not right.

If only she didn't have to kill them to give them life . . .

How could she dispute the man when he told her they were better stuffed? She was not an idiot; she'd seen creatures slaughtered and mutilated by the thousands in the wild, the skins taken, the carcasses left to rot, and it was not just the work of man. She's seen animals born crippled and deformed, at the mercy of the elements, or preyed upon by other animals. She was not a child. She had seen what nature could do.

Each day she practiced the arts of taxidermy, she felt more endowed with its victims' knowledge. She was sure that they could make this suffering inside her, this questioning, vanish. That finally she would strike on the question that, once answered, would make all the others cease.

THE FIRST TIME THEY PAINT TOGETHER

She had to stop him from touching her hands. They were so ugly, she thought, how could he stand them? She would have to chop them up and throw away all the pieces, she resolved, as she watched them grotesquely enlarged as the man held them down under the water. She would have to cut them up or she would have to give them to him. Either way, she knew she'd lose them.

He said to her, "Come with me," and together they walked the river. He set up his paint box by the bank, on the edge of a slippery overhang. Miranda took up her skirts, white and seamless cotton, and sat down on a rock behind him. She watched a family of snapping turtles stretch their necks in the sun and fall into a dazed snoozing on the scum of the water. She imagined she heard them lightly snoring, but then she realized that it was the yellow bees spinning around, fruitless in their search for pollen; for no flowers grew here, not even weeds. It was all rock and river, hard or liquid, and only those two extremes.

She watched him work. Like work was a miracle. She helped him mix the colors, set up the easel, spread the canvas. He had his brushes out, bunched together like a bouquet of flowers in an old mayonnaise jar, which he submerged in the cool, murky waters while he prepared the paints. He took off his jacket and exchanged it for a painter's smock. Miranda began to unroll the canvas by her feet, chasing it crosswise until it covered the expanse of rocky riverbank and hung majestically over the edge like a waterfall. With a big, thick brush, she dusted the canvas with chalk powder and slapped down a coat of rabbit-skin glue. She laughed as she worked, but he was so silent in his preparations that she was not sure he would be there when she looked up.

"Am I doing this right?" she inquired, as much to hear his voice as to assess the quality of her handiwork.

"Hmm," he muttered, not looking.

"Funny," she insisted, "I've never done this before, but I just know this is the way. Look how creamy and smooth it is; you can barely see the rough underneath."

He looked up, not at her but at the canvas, and he smiled.

"You're right, Miranda, and so quick. Why it looks like you've got fifty feet ready at least!"

She turned away, humiliated by the praise she would have of him.

He started to laugh at her, and the sound of it rumbled through the space that contained them—the river and its bank and the two of them—as if the whole comprised a canyon that his laughter raced down, escaping them through the crevices of rock and water to destinations as far away from her as the distant planets. She liked what happened to the sound of his joy, although it gave her a sense of abandonment that was, to her more rational self, idiotically morbid; for what stood before her now, looking down, was a kind and handsome young man who wanted to keep her company.

"Make me a sun to go with my painting," he said playfully, and she shivered.

"No," she answered quickly. "I wouldn't know how to paint on your painting."

He shook his head, disappointed. On his palate were undistinguished blobs of white, blue, and green.

"Besides," said Miranda, feeling as if she needed to justify her resistance, "I don't paint so well from real life—the light's too bright."

"Miranda," he called to her. His hand was now imperceptibly open and a small sable brush lay between the fingers. Suddenly beneath this brush there was growing the river and the bank on which they sat, except they were not in the picture, nor were the reams of blank canvas the girl had so diligently prepared. Each image he made was remarkably true to life; even the temper of the day seemed accurately reproduced, clearheaded and on the move, with a hint of an approaching storm. Then the brush fell from his hand, and he lay on his back, staring up at the clouds and imagining in them an audience to his impressive depiction of a mysterious continent and its mercurial changes. He got up and kneeled to her; he took the brush and pressed it into her hand and closed her hand around it until she could not let go.

"Make me a sun to go with my painting," he urged her again. And she said nothing.

"Go on," he urged, "you know how to. If you want you can close your eyes while you do."

And she did, because to make the brush perform was to her an act of such confusion, fear, and shame, with a result so totally out of her control, that the moment she began, it occurred to her that she must be in love with this young man or she would not do this thing, wide-awake and in the light of day.

She put her sun to his painting. And she could see right away that he hated it. She had created an object so out of keeping with the style of his work that it looked pasted on, this child's sun, mustard colored with no subtlety of shading. It was the shape of a deflating balloon, set low on his exacting horizon, with swirls upon swirls making up its volume, creating such a whirling dervish effect that one might think there were souls burning up inside this sun.

He said nothing to her; but his hand, confident and quick, took up the brush and fell on the canvas.

"Don't do that!" she screamed. "Don't you cover up my sun."

He stopped, startled by her outburst.

"Miranda," he said kindly, "I'm just trying to make it fit the composition. The way it is, it just isn't natural."

"If you don't want my help," she cried, "don't ask for it."

Gone were her rough swirls and thick strokes. It was as if they had never been there at all. The sun was now a vague object in the background of Benjamin's cloudy, tree-dense sky; the river he painted was too muddy to reflect its rays.

"Isn't this more the way it really is?" He held her wrist tenderly and firmly.

"You made a bad mistake," she said softly. Pulling herself from his grip, she took off down the rocks as fast as she could. She shook her head back and forth, hard, as if to make the image of her mutilated painting fall out of her mind. Where was the sun he asked her to make? And the faces in flames there? And her bright colors? Watered down, hidden under horrid green trees. She resolved never to paint him another thing. Her heart was running.

Benjamin did not run after her. He knew that some griefs must be endured alone, until the heart grows sick of its loneliness and surrenders its sense of justice for companionship. He knew, too, that the panorama begun must not be stopped, for the oil was in danger of drying if he left it now. But looking down, he could not help noticing that the mixture of the girl's work and his own made for a most intriguing painting.

LEAVING THE GLASS HOUSE

Her right foot was out the door before she realized there was nothing to walk out on. She slipped backward into space, her red hair flying up, her eyes desperate for a fixed object as she plummeted down. Then to her mind came the flight of a sleek black bird with a golden beak. And she stopped falling.

The day she walked out of the glass house, she fell into a despondent land. People all over a crowded expanse. The world outside the glass house was homeless. But the people couldn't even wander, which is the privilege of the homeless, because there was no room to move. People even slept standing up. Rose tried to talk to them, for she understood their language, the universal exile tongue of hunger and desperation. But they acted as if she was not there.

She saw a wolf pup sitting on top of a dead, upright body. The pup was sleeping, but his eyes were open. She called to him, in silence.

"What's going on here?" she asked.

"The same as always," the young wolf replied.

"That's not true. It was never like this at my parents' Hotel, it's not like this inside the glass house. Such misery."

The wolf pup laughed. When he laughed, he raised his long snout to the sky like a giant funnel sucking down all the light. The sky turned to mud.

"It is too like this where you come from. Maybe you can't see it, like living in the North and trying to see the South. Or you might be right in the middle of it and not feel it yet; like being in the eye of a storm. Who on earth sees with their own eyes that the ground they're standing on is not flat but round? That's the problem with your family's Hotel and your little glass house in the sky; you could be stepping over the bodies of a million people; they could be stepping all over you and you wouldn't know it. You'd feel it, like a choking in your chest, an itching in your throat. But you wouldn't know what it was. That's why even when we sleep we don't close our eyes, not here, not anymore. We can't."

"Tell me what to do." the girl asked the wolf. "Tell me what to do, if misery is so complete."

The wolf grinned. He said, "Do what most people do: ignore it. When things are too much, the mind sleeps, the tongue rolls."

"but I can't do that."

The wolf just laughed. He laughed so much that he howled.

"My dear," he chortled, "what do you mean you can't do that? You're the one living in a glass house, not I."

His howling made the corpse he was sitting on wake up and the one next to it and the one next to that one, like a toppling row of dominos. They moved the little that they could; they laughed as much as they were able; their throats choked with other bodies and the mud of the earth that had nowhere else to go. Rose could feel them pressing in on her. There was no distance left.

"Wrong person," she wept to herself, "the wrong person to be seeing this, with my paralyzed tongue and failing wings."

Birds aren't angels, she thinks to herself; their wings hold up nothing. If chaos to be transformed into clarity must be enacted of violence, then this is it, the beginning . . .

The wolf says: "You should eat something, Rose, you're getting flimsy in the head."

He hands her a chunk of raw meat, tears it from a body who screams, puts it to her mouth. Rose eats, gingerly at first, and then gnawing thoughtfully.

"That's better," exclaims the wolf.

"Yes," says Rose, "now I'm not so starving. I can think."

She gets up, starts walking through the corpses with the wolf pup yelping at her side with its blue glass eyes.

"Isn't sight a blessing," he says to her as they walk and walk and walk.

ROSE AT TRAPPER'S DOOR

"Let me in, Trapper," the desperate child cried, "Trapper, let me in, let me in."

But she could see through the window that his coat was not on its hook, his boots were gone from the side of the fire, and the fire itself had not been lit at all that day. So she took herself around the side of the cabin, and as he taught her, she broke in.

Maybe, thought Rose, even though he isn't here to give me one new word, one more piece to this puzzle, maybe if I just sit there with them, a girl and her stuffed animals, I could stay away from the glass house and stay a girl on earth forever.

In the dim leaf light of the cabin, the stuffed were strewn everywhere—standing, crouching, lying—the panther, the heron, the rattlesnake, the bear cub that was her first. Looking around the creature-filled room, it seemed to the astonished girl that there was no life there. The animals who talked to her were silent. And when she pulled on their mouths to make them speak, she found they had no tongues.

"Why isn't he here to talk to me?" wondered the girl.

She knew what he would say if she told him that the stuffed animals had all suddenly died, for that is what it seemed to her now. He would say she had lost her senses, why, he could hear them carrying on right this minute, he could hear their blood, touch their breath, smell their thoughts. But would he tell her what she should do, what she should believe? She had to know how to believe again. She had to believe that any moment he'd be there, whispering in her ear "Don't you remember, remember?" And he would be more tender than ever she could remember. He would fill her head with more secret words of embalming and she would believe that with this special knowledge, she would be saved from the unspeakable glass that forced her to watch things she could not wholly enter or change. He would put his arms around her. He would take her in. Feed her. She would understand. And they would go hunting again.

But he wasn't there and she didn't know when he would return—two hours, two years. She didn't know, couldn't wait. Surrounded by the stuffed trophies of the hunt that she could no longer hear nor feel, she took the knife that lay by his bed.

She pulls down a freshly killed creature—an otter, she thinks it is. To stuff one of the animals alone—if she can do it alone, she reasons, she will not need him. She'll throw him away like old meat, she vows. This is what she dreams of doing. She dreams of not needing him to understand, to listen, to teach. She would sit alone with the animals that she alone had stuffed. There would be a constant deep spring between them; the air would smell of promise and she would not have to struggle anymore. The knife raised in the air, she looks down at the dead thing. It's curled in the nursing position, its back paws splayed the way an animal does when asleep, it's dreaming. She knows it has its secrets. That its silence carries secrets. She's tired of not knowing what they are.

Her arms are in the otter's belly; up to her elbows, she's warm with blood and feces. She thinks her hands will stay in there forever; rot in there like fallen leaves. One hand then the other pulling out the viscous mess. One hand holds the needle, the other aligns the thread, and it is done, the sewing up unto itself.

"Talk to me," Rose demands, "talk to me . . ."

But the animal before her now was still and silent. How was she, Rose, to change if the creature was silent?

Maybe for it to talk to her, she speculates, she must wait until the embalming takes. Meanwhile she is dreaming a paradise of knowledge. It turns the gruesome work into a sort of gardening: all the parts that she's thrown out are weeds, the soil she tends is its emptied body. She sits up for as long as she can with this the first animal she has stuffed alone, waiting for it to start talking.

It seemed to her that waiting was killing her; that seeing and experiencing too much while knowing too little was going to destroy her; that the Rose who stuffed, the raven who flew, and the girl at watch in the glass house were all enemies of each other. She waits and she waits, until sleep is irresistible. When it comes, it's not like sleep at all; it's like death. So when she wakes, it's not like waking at all, but like being brought back from the dead. When she wakes, it's morning, before light. The animal is lying on its side exactly the way she left it. It is saying nothing, nothing, and not only that, it stinks.

She takes down the stuffed bear cub from its place of honor on the shelf over Trapper's bed. She holds it in her arms, rocking. It looks so beautiful. It smells so sweet. She yearns for the times they did it together. When they did it together, she knew what he knew, believed what he believed. She rocks faster and harder. It's almost like running.

She was scared he would come back and find her there, looking down in her arms at what she had done. What had she done? What would he do to her seeing how she had acted in his absence? In her frenzy she'd pulled the little bear apart; its legs ripped off and hurled upon the unmade bed, its head in the dying fire, chunks of its fur in her teeth. She had to do something, do something. Put it back together somehow or surely he would kill her. Trembling, she gathered up the pieces, rescued the head from the ashes, combed out the fur, sewed back on the limbs, so that once again the creature seemed peacefully asleep. But the eyes, the eyes were shattered, little bits of glass gone everywhere. To put back the eyes was impossible, so she gathered their splinters in her pockets, hoping that he would not find them when he returned. She sewed up the vacant holes that were now the creature's eyes—it was supposed to be sleeping anyhow—then hid its body behind a leering puma. She realized all this was fruitless, that he knew the exact position and condition of each of his trophies; that when he came back he would look and nothing she could do now would stop him. She had gained nothing by her solitary attempt but rot and mutilation. And the promise of the man's sure, swift punishment when he found her out.

BENJAMIN AT THE ATTIC DOOR

"Let me in, let me in, Miranda," he cried, "Miranda, Miranda, let me in."

She could hear his voice like an earth tremor underneath, as she stood, her arms out, grasping the willow branch, in the middle of a fresh floor painting.

"Leave me alone," she screamed. "You hate the work you say is mine. You made me own it and now you say it is nothing. Leave me be."

Beneath her feet lay a road of tangled red arteries and blue veins with a giant grandfather's clock growing out of it. The clock had people's names that she couldn't make out scrawled all over its face instead of numerals.

"I don't hate your work, I love your work," he coaxed.

"It's not my work. Some monster made it," whimpered the girl, spread-eagle on the floor, as if to smother the hideous thing.

"It is your work. I love your work," said the young man again. "Miranda, I love you. Please Miranda, let me in."

On the road of veins beneath her feet, in faded shades of black and gray, there stood two children: a girl and a boy holding hands and swinging them as they went forward. In her free hand, the girl was leading a heart by a ribbon, like a dog on a leash, and in his, the boy held out a map of the world. Fish swam above their heads and stars moved below their feet. It was their names, Miranda's and Benjamin's, that were written all over the clock and as the brass hands ticked, it was as if time itself was cutting through them.

This is where Miranda stood shuddering in the first light of morning with Benjamin knocking on her door. She crept off the still-wet canvas, her hands stretched out, her poor heart heaving. Her hands were the color of mud and she smelled of freshly turned dirt.

She went to open.

ROSE IN THE CITY OF SHAPES

Rose climbed up, foot over hand, so fast they blurred into wing, a small hard girl like a hazelnut making her way up a huge oak tree. When she reached the top she took off running until running became flying; a slight transformation of necessity by velocity, and she was a raven; glossy, fat, and sleek, her eyes endless magnetic bubbles, black holes in space, against her chaotic feathered head and peninsular range of beak. Then she crashed through the glass, a reflection she could not see, and became a girl again.

Shipwrecked in the glass house, the body of the girl and the sensibility of the bird merged. Rose hated the confusion of images that the eyes of flight and the eyes of gravity perceived together. They saw simultaneously dimensions that one hardly thinks of in the same breath: the historical and the geometric; the primitive and the microscopic; the architectural and the planetary. She saw the bones while she was seeing what lay inside the bones and how the cells of bone multiplied themselves to take on form and function in a world that was at once vuluptousness and floor plan, concretization and dream.

She saw an ancient aqueduct spinning around in the sky with its life-sized blueprint veiled over it like a fisherman's net. She saw fire raging in a war-torn city while a series of one-dimensional squares and triangles, flat as flounders, stood ground with the thick debris of murdered bodies and the exploding abundance of neglected gardens. Neither had the people of the city any fixed identity. She saw the face of an emperor, of a martyr, of a slave, changing one into another. Each proclaimed themselves to be the true face. Many of them had histories that had been erased from human memory. But when Rose tried to approach them, they ignored her so completely she began to believe herself that she was not there.

And now, after she left the city, she could barely remember these people, as if once they had come into her time frame and passed through her body, they no longer existed in their own particularity. And she wanted them in their own, needed to see them living in their own immutable beings. It was for this that she had ventured into the world past the tree. But the more Rose went to the city of shapes that existed beyond flying, the more she began to have the odd feeling that she was being walked through by its inhabitants, that their separation was a lie, that all solid matter, all boundaries between things were delusions of survival. The beings outside the glass house passed through her like a shortcut through a field. Were they people at all, she wondered, or were they only the dreams and memories of people imprinted on the glass-boundaried landscape?

She had no molecular solidity as either girl or bird in this place. Here she had a third identity, a transparent one. It was as if she were that unseen pivotal point in religious postcards where the images whir back and forth between two disparate pictures, folding one over the other, with no respect for sense or clarity, insistent only that they occupy the same field of vision at the same time.

CORA'S HOUSE

Ready for auction, the stained-glass window that once stood thirty feet high in the main stairwell was lying flat in the middle of the ballroom floor, with the sun beating down on it and nowhere to reflect the colors it was striking.

Cora smiled, remembering the Cistercian abbey the panel had come from and how many letters back and forth across the sea it had taken for it to emerge here, packed in straw on a flatboard wagon drawn by six exhausted oxen on a maize-summer day at the peak of harvest; and how they had needed to cut out an extra ten feet from the Hotel's brick exterior to fit the window in and how this had necessitated the complete resituating of the mahogany central staircase, which took so long that the children learned to climb the four stories up and down the stone outer wall like mountain goats before they had any idea what it was like to use stairs.

Now the medieval stained glass lay dull and dark on the floor, the apostles Mark and James staring up blankly at the place where the Venetian crystal chandelier had been ripped out. A few green horseflies flitted around looking for some debris to feed on, and finding none, frantically sought a way out. But they were trapped; for Cora had shut up all the windows and doors.

The auction nights were feverishly long. At first, just a few curious transients came to loiter, then the local towns folk showed up for a lark. Soon people were catching trains and wagons from all over the country to attend Cora's auctions and marvel at the riches she had for sale. But no matter how hard she tried, she could convince none of her eager customers to bring their own goods to sell. The objects of the Hotel, meant to be merely bait to bring other people's goods upon the block, remained the only articles offered up at the auction house. But Cora was sure she had to keep selling—that it would lead her to the future.

"The more that's gone," she declared to him as she pulled Emmanuel's picture off the wall for the next day's sale, "the surer I'll see my way clear to saving our Hotel and the family. Even if it means selling every single thing we own."

THE HUNTING

In many languages, Trapper explained, "to sacrifice" and "to send home" are the same word. Gods like to visit the earth, and to do it, they have to put on an animal body, but then they are trapped in their animal disguise. They give their flesh gratefully to those who set them free. An animal is a visitor from the spirit world, to which we are kindly returning it by killing it, he said.

This time they go after a wolf "because," he said, "you've never stuffed a wolf before. It'll be good for you. Each animal is different and thus must be known singularly. I hope by the time I die, I have myself killed a pair of them all."

"Then will I be wise?" asked the girl hopefully.

"Yes, Rose," the man smiled.

The steel-jawed trap did its work, but the creature was still alive and in such pain that she wanted to finish it off with a gun. But Trapper said that would make an ugly hole.

"If you're going to make them live forever, you'd better make them pretty," he said.

He forced her to break its neck instead.

"That doesn't leave any marks on the pelt," he told her. Then he winked and said, "Next time, little lady, just set the jaws right. If you had, he would have died on the spot."

"But I don't like to hurt anything," she said.

"That's why you need to do the best job," he said, tenderly pressing her down upon his knee, "shoot the best shot, set the best trap—the ones that drown or break the neck—then the suffering amounts to nothing, just a moment's itch for the reward of eternity."

He looked exaltedly around him. "Listen, Rose, it's logic, pure and simple: You can't have my kind of power unless you do the dirty work too. Now clean this mess up," he said and left.

❦

The creature tried pathetically to get up and escape the human form looking down. It was then that she recognized the wolf who had befriended her and led her out of the glass house into the inhabited sky.

"Why did you do this to me?" he whispered.

"It was a mistake. I didn't mean to get you. I was trapping."

"Why do you do this?"

"For the animals."

"For yourself."

"Let me help you."

"I helped you."

"Here now, don't move," the girl said, trying to stem her panic.

The animal stared blankly. Its eyes were now the eyes of all the brutally broken young who have no chance but to continue life broken.

His eyes were like hammers, thought Rose.

"I helped you," yelped the wolf.

"You weren't supposed to be here," answered the broken girl. "You don't live down here," she insisted. "You live up there."

"I suppose now you'll want to stuff me, Rose, give me a taste of your everlasting medicine."

"I'll fix it," the girl lied. "You are not going to die."

She gathered the thing in her arms. Trapper would fashion new bones for the wolf, and the wolf would run again; hide, play, seek, he would be himself again, predator, friend, guide. "Better than new," she promised.

At night the young wolf enters her dreams. He lies in her sleeping arms, licks her face, tickles her feet, paws at her to follow him. Takes her traveling in the black sky, teaches her to jump star to star, shows her how to hang from cold spots in the atmosphere; how to travel time, how to enter different eras from different points of view and how to leap out of them to no time, which is the border between times. He begs her not to stuff him, but to carry him up the tree in the river, lay him to rest in the tallest branches; *the least you can do*, he says, *for a friend*. His body on her back, she scales the trunk. In the morning she finds herself alone in the tree.

"Can't even snap a neck right." She heard the man. "The wolf is dead," he cried up from the ground. "A hole through the head, I put it out of its misery. It was too mutilated to stuff. So I buried it. For good luck."

THE JOURNEYMAN

She listened again to what he had promised; that they were not really dead, but preserved perfectly in a better life. He told her the wolf pup had just been a bad dream. And she believed.

She could barely remember a time anymore when she did not kill, did not stuff. She would talk to them after she killed them, like nothing had happened between them, like they were the best of friends, like they were going to have a grand old time, like they were going to be together forever and ever.

After the girl and the man made love, which they always did on the ground after a kill, she would help him drag the creature back to the shack, where they would hang it upside down and slit it down the middle to drain its blood.

"Blood goes bad when the life's gone," he told her. "An imperfect substance, blood," he said, sadly shaking his head as he mixed the chemical solution to replace it.

He would let her choose the color of eyes, the type of mount, the rock or piece of tree trunk that would serve as the natural habitat for each new specimen. And while he slept, because the work was hard and long and he was old, he would let her play with the stuffed animals in the shed. With Trapper at her side, they had begun to talk to her again. They told her everything about their lives; what they did all day long in the forever, what they ate, drank, thought, how they played. What they knew.

They asked her when she was going to join them in the still life, the afterlife that had no end. They kept asking:

"When are you coming?"

And she, nervously, "As soon as I can."

"When's that?"

"As soon as I know everything I need to."

"Why do you need to know anything?"

"Because when you don't know, you don't have a leg to stand on in this world."

"Why do you need to stand," they teased. "We heard you can fly."

"Who told you that?"

"Its a secret."

"Don't tell him, he'll kill me if he finds out."

"Why should he kill you for not being human, Rose? Why would he kill you for being a bird?"

"How do you know?"

"We know . . . Why do you think he'd end your life, when everything he does is to bring back life?"

"That's right," the girl stuttered.

"Then why are you afraid? You were never afraid before."

"Because I won't be Rose anymore. He'll shoot down the raven to give it forever-life and Rose, Rose will be dead; there will be no more Rose and I'll not have learned how to do it myself."

"Do what?"

"Preserve life."

"He hasn't taught you yet?"

"He says it takes a long time."

"Maybe he's not teaching you right. What makes you think we're alive?"

"You talk to me."

"We do?"

"Don't do this."

"Why do you think?"

"He promised me."

"Then why aren't we moving, Rose? When a thing is alive, it *moves*."

"Because . . . because you don't need to. You can get everybody to wait on you, so why should you? Why should you move at all if you don't have to?"

"That's what he says."

"That's what he says."

"Maybe he's a liar."

"He never lied to me, he loves me."

"Then why do you think he'd shoot you dead?"

"Because he wouldn't recognize me. I'd look like any other dumb black bird."

"So why don't you tell him. Warn him."

"Tell him?"

"Yes."

"I can't."

"So you think you can stop changing back?"

"I don't understand."

"Don't play dumb, girl. You think you can stop changing back into the scavenger bird you've become?"

"Yes, I can!"

"No, Rose. You can't."

UP AND DOWN THE RIVER

Every night for dinner, they came home; but the days, no one knew where they went. When they left in the morning, it was as if the landscape had devoured them, or they had grown chameleon skins and wherever they traveled they just blended in.

They walk for miles, as if miles were minutes. Easels, paint kits, picnic basket, camp stools, and umbrellas squeezed under their arms, grasped in their hands, strapped to their backs, but they feel weightless. Chasing each other back and forth as they go walking. The smallest thing they see astounds them. They point, they gasp; behind their hands they whisper:

"Look, Benjamin."

"Look, Miranda."

Sometimes it's a cloud in the sky turning like a ship on the sea. Sometimes it's a beetle creeping up a towering weed. Sometimes it's a rock, alone, in the middle of a field.

"Look, Benjamin."

"Look, Miranda."

One hand points while the other drags out the instruments. Now they're both on their camp stools, at their easels. They work quickly to catch each image at the second they see it; before the light changes or the deer moves or memory lies. Their eyes look out, their brushes bear down. The hand of hers that does not paint burrows itself under her apron where it clenches and releases, again and again; it won't shut up.

"Look, Benjamin."

And he answers:

"Look, Miranda," as his mouth moves in a sucking motion, the lips and the teeth chewing on each other until they draw blood.

Many sounds accompany them, insects being the loudest, as honey bees, crickets, and locusts compete for sonic space. There are also the background shadow noises that follow them: natives singing, mothers calling, the engines and factories of town, the vague roaring of oceans far away and pressing in on the continent's two sides. Then there were the sounds that have no origin and no description. These were the ones that awed them, as if deep valley plus side of rock were one sound, fog and tree line another. These were the combinations that Miranda and Benjamin loved best to paint. Sitting side by side in the heat of the day, they tried to depict these things half vision, half reality, with ample space in between for the observer to step in and dream.

When their work was done and the sky began to darken in that late-afternoon way that makes the trees and rocks look paper-cutout bold and disembodied, they would share some smoked beef, a hard cheese, and a slab of Emerald's nut bread. They would eat like wolves, tearing at their food, swallowing in gleeful chunks, without tasting, barely chewing, as if the only thing they cared about was the transformation of its substance into the energy that would urge them on to more activity. Then, full in the stomach, they would pack up and head back, following the river until they had no choice but to leave it and climb up the pine trail to the Hotel.

After dinner they would steal out to the back porch and light the citronella candles that repelled the mosquitoes and attracted the gypsy moths, whose shadows would spin and flutter over the lovers' golden wax-illumined hands. Together, in the yellow light, they would look at what they painted that day.

Each held a hand, the painting one, behind their back, shouting in a whisper: "Go—one, two, three," and throwing out their fists—"You're it,"—to see who should go first. This time she won and out the other hand came, fingertips in a light, careful grip over the edge of her canvas.

"Here it is," she says, with a discernible expression of pride.

He's very close to her now, so much so that she feels her body has expanded, that it holds the territory of his chest, his arms, and his legs in her own. She thinks she should feel full, and she supposes she does, but she also feels herself reeling, the way a body does in a sea that has just buoyed her up and suddenly pulls her under. He bends close to the canvas, as if to counter its shadow and her reflection, his arms thrown out for balance and framing.

Fascinated by the painting, he has forgotten her entirely. The girl knows this. This is where she starts to drown.

He sees in the painting a low, gentle mountain. Somewhere in the stretch of it, a tall white lighthouse emits a green flashing light. Benjamin traces the journey of the light and he discovers that it doesn't lead to the sea at all, but to another mountain barely visible in the background. At its precipice, a young, beautiful woman is standing with her eyes shut, in the wind. Her dress, which reaches and blows around her knees, seems more alive than her body. In fact, she has the features, even the poise, of the dead.

Miranda kneels beside Benjamin, the canvas between them. Their eyes form the well of a valley; they're plunged exactly like two suicides. He can see nothing but her eyes looking in the same direction as his. Her violet eyes, wild, hungry as teeth. As she stares, he fears they will consume the canvas.

"Now let's see your picture," she coaxes him.

He takes the canvas from behind his back and stands it up on the seat of an old wicker armchair.

"Here it is," he says proudly, standing back for her to see.

It was a landscape, true to life in its most excruciating details; but what caught the girl by surprise was the focus in the painting. While there were the mountains they had walked, the meadows they had crossed, the animals, the river, the trees they had seen, all minutely reproduced, the painting itself seemed all sky. It was as if all the details he had recorded faded in the immensity of this sky. It made her want to walk around on the clouds, as she was sure her gypsy heart did many a night while she herself lay tight and paralyzed on the attic floor. Her eyes now found proof of what her heart had always hoped about the atmosphere: that it was a rich and buoyant environment, that it would float her; she would not go down.

Frenzied, in a kind of ecstasy, she dragged her own painting back up into the light, placing it on the wide porch swing. She ran to the chair upon which Benjamin's canvas lay and pulled it over to the swing until their two pictures formed a single line. Rain began to fall lightly and cloud came fast over cloud, striking shadows over the backyard willow so that it looked like a woman cradling something in her arms and rocking in the wind that was building up over the ridge as the rain started to come down harder.

"We must go in now," he said, grasping her arm.

She shrugged him off sharply, as if he were a tick. She went to his painting, lying on the rocking chair, untouched by the rain as rain fell all around them. She pushed it hard, and it lurched into motion. She pushed and pushed, and in a path of jerks and stumbles, it careened but never fell. Then Miranda's painting, which was sitting serenely on the still porch swing, suddenly began to sing. A wind came up and caught the sound:

"*I was once a-young like you,*
all men's pleasures did a-find me . . ."

The one painting silent and swinging, the other singing and still as stone; together they made a moving picture, a picture that leapt, that sang. Miranda gazed at their two compositions. How much more wonderful they were this way, she thought, each one unique and animated. And she wished the paintings could always be revealed like this, rather than as flat, lifeless entities pasted and sewn together to make the panorama roll.

Lightning cracked open the sky as if the sky were a jar of paint that broke to pieces and poured down. In the rain running over them, they pressed their bodies together to protect the work and their lips made a covered bridge over the paintings to save them. But they were too late. The bright colors bled onto the floor as their mouths ran over with paint and rain. The pictures were ruined.

For the first time since she could remember, Miranda slept through the night, and when she awoke in the morning there was nothing on the attic floor to alarm her. When she awoke, she saw only waves and waves of pure white canvas below her as if she had been sleeping on clouds.

EVERYONE OUTSIDE

From where she was lying, half-hidden in the high grass that had taken miraculous growth in the brief, hot spring, Rose could see her mother and sister working. They were concealed from each other by the tall, frazzled side hedge that divided the yard. Nearest to her, she saw Cora, in a crisp pair of men's overalls and a long baker's apron, down on her knees digging up the mosaic tiles that wound around the wide veranda. On the far side of the Hotel, by the backyard willow, Rose observed her sister bent over the slight figure of Benjamin, who was peering into a half-finished canvas.

Cora was holding mason's tools in her hands, a trowel and a cutter. She was meticulously dislodging each tiny tile in the mosaic floor so that the whole thing could be auctioned off and put back together somewhere else. This task was far from easy, as the tiles depicted a maze and were somewhat constructed in the fashion of one. Cora sat down in the midst of her labors to weep.

"What am I doing," she asked herself, "selling off the very floorboards of our home?" She looked over the sphere of her destruction, staring confusedly at the cutter she clutched in her hand, the grout that lay scattered in a haze around her feet, the half-destroyed mosaic maze that encircled her bent-over body.

Her mother was a rage of activity, Rose marveled as she watched Cora's cramped but constant movement over the palette of porch. While dust and dirt whirled around her, Cora herself managed to remain immaculately neat. Only her hair, bursting from its construction of braids and bun, seemed to have any relation to the destruction she was wreaking.

Cora remembered instructing the children how to walk the porch maze, for it was the only way anyone could enter the Hotel. It worked like a lock against all strangers, even those earnest ones who might wish to stay there, but feared getting irrevocably lost in the labyrinth of the veranda. Cora remembered her daughters' terrified screams when they would find themselves paralyzed in the serpentine space, having lost their way; and how she would tell them, firmly and without stepping one foot in the direction of their aid, that the only way to get through it was with their eyes shut and crawling on their hands and knees until the impression of the tiles stuck to the body, and talked to the body, told it how and when to turn and reach. She remembered her pride as the girls learned to maneuver through the mosaic until they no longer got frightened or lost in the wide front porch, but tripped through with the ease of practiced thieves.

Cora looked down sadly at the floorboards that lay rotting underneath the tiles. For years, the vibrancy of that mosaic floor had reflected and recorded the memories of her life on the frontier. Now that it was gone, what would happen, she wondered, to all those memories the maze of mosaics had chronicled and preserved while she herself had forgotten them? Where would they go? she wondered, hunched over in the scraped out, vacant place.

Rose watched her mother work the way one watches a child at the beach who cannot swim. Every time she slumped over and dropped a tool, the girl sat up, alert. Even from a distance, she could see that her mother was miserable in her obsessive surgeries. As Cora tore up for auction the priceless floor, her eyes darted hungrily to the heavy white columns that held up the entire Hotel, and Rose could imagine her calculating their worth on the market and what it might take to bring them down. Cora's project of disassembling the Hotel had transformed her motion and will into an incessant urge for unraveling. Rose wondered how her mother's quest would end, as she pioneered a path that was made possible only by her clearing it of every object, every substance she had ever treasured in her life.

Inside the Hotel, it was even worse. Cora had stolen the beds one morning, all of them, and the girls had seen them up on the block that very afternoon. The whole family was reduced to sleeping on the bare floor, without quilts or pillows or sheets. Rose had simply moved outdoors, spending her nights as a raven in the trees or a girl in Trapper's shed, because it seemed that she barely had a home anymore. Sighing, she raised her dirty elbows off the pressure of earth, and turned her body over slowly, until her back rested on the ground.

Stretched out and averting her eyes from the noonday sun, Rose could see her sister and the stranger standing under the willow tree, surrounded by canvas and paint. He was singing a chantey and when he got to the lusty parts, he would pause, and she would laugh and laugh, until the canvas fell from her grasp and rolled along the ground. He would reproduce in paint exactly what he saw: the great pines, the river shallows, the long canoes that still sometimes skirted by, the steamers that raced away at a distance, the wild geese, the mountains. As long as she laughed and pointed to what she saw for him to fol-low with his eyes, he kept to his work, but when she stopped for a second, he would drop his brush and start the kissing. Up and down the face and neck they went, chasing kisses; then suddenly, she'd lower her head like a horse avoiding the bridle and snap up the fallen brush from the soil and swoosh it clean in one of the large, deep jars of turpentine that stood all around them. She would hand it back, and, firmly turning his face to the landscape, she would point, "Here, here, and here."

Rose could see them, sure as through a spyglass, though they believed theirs was the utmost private act. She disliked watching her sister growing daily closer to this young man. Something about him made Rose shrink; something about the two of them together made her want to mash their faces in the mud. Before he came, she had a sister, and now she was com-pletely shut out. Now, as the wilderness began to swallow them up and their Hotel verged on disintegration, Benjamin was the only one Miranda cared for.

He had surely come to save her, thought Miranda in the nights when the paintings rushed out of her body onto the attic floor. He loved the paintings as much as they horrified her, but for his sake, she began not to hate them so much. She believed what he said to her, not for what it meant, but rather in the hope that it would keep him from leaving her. She wanted to be close to him, to give the paintings to him, thereby to purchase her place by his side, itinerant as he, but latched to the security of his belief in their mission. It hurt her to see how he had begun to toy with her paintings, the way he scissored them apart and sewed them on to his own. But each time he came to her in the early mornings and rolled up her night's labor, she felt herself transported out of chaos and insubstantiality; a gypsy heart still, but with a pair of sturdy feet.

Rose saw that everything that was vibrant and alive in Miranda seemed to be daily draining from her face and animating his, until he began to look more like her than she did. At the dinner table where the young man was no longer a stranger, Rose took to holding the blade of her dinner knife up to her eye like a mirror. Reflected in skinny miniature, she stared in disgust at Benjamin. She turned the knife slowly, until he disappeared into its cutting edge. She decided she would get him to take a walk with her into the mountains, and there put a bullet through his head. She liked the idea of a slender trail of red running down the mossy slope, his blue eyes open wide like a mounted hawk's, his expiring hands hefting the grass.

Alone like this, more and more, Rose found herself perched on the tree in the river or rocking in the glass house. She believed she wasn't much of a child anymore with her life at home and her life in the skies. But what is a child anyway, she sighed, if not fragments of life in transition, from one stage to another, from one sphere to another, somehow held together by a body that is itself in the midst of metamorphosis? She came to believe that she swam in a thin capsule of dirt in the middle of the earth where she could breathe, always alert, always awake, but growing more and more unconscious of her present life and her past, until her only conviction was in the future, where she sat rocking back and forth in the glass house. She began to believe that she never slept. People in the future, she sighed, do not sleep; if they did they'd never get there.

Rose couldn't bear to watch the lovers anymore. Her gaze turned back to her mother, deliriously chopping away at the mosaic floor, her body layered in Roman dust. Rose couldn't stand looking at either of them, sister or mother. It was as if, without going anyplace at all, her family had abandoned her, her mother to the obsession of selling, her sister to the hunger of love. She couldn't stand to look either left or right, so she kept still and stared straight up at the blinding sky.

BENJAMIN AND MIRANDA
WALK THE HARVEST

Their days were full, but his dreams were fuller. He pictured himself on a large ship, his hand saluting his eyes as they strained out over the blue and blue. Benjamin and Miranda, standing with their razors, their scissors, their glue pots, and stacks and stacks of painted sheeting, deciding the final sequence of events for the panorama. Mixing and matching the fat cylinders of imagination and fact. Cutting them up and pasting.

From where they were, they could hear only the harvest. The shovels digging, the dirge of tractors, the saw, the hoe. The tools of reaping focused all awareness of sound on the buzz, the hum, the rilling. In the low sky, dragonflies and yellow jackets circled in their last life. Any time now, the first frost was due. Hard to believe, thought Benjamin, stripped to the waist and bristling with sweat that made his chest a prism.

The sun was a harsh dot in the cloudless sky, but the winds confounded everything. He found himself feeling cold, then hot, over and over like chill and fever. He counted on his fingers how many more days it would take to get the harvest in and how many paintings he and the girl had left to make of the river. He could envision the panorama all packed up and sleeping through the long, restless journey across the sea to the Old World, there to be displayed like a beautiful young debutante, to be unfurled and stretched out before an amazed public. He made a mental note to put in a few more attacks by hostile Indians as well as some ominous but peaceful moonlit prairie scenes. Out he rolled the heavy canvas sheets like sheep being readied for the fleecing.

He threw a light shirt over his shoulders, to give his sun- and wind-burned back a rest. He watched the girl, fifteen tableaus away with her razor blade, trying to decide what to cut next. "Should I put this one here, that one there?" she questioned herself.

She was looking at one of her attic paintings. It portrayed a large, verdant lizard with a provocative intelligence in his eye. She felt it would fit nicely sewn into Benjamin's picture of hooky-playing boys fishing off the bank of the river. Her head nodded yes and her hands in swift response carried out the execution. The boys seemed to have no expression on their faces; their eyes were blankly fixed on their poles. The lizard, in contrast, had a sagacious air and looked out knowingly from the canvas, which made the boys appear even duller. Benjamin commented that perhaps it was a bit too harsh; this pastiche of river boys and a giant green lizard made the human element look mentally deficient. Miranda laughed so hard that her skirts billowed out and whipped around as if a hurricane were blowing.

"Oh, Benjamin," she laughed, "you might as well show people what you see."

And this was for him the problem, for he was not sure anymore the difference between what he saw and what she saw. The images of the panorama could be winnowed out into hers and his, but the way they fit together and what that juncture was, could not. Between them now there was posed a world in which fishing boys really did live side by side with giant lizards; this had become for him the most normal of things.

He was bothered, too, by memories of his family, a family whose backs were as straight as their chairs, their faces as dour as spoiled fruit. He missed them despite his memories, longed for their crampedness in this endless spread of prairie. As he held his brush to the canvas, he longed for their heritage, the shapes they were molded from, long ago and across the sea. He would return to his ancestors, he vowed, transcend the geography of his living family and go home to its blood root, Europe. He was sure that the continent he had never seen and the relatives he did not know meant home for him, and he would bring the panorama as an offering to them.

Then he thought of Miranda; the months, the paintings they spent together, the ties that had grown between them.

How could he leave her? How could he take her? He wanted—
no needed—a self of himself, something as clear to him as a
faithful rendering of reality; and he felt muddied by her. She
influenced him in ways he did not wish, as if he had become
one of the monstrous amphibians that danced through her
paintings.

ROSE ARRIVING AT THE GLASS HOUSE

And sometimes it was just the girl's eyes that surfaced and thieved among the visions of the bird, until what the bird alone saw was obliterated. But then the girl's sight, too, was turned to a wasteland; its fields and summits went flat and gray.

She was flying, and flying hurt. Natural as it was to a bird, it never felt natural to the changeling girl. The muscles at her shoulders, the wing tips at her hands felt painfully stretched, as if forced to alter their chemical composition. And then there was the trouble turning back into a girl again. Turning back was as hard as becoming in the first place; turning back could only be accomplished at certain altitudes and speeds, and certain places she could not always reach.

Since the killing of the wolf, she no longer went to the city of shapes outside the glass house. Still, she could see into every corner of it just as if she were walking its streets. Now, in the glass house, her vision is expanded until she can see 360 degrees but a certain paralysis creeps into her bones. She becomes afraid to move, is left to rock back and forth in the middle of the sky and watch a world of disasters for which she can provide no healing, which captivate her in a hypnotic cowardice. In the city of shapes she sees from her frozen place it is not uncommon for people to torture each other for no reason but to watch suffering, or for children to toss other children out of windows just to see how they fall. Cruelty walks everywhere here. It is as close as her face but she cannot touch it. Stabbings and gunshots are the music of the land; destruction is its art and hatred its vision. Sometimes there is nothing at all to see in the city, as if nature itself has gone into shock and drawn a blank.

She knows it is wrong to keep silent about what she sees outside the window, that while she did, thousands of lives were lost. She knows there is a kind of screaming she could do that would not lead to more pain and death but to freedom, a certain frequency that evil could not hear. But her rebellion never went any further than a passive insolence. For this, her paralysis, she suffered the most. She lived with the horror of doing nothing in the face of horror. This suffering that she was hiding from was walking through her like she herself was a clear glass house.

"I'm never coming back here," says the girl who is staring out and weeping. "I don't want to see anymore the atrocities made beautiful by distance and framing. I'm never coming back!" the girl vowed. But the raven was lying.

PART III: THE FALL

Hearts Harvest

THE ROOTS OF CARTOGRAPHY

A map, I make a map of the heart: the coordinates of its circumference, the natural boundaries that cordon off its chambers, the rivers that comprise its bloodstream, the colors we use to describe its weight, the lines we draw to hold in its longitude and latitude, where the mouth of tears lies, and the tearing up of grief at irreparable loss. Trace the marbleized edges of veins upon each of the map's skin-thin pages, the tightening ropes of the arteries where reason must sit in the bowl of blood-passion and from which the heart attacks its prison-home, the insensate mountain of flesh and bone. Here is a map of my sister's heart. North is not a constant here, but a variable of emotional climate. The only thing you can actually map of her—that is, depend upon for stability—is her hands. They go up and we are in the land of praise, they touch her lips and we are in the valley of fear, they reach out and we are in wonderment. This is where the body hurts, the hands tell the map maker, and this is where it heals and this is the road of yearning and the range of hoping and the trail of tears and this, this round spot is the faith of children, and this indentation is also the faith of children, but in specific, those children who have nothing, who are nothing, who will neither be heard nor be saved.

THE GENEALOGY OF MAPS

—What lines can be drawn to draw shape out of the wilderness?

This is the why of a map.

—When and in what proportion to employ the head, the heart, and the will?

This is the how of a map.

—To go to undiscovered places and return home again bearing knowledge.

This is the where of a map.

—Questions and decisions and more questions.

This is the what of a map.

from *The Book of the Cartographer*, Chapter III

FALL

Love with its kind smile and its dragons back.

As the first frost covered the fields and made the roofs gleam, Benjamin's restlessness grew. They walked together every day now, hardly ever stopping to paint. His black coat slung over his shoulder, her paisley shawl laid loose around her arms.

"I think we should leave soon," he'd tell Miranda. "The panorama's as good as finished. Now it needs an audience to make its life complete."

"Oh," she'd say, wondering what an audience had to do with it.

Then the cold weather started setting in. There were days when the chill and wind were so high that walking the land was impossible. Then they would stay inside, lighting fires in the library and browsing through the many strange volumes there, most of which had never even had their pages cut. The girl was happy to sit and read with her beloved. But the man felt fettered by the books and the fire and the glittering glass windowpanes, which were too frozen to let any image of the outside in.

He started to disappear a few hours at a time. He said: "to go to town. To make our travel arrangements," he announced, passing quickly out the door.

"Let me come with you," she'd say, putting down her books and slipping on her boots. But when she reached the veranda, he would already have vanished.

She would wait up for him, as many hours as he would take, most often making a tiny lair for herself in the library where she collected pictures in her mind from the words in the books. Sometimes, when he was gone a long time, she'd climb up the spiral stairs in the middle of the library to the tower,

which was her father's room of maps. There, upon the faces of
the charts and globes, she tried to picture the places they were
to travel. She'd sigh with pleasure when she recognized the
name of one of the cities Benjamin had mentioned as a stopping point for their panorama, and she'd take a pin with a colored head from her sewing kit and stick it there to mark the
spot. She pulled the enormous old atlases off the shelves,
searching for pictorial representations of the places he
promised they'd visit. She pictured the fabulous theaters that
would be constructed just for their panorama. Oh! the buildings that would be destroyed to construct grander buildings for
them; the overgrown, untended gardens that would be restored
to make a fitting showcase for their creation. People all over the
world would wake up from their sleep of indifference in the
light of what they had done. She could see it all in her mind;
it would be as Benjamin had promised.

"The people will love our work," he told her. "When I
introduce you and you take your bow, they will throw gold and
silver coins at your feet." He laughed, and she laughed too.

But she took the greatest pleasure in imagining how it
would be, just the two of them working and traveling together.
After the shows, they would share meals alone in dark cafés full
of crowds and cigar smoke or in grand restaurants with rows of
waiters in full-length starched aprons, damask towels draped
over their outstretched welcoming arms, for Benjamin had told
her such places existed, that people were flowing in and out
their doors at the very moment that Benjamin and Miranda
were dreaming of them. They would drink champagne and eat
frogs' legs, caviar. His nostrils quivered as he told her, and she
believed him when he said this was something she would enjoy.
Mostly, she loved the idea of going with him. Never had adventure felt so comforting.

He warned her not to tell anyone what they were planning.
It was best that no one know until they were safely departed.
One day he came back after a particularly long absence. She had

neither eaten nor slept while he was gone, as if abstinence might make his return come sooner. This time he had the tickets of passage in his hand.

. She looked them over, turning them over in her hands—simple black writing on cheap scratch paper, palm-sized booklets with a cursive Gothic script denoting the steamship firm in the lower right-hand corner. Inside the booklets, their names, class of travel, number of berths all scribbled by some rushed bursar. She held the paper against the lamplight, trying to ascertain its method of transformation; how it would change her from a timid girl with mutilated hands and a murderous gypsy heart into someone for whom the joy of exploration and the security of home would live in harmonious accord. This Miranda, transformed by the ticket book in her hand, could roam courageously all over the world, absorbing its visions and releasing them into new spheres. Since Benjamin, she had developed a sense of mission; and like a bird or insect whose instinctive job it is to transfer pollen and fertilize seed, she understood her work to be the transmutation of ephemeral vision into visceral shape and form.

The four globes in the map room sat sentoriously still, one each in the four stone corners, cupped like giant eggs in their oak pedestals. One had a sea of monsters with very little land, another had a fleet of sailing ships with more ports than water, still another seemed to recognize only the existence of the Northern Hemisphere, while the last, wedged in back of the clavichord, was only cognizant of the South. Miranda could not see by evidence of the ship tickets which of these regions she was soon to encounter, because they curiously left the place of destination blank. Into this dotted line of space, she crammed her dreams of where they were going.

Her one valise became a mess of packing and unpacking, although Benjamin had told her to take very little, as everything she could hope to want or need would be abundantly available in all the places they were going. She tried to listen to him, but her worry outran her. She packed dozens of dresses and shoes, reams of underthings, jars and jars of pigment and paint, and, of course, the willow branch. Then, there were all the books she could not stand to leave behind, and suddenly she was running back to the library again, her arms piled with natural histories, lives of the saints, monoprints of the old masters, sheet music. These, too, she pressed inside the bursting suitcase.

Finally, she sees him coming up the path, his arms held out for her. With their tickets of passage still tightly in her hand, she runs out to meet him, coming so fast and hard and tearing off his hat that he didn't know what hit him as he lay panting on the frozen yellow ground, the wind kicked out of him by the girl who holds the tickets up to the sun, watching the pictures of their future travels within.

"Give me mine, Miranda," he whispers, roughing up her hair, grabbing at her hand. "We leave tomorrow."

THE SECRET ADMIRER

The arteries pink, the veins blue, the dusty clippings of finger-nails, the excrement that is the brown of fertile soil flecked with the golden leavings of corn and the harsh orange gratings of carrot. She thinks of no one, sees no one. All concentration is of sweat; to make a body of work.

She had never let him spend the night. As soon as it was dark she would push him out the door. This last night before they were to leave, he couldn't take it anymore, all her secrets, all her without him. He had to see just once how she . . .

This is how he comes to stand here on their last night at the Hotel, spying in the shadows of Miranda's attic.

He knows she'll never let him in, up the stairs, through the door. So he climbs out his bedroom window onto the blue-tiled ledge. From his bedroom to the attic there are two floors in between, and the higher he climbs the more his thoughts are on the earth, for there are no footholds here, just slight indentations between the stone slabs. He pulls himself up past the ghost-inhabited servants' rooms and the bloated ballroom of the auction hounds. He passes room after empty room, hanging on for his life.

The moon is on a narrow course, barely squeezing through the heavens on its crescent back. A little rain is falling out of the bloated sky. He is in front of the attic windows now. He's dressed in black, and with the rain getting steadier, he knows she'll never see him looking. So he edges slightly closer, his nose to the pane, his hands holding onto whatever they can.

At first he can't find her in the labyrinthine room. Only the white canvas spread over the floor gives her away as it breathes slightly in the wind. He sees her heaving as she shakes the willow stick over the floor like a diviner's rod. Suddenly the meal they ate together that day she is throwing up onto the white canvas floor: the bits of lima bean, the slices of cheese, the curlicues of tangerine, half-digested, all mixed up. Her stick stirring the stuff up as if it were a hearty soup, she stirs and heaves, stirs and heaves, until all she brings up is a thin gruelish bile that she delights in, that she spreads through her excretions like paint thinner, mixing and muting the colors until they are a warm blend of earth tones. Then she holds up to the frail light of the oil lamp her injured hands, squeezing at the tortured fingers until their blood is just another color of paint. She moves to one side of the canvas, where she squats and urinates, while in another corner she sits and defecates. Then with her willow stick, she mixes the wondrous colors that have made him so envious. The colors that are the waste and lifeblood of her life.

Everything that her body rejects or can be robbed of is in these paints. Everything that the body gives up, grows tired of, cannot live with, is here, he thinks, making painting. The mud depths of her hell is the excrement of her body, the red clay of her heavenly hills is the blood of her body, the green grass of earthly paradise can only be her bile, and the yellow rays of sunshine the drift of what she has pissed away.

Now he must realize. The delicate gradations of her skies are the lining of her severed veins and the ledges of her purgatory are the clippings of her fingernails that have ripped up her own flesh, and the foam of her spit is the eternal seas that are the effervescent bottom ground of all life. The golden phlegm, the mossy mucus, the clear river of vagina, the milk of the breasts mixed with sweat. Now he knows.

Hanging onto the window ledge, he is watching and hating her more than he believed it was possible to hate. He is horrified at what the pictures are made of and he is repelled by the girl who had so fascinated him before he knew. This.

He's disgusted and wants to run. Disgusted and wants to kill. So sick he can barely hang on. Dear life. And the stars seem closer than the solid ground of the ledge he's holding on to. The stars are clean, he reasons, they make sense, not this battleground of paint, not this disgrace of body.

The willow stick in the girl's hand flies over the crowded floor. It traces the outline of a shrinking woman, the ghost of a starved body. Then it makes pair after pair of eyes but forgets to give them faces. He wonders what is holding these eyes in place, like cats' eyes, disembodied in the dark and cast out. The faceless, pale woman-thing has the trunk of a willow tree for a body. It waves back and forth, teeming with vegetation, a swamp life growing out of the holes left behind from its chopped off limbs.

He watches her work, watching and hating. The stick from her willow tree flying over the canvas floor he gave her. She presses the stick down her throat again, a swallower of swords.

What does he see of her in the dark as she brings up her guts? Him in the dark, watching the insides of a human being he believed he loved pouring out. Emptied out, she seems to glow. Her whole body, a filament, goes blue-purple-blue. He has his arms out, as if he would catch her. But he is still hiding. He knows if she caught him spying, she would push him off the ledge.

BENJAMIN TRIUMPHANT

He wants to cut up all her pictures, divorce them as much as possible from their source. And in this manner, to make them clean.

Back, back a time, he could feel her making sense. But he did not know then that her sense was made from this: the refuse of the world transformed by the alchemy of the body, turned into a portrait of the soul she suffered, this image that was so indifferent to her desires and her shame; that did not care if she lived or died as long as it could excrete itself. Now, as the man looked, the wondrous attic became a dungeon: dark, full of the carcass ribs of rotting beams and the stench of human excrement.

And he wants to erase this art of hers, wants to erase her. If only he could bring himself to kill her for deceiving him, for not telling him how it was she made beauty. He wants to take the willow stick, her magic wand of garbage, out of her hand, take her life out of her hands, wants her to be the bloody chopped flesh that she has rearranged into flowers, into fields, into silver-dollar babies. The liar, seductress, cheat.

He moved from the shadows of the ledge, where she could not see him and, as if muffled by his extreme anger, slipped noiselessly into the light. She was concentrating on a black shadow— a man she was painting on the floor, made of her shit and outlined in her blood. As she raised the willow stick, he grabbed it out of her hand and turned her to him as if to restrain her; but he found he could not restrain himself, and he brought the stick down on her head over and over again until she was bleeding afresh into the pools of distracted colors on the floor. He bends over her like a willow tree and hits, hits, hits.

Floor. She lies unconscious in a black-blood puddle on top of the shadow she has painted. Now it's her face that is the face of the shadow. Her face that gives the thing a semblance of any life at all. When he sees this, he stops beating her. Keeps crying, stops beating, keeps crying.

ROSE'S REACH

One day, impatience overtook her—like a wounded bird who, though healing, is not yet capable of flight, but is in spirit overripe.

Girl flying, girl flying. Houses down and falling, trees flying, mountains spinning, she atop her losing memory, a top spinning. She's been to the future already; she says it's coming back.

Oh my God. Her arms are open. The light in the corner of her arms is open. Why is she flying into the glass? Why can't she see what will hurt? There were two of them, once there were two—twins—and in between the water and the dirt, their time together by the riverbank, before the stranger and the auctioning, before the tree, before the glass wing.

But now Rose's hand through the window can't reach her sister. Her sister, her sister's in love. Her hand through the window. Sees her sister lying. In the arms of the stranger. Rose's hand through the window can't reach her sister. Her sister, her sister's in love.

His body has made itself a wedge inside her. He is moving so steadily, it seems he is not moving at all. But Miranda is all struggle, sharp angled and breathless as a trout leaping white water. The rush of foam spinning her up, up, up over the liquid breathing. She dives airborne. *Take your hand out the window, Rose, the glass is doing it no good.*

She wants him; inside teeth, inside nails. Oh yes, and heart. There he is, marvels the girl, scraping the barrel of love! Look! Him inside her, unfolding, just like a panorama, unwinding the landscape of her womb; the mountains, the rivers, the sea cliffs of love reeling through her twin, a blank of celluloid. *Take your hand out, Rose, to death you are bleeding and she won't notice you dying.* You're just a sister. A fatal repetition, that's what a twin is.

Poor Rose, to be the younger, not the wiser. To be the less-girl, the more-bird. *Take your hand out the window, Rose, the glass is doing it no good.*

BENJAMIN DEFEATED

"How to escape you," he wondered to himself in a dazed panic while the girl in his arms slept, "without tearing off a part of myself?"

Why was he not like a starfish who could leave his limb behind and know he would soon grow its replacement? The idea of his mutilation he could not abide; he wanted himself whole as well as free—after all, that was the reason for his river journey. What spell could he chant, what insult false or true could he say to Miranda's face that would set him free?

So he went through her character like a catalog, scraping down what he knew of her, as sharp and dedicated to his task as a master carpenter, to see what attributes of hers he could not do without and still retain his own form. He saw that he could do without her love, for he had been trained from birth to do without that; he could do without her counsel, because he believed in his own strength of will to make his way; he could do without her company, because whomever he was with, he was still a lonely man; he could do without her devotion, because devotion denoted history and he was bent on escaping what had thus far constituted his past, because what he wanted was to go even further back than that. What was left, he wondered, marveling at the ties that bound him to her.

"Why am I not yet a free man?"

He looked down to see that Miranda's paintings had grafted themselves so completely onto his own that they had changed the panorama utterly. He had to keep them, he could not give them up, they were part of the story now. They would travel with him all over the earth, evoking the image of a new world. Someday he would return the panorama here, to the land that inspired it; and he'd transform its history, too, until its past was the one he decided to give it now, after the fact and forward unto hundreds, thousands of years past his own demise. This panorama must be his, he decided, solely his legacy.

"Cut her off at the paintings," he told himself firmly.

Which one of them would bleed more from this was the only thing that he wondered. Which one and how much blood must it be.

THE NECROMANCER'S DAUGHTER

I was sleeping in my grandmother's lap, her long red hair flowing through my mouth as she told me her ghost stories. I would fall asleep and she'd begin another story for me that I believed was not a story at all but a dream I was having.

There was once a man who loved his daughter more than all the gold in the world, better than all the air in the sky, even more than his own life he loved her—and his was a special, magic life; he was a famous necromancer. He loved her so much that from the day she was born he never left her side. But one day he had to go away, for there was a plague raging in the land and the king thought this necromancer could stop it. He said goodbye to his daughter sadly and he told her:

"I trust you with all my love and all my life, and I know that what I will tell you to do, you will do for the love of me, and what I forbid you to do, you will for the love of me not do, for I have loved you so much your whole life that I have never once left your side."

The daughter nodded her head silently and cried, for she did not know how to be alone. She was sure it meant she would die.

The necromancer placed his hand on her head and continued, "While I am gone, you will go to my workroom every day and you will care for the things we have created there: the half iguana man, the dog with a fish's fins, the cherry-plum tree with bear-claw buds, the lamp that eats only carnations. You must care for these things we made and tenderly you must love them.

"But you must not," he said sharply, "not ever open that." He pointed his finger through the laboratory doorway to a dark mahogany closet; a creaky thing, with its thick double doors shut tight.

"Not that there is anything secret in there," he warned her, "not that there is anything to worry about in there. It's just an old wardrobe, you see, that has sentimental value for me, so I find I cannot get rid of it. The door opens out into another world, that's all, just another place in time. And a very boring, ordinary world it is. But if you open that door, you let that other world in here, where it has no place, where it will be hungry, and being hungry, it will roll over you like a giant wheel, roll through our doors, through our house, and outside into our neighbor's yards and into their houses, devouring everything in its path. But it will not be satisfied here; its hunger will be never-ending here, because its nourishment cannot be found in our world, where it does not belong. It will roll so far out into our world that it will never know how to get back to where it came from and it will be with us, forever and ever. Wanting to make things better, wanting to put things back to the way they used to be, you will open the wardrobe door over and over again hoping to see this piece of wayward, wandering earth reunited with its own sky. But you will see nothing. Just an empty black hole."

"This," he said, "is the way evil will come to stay in our world, the never ending hunger that is both greed and true neediness. So do not," he glared at his quaking child, "do not disobey me in this." Then he left her for his journey.

The necromancer was gone for many days, and the daughter did as she was told. She fed and watered the things they had created; she walked the aisles of their laboratory, to learn its contents by heart so that she could help her father mix new combinations of matter to make new living things when he returned. She was very busy for many of the days he was gone. But then there was day after day after day that she had cleaned and tidied, learned and memorized all that she could and still he did not come home. She was filled with an agonizing loneliness, an unquenchable boredom.

One day she decided to polish every inch of wood in the laboratory—the walls, the floors, the stools, the worktables—and as her tireless hands rubbed and shined, they came across the huge old wardrobe. As she rubbed, its door popped slightly open, just enough for her to peek inside. And she did look in, just to see if everything her father had told her was right. But it wasn't all right, no, the whole laboratory came alive with stinging winds and filthy rain. All the glass beakers fell to the floor and shattered, leaving a thick, sticky, stinking residue that held the necromancer's daughter glued to the spot. She could go neither in nor out. Neither into the laboratory nor out through the wardrobe. But she could see everything that was happening in both places. The place she had opened up could not be shut again and it swept through in its hunger. And nothing satisfied it but more hunger, and so it made the necromancer's daughter hungry too, though she could not move to satisfy this hunger.

"Help me, father," she cries to the figure of the necromancer, who stands in the fury of the open door. "It was an accident," she screams. "Save me. I was only cleaning up!"

He is calm and he is grave. He looks down at his necromancer's robe, rimmed blue with the constellations and fringed gold with the rays of the sun. He says: "Daughter, I can't help you now. Daughter, you chose."

The land of the necromancer's daughter is stuffed with hunger—the people, the animals, the plants, even the rocks— and there is nothing, nothing she can do. Even after he is dead, she's stuck forever, listening for his magic words, hoping to save them. She's glued to the spot, waiting. Among the miserable people and the evil wind. In her famished exile she wishes to death that it had been she who had tricked him.

THE LAST ONE

"You want to learn the secrets, Rose," he said to her, his broad back turned against her as he sat hunched over the rough, narrow worker's bench, his hands carving the eye holes on a new trophy. He sculpted with enormous care and agility. The sockets were deep, nearly sunk to the level of cheek.

"Do you want some cut off here?" he asked the specimen gently.

"Yes, that's what I thought you wanted," he cooed to the creature as he lopped off a piece of it.

It was a deer, a young doe tied feet to feet on the long wooden table. It seemed to Rose as she looked around the rosy fire-lit den that all Trapper's specimens were young; not one could be called mature.

"It's because I believe in the young," he had told her once. "They are our hope, our future; they must be preserved."

Something in the memory of his voice held her cowering to the wall.

"Come closer, Rose. You can't see what I'm doing at all from back there, the light today is bad."

The girl edged forward, watching his arms gently raising and then dropping the flanks of the doe. She saw him carve away the layers of fat without disturbing the skin. He used the knife as if he were a sculptor and the deer his block of stone.

"Speak to me," he whispered, and Rose began to mumble.

He silenced her with a grunt: "Not you. I'm speaking to my girl here so she will tell me what she likes and I can do my best job."

He glared at the child at his back.

"There, there my sweet," he whispered, his attention riveted on the deer.

"Ah yes," he sighed "you want it there and there and there."

He began to break all the leg bones until the rigor-mortised body went limp.

"You love this feeling. You don't have to tell me," Trapper whispered in the doe's ear. "I know how to put you to sleep. I just want to make you happy." The man wept softly.

Rose bent forward to observe the position of the fractures. She marveled at the sense of agility and speed they'd given the dead thing.

"Don't get in my light," he growled at her.

"But you said stay close," she whined.

"Don't sass me." He thrashed out at her face so hard that her only sense for a while was a shrill ringing in her ears. When she could see again, the deer's muscles were stripped off and hanging by her head, from coat hooks over the bed.

"Makes the best binding in the world," the man said almost kindly as he tied them to the wrists of the girl, who found herself lying on his bed naked, half-covered by an old soiled patchwork quilt.

He approached her softly, dragging over a little bench upon which he had placed a glass of milk, a sweet biscuit. Next to the food lay a scalpel, a saw, and a small, severed squirrel's head with the remnants of a spinal cord trailing to the floor. He held her face in his hands; he licked at her eyes with his tongue.

"I want to teach you love," he said, "the hardest lesson of all."

His hands came off her cheeks and neck; he fumbled around his belt, which he slid through its loops. His hands gathered up the squirrel's head, its fur matted from dehydration, its eyes bulging in a dried-up retinal jelly. It stank.

"I want to teach you love, Rose. I want to . . . transfer what it is I know about animals, about nature, to you."

His fingers had crossed under the bedclothes now. She felt a terrible, sharp pain in her belly, yet she leaned the arch of her hips toward his movement. His hand found her open and wet.

"We must put the head here, Rose," he said softly, almost weeping, his whole hand stretching her open until he could fit the other. She could feel the bony ball of skull inside her; pushing and jerking until it could go no further.

"This is how we give them life," he said to the girl. "The squirrel's head will live now. It will grow feet, a tail, and perhaps it will grow hungry, Rose; then it will bite—because the living must eat, Rose, and it won't think that it was you who gave it life or maybe it will, but it won't care."

He jerked his hands free of her, leaving the head of the squirrel inside. While she felt a swollenness, she was paralyzed to remove it. He spit on his hands several times and returned to her body, massaging the labia and clitoris. He was sobbing now, to such an extent that her chest was dank in his tears.

She wondered as the pressure built inside her, when would the head live again; and when it did, would it bite her to death?

"We must do it this way, Rose. There's no magic, no eternal life, not for any of us if we don't do it like this."

"Get up," he yelled at her. "I want to see you walk."

"I can't get up," she whimpered.

He dragged her up, forced her to stand, his thighs behind her, flanking her knees, her belly distended. He ripped down the deer sinews from the wall and roped her hands behind her back. He shoved her toward the workbench.

"You think we can have this never-ending living without suffering, Rose? Answer me! Are you a coward?"

"No," choked the girl.

"I think you are a coward. I think you are unworthy of learning taxidermy. Answer me: Are you scared?"

His fingernails were digging into her buttocks. The thing inside her felt as if it were expanding, and she faltered. "No."

"No?"

"No," she said to him.

He drew his fingers up in between her ribs and squeezed diligently. "Yes, Rose, yes, you are a coward. You think you want things and then you don't have the courage to go after them."

"I did everything you told me," wept the girl, her chin crushed on top of the tabletop, next to the skinning knives, the doe's soft muzzle with its begging expression barely an inch away from her eyes.

"I do everything you say," said the girl, "and still they never come alive. They look alive, but they aren't. They don't move, they don't eat, they don't shit, they don't howl."

"Idiot! That's not what eternal life means," he said, pulling on her strawberry hair. "Those vulgar things have nothing to do with immortality. I try and try to teach you, Rose, but you don't learn anything. You're too greedy for fast . . ."

He reached around her and scooped up a gob of jaundiced tallow, filling his right palm.

"You believed me before, Rose. Remember? Remember how it was when you believed me? What is happening to you to make you think I'm lying?"

He pushed apart her buttocks.

"When will you see that if you fill an earthly vessel with the proper foreign substance, it transforms the vessel, Rose, transforms it into something that can endure anything and forever. This is called learning. You pull out the guts . . ."

He shoved the deer fat into her ass.

"Look at the deer, Rose, not at me. There's nothing in me to see. You pull out the guts and you stuff the empty cavity full of another substance so it can become another thing. It can't change, little lady, when all it's got inside is its own body. Then it just rots."

His fingers, first two, then three gouged and twisted their way up her anus. The girl staggered, but she had nowhere to fall.

When he withdrew his hand suddenly, she automatically relaxed. But he had done so only to make room for his cock. "Why do you think I'm lying?" he begged.

The girl could not scream because pain and fear had so stuffed every inch of her that there was no room to scream. She imagined this was the end of her now, that somehow all her carping after this knowledge, her obsession with the eternal possibilities of nature was going, in fact, to kill her. That the life forever after in which she had so blithely believed was a lie, as hollow as she was full to bursting. At that moment she became a being who no longer believed. She saw the dead for what they were; she could no longer envision the spirit of a soul or the lost dreams of a living ghost. That part of her, as he plunged into her ragged cavity, was indeed dead, dead as the deer by whom she lay, head to head.

It seemed to go on eternally; this movement of objects within her holes, one ruthlessly living, one festering dead, longer than she had lived. The girl began to believe she had never known anything else but this. She became conversant in the gradations of pain; she resigned herself to accept some, only to dread others and resist the worst forms of agony, which was impossible and therefore made the man's actions even more excruciating. After a certain point, the pain itself became a distant thing that some other poor soul was suffering: swollen, ripped open, bleeding.

"Oh my love, my heartache, why won't you believe in me?" the man cried, tearing at her hair, lurching back and forth inside her as if she were a cradle for rocking.

Rose didn't exist, she told herself, not anymore. She was a raven now, coasting over the scene, her black sparkling wings catching the light, drawing the air downward, until she came to rest on the bent-over back of the sodomized girl, now fainted. The raven looked at the man raging into the body of the child as if to gut it clean. The man was startled, he drew back, stopped thrusting, but he would not come out from the body. The bird stared at the man hard; it had eyes like a diamond drill. The man got dizzier and dizzier as the raven eyes bore down between him and the girl. His cock went limp suddenly. He fell off the girl, like an old skin. Pulling up his pants, he ran out of the cabin toward the river. He ran and he ran, but the image of the raven chased him relentlessly.

The raven ate the squirrel out of the girl's womb. It pulled and pecked until there was nothing left except the two hard acorn eyes, which the raven stowed in its throat and took away as a trophy for its nest. It flew over the river and whistled until the tree appeared, a green profusion growing up out of the wasteland of water. Then it flew to the highest reaches and kept sentinel.

The girl slept collapsed on the cold floor of the cabin that night. She dreamed of the bird.

"My, how high it flies," she marveled while she herself could only lie in a heap on the packed earth.

She dreamed of the raven, circling the earth with the squirrel's eyes clutched in its mouth like precious jewels. She saw the shiny trinkets that the bird had stolen from the Hotel laid out like a museum on the twigs and mud of its nest.

"I want to steal things too," thought the girl in her dream. "I can't give anything eternal life. I can't. But I can steal: caterpillars in a jar, fireflies in the hand, a kiss, a secret, a look." And she watched until the shape of the bird faded into the horizon.

When she awoke, she crawled over to the fire, where the embers still glowed although the flame had extinguished itself long ago. It was morning. Over the pine trees she could see the oak tree flourishing in the river and on the highest, barest branch a raven perched, its black eyes staring out, its mouth stuffed full of treasures.

TRAPPER UNDERGROUND

He ran out of the shed, leaving the girl half-dead in a heap on the floor. "Pale as milk," was all that he could think of her.

He ran. Ran until there was nothing left to do but swim. He hit the river hard, belly up. Tangled roots of ancient trees grabbed up from below to drag his body down.

"But," he chuckled to himself, "I'm too mean to drown."

Dripping with mud and encrusted with weeds, Trapper came up out of the water onto the banks like the first reptile on earth. He crawled to the brush where he kept his pile of traps when they were not in use. But where the traps should be, there is only a hole that he doesn't remember. Freshly dug, he thinks, maybe for a corpse, he thinks, his imagination's eye on the girl heaped on the floor with skin as pale as milk. He thinks she would fit this hole very nicely. Then he thinks maybe somebody made this hole to hide his traps, some Indian trying to trick him or some other trapper stealing his stake. He takes out his hunting knife, makes sure he's got his flints and steel, slides down the hole feet-first so he can kick his way in. To see what's down there.

He slides down the length of a man, thrashing his legs like the tail of a shark. When he stops sliding, he starts falling. The hole is so narrow, it's a miracle he can fall through it at all, except that the sides are so soft they can't hold onto him as he plunges down.

"How far am I dropping?" wonders the man, his sense of time changing with the velocity.

When he stops falling, he has a sense of things still falling, as if his torso is plummeting through his body while his body is caving in.

Bits of beard and mud invade his mouth as he falls into the earth below the earth, below the river into the part of the land that was once sea and before that, was the largest mountain range on the continent. He lands, finally, a half-mile down atop this buried mountain that is now the floor of a gigantic cave.

Trapper loved mountains. High above the earth or deep below, it made no difference to him. He loved the rough, hard immensity of mountain space that made him feel so astonishingly small. He enjoyed feeling small for a change, the bigness of him turned flower-fragile in the sea-buried landscape of extinct volcano and glacier rock. He could imagine his kind a millennium past, rejecting the life of the gills for the lungs of a creature who breathes and burrows through the mud.

He tries walking, but the hole is so narrow that he can only do so in place. He looks up the extreme shaft to the eyeball of light that remains; the only way to go forward is by crawling. He laughs about his wonderful sense of direction, because it won't do him a damn bit of good down here where he can only go or stay.

"*The girl*" he thought, "*the girl, the mother, the mother, the girl.*"

He had her blood on his cock and the sickly smell of her fear on his hands. He had bits of her skin under his fingernails. He wanted her to love him so much.

Bam bam bam. The rock walls, his fist, his feet his head, *bam bam bam* in his head as if all the animals he's ever hunted are stampeding in there.

He lies at the bottom of the hole, his body bloody from the self-beating, staring up at the distant catch of light. He hears the walls whispering to him, buzzing through the deep ache of his swelling head, cutting through the stars that are dancing before his eyes. He crawls to get away from the noise, the darkness, the narrow space. Suddenly he finds he has room to walk like a man. He stands upright and lights a piece of wood he's found, wraps it with a rag so it will burn awhile longer. He turns this torch to the walls to see where he is.

It was as if the whole intention of the cave's natural darkness was to glorify such shadow and light, as he discovers himself surrounded by walls painted red, black, and ochre with the images of charging beasts. There are bison, deer, ibex, mammoth, antelope, all running on the cave walls. He knows he should find this beautiful, but all that comes to his mind is that he is trapped, finally, himself, trapped for all eternity with prey he cannot kill.

The man thinks: "I'm going to starve to death in this sanctuary of flesh I can't eat, that my traps, my knives, my guns can't kill. I'll starve to death in this cave of painted fur and meat."

He swears he sees a thousand black birds flee down the narrow hole through which he had so recently fallen. They flock around his head and he yells, "No, no, no, you aren't real; birds don't live underground, birds don't breathe dirt. They suffocate in it."

And, just like that, they vanish, until all that is left of them is the sound of their wings. He says to the walls with their angry beasts, "You don't exist either, you're just dreams for the dead."

All around the walls stampede the hunt. The forms of the rocks decide their images. The natural contours of a boulder suggest a muscular chest and an eroded chasm is the perfect hollow for two preternatural eyes. But at this moment, all the man sees is the floor that he sits on, with its piles of warrior bones thousands of years dead. They're pretty, thinks Trapper, the way the skeletons are all dressed up in shells and beads.

He can hear the old ones singing. Songs of great deeds and heroes' courage. He was trying to think about something but he's forgotten what it was, and all that comes out of his mouth are fragments of thoughts, like shipwrecked pieces—"blood" is one, "sharp" is another; "finger," "knife big," "love," "cherish," "obey." But the old voices drown him out with their singing and his confused thinking rattles along on the brutal floor.

He had meant to do some stuffing that day but ended up raping the girl instead. He meant to go trapping, which is just a kind of walking and thinking; but he ended up here, trapped in the bowels of a cave. He remembered how Cora once had told him he was a violent man.

He asked her then, a little boy in his voice: "What does violence mean?"

She said: "It means thinking with your fists and teeth."

He bent his head, wanting to pray, but it was true, what she had said. The woman and the child converge in his thinking, which is limited to what will fit the rhythm of the warriors' song. He claps his ears to stop the sound but he can't do it.

He laughs. "She's damn right."

He's thinking with whatever pieces of him can cut—his teeth, his fingernails—and the parts of him that can snap and crush—again his teeth; but added to those, his hands and feet. How many parts of him can be deadly, he wonders; and after counting up the obvious ones he wants more. He wants poisonous ears, killer eyes; a belly button that strangles; a penis whose semen makes its victim stop breathing; and he wants a heart that can oppress unto death and a backbone that will strike and cripple. He wants to kill everything and make everything live again in his image.

In the rage that comes from the body's self-deception, he wants to kill, which he considers the ultimate ownership. He wants to eat what he kills so that it will be part of him; his power, his triumph over annihilation. This is the true meaning of beauty, the man thinks. He wants to possess land and more land and everything that grows and breathes upon it. And to keep others off his territory he will burn it, waste it, make it unlivable even if it means that he, himself, will starve. Even if it means that the only animals left in the world are the ones painted on these buried walls.

He gets up and walks to the far end of the chamber and looks back. All the animals he has ever killed are stirring in this ancient gallery, over the bones of the warrior dead. "You don't frighten me," he screams, "you don't frighten me!" as he tries to climb the walls to get out of this cave. But he can't keep from slipping back, from falling down. He can't stop the stampede in his head.

MIRANDA AND BENJAMIN: BEFORE LEAVING

He loved her. In ways that made him forget he loved her. In ways that made him promise to go with her up to the bluffs and forget to show up. For he had the panorama to finish, and he had heard of a group of Indians camping on the other side who would make wonderful portraits, and he hadn't had time to tell her or invite her. So . . . he just went.

Then later, he would describe them to her, and she would lock herself in the attic and paint everything he had told her. And what she arrived at was more real than anything he'd described to her or, perhaps, anything that actually occurred.

He loved her for her vision and he wanted her for it, more than any promise of fame or measure of wealth. But because those were the things he believed he wanted, he never believed he loved her, even when he swore it, even when he forgot it, even when he swore never to forget. He never believed what he meant to believe or understood the difference of their love from his other loves. And when he came that night and watched her work and did understand the difference, he couldn't stand it. So, instead of staying, he stole from her whatever love could.

Because in the end, he figured love made them—these paintings—out of an awkward girl with beat up hands stalking the refuse of her body. His love of her made her work. So, he reasoned, to take her paintings was not theft at all. They were, by all rights, his.

It was a full eclipse of the moon the night he went, first in fifty years. So no one saw him leave. He carried them off, the rolls of painted canvas, slung across his back like a trapper with his kill. Dark as the devil that night. And the rain! Poor boy. Stole down to his boat, practically drowned in the mud. Crawling back to the Old World on his hands and knees.

THE RAVENING

Forget about being a girl, Rose, said the ravens. Save us, and we will take the squirrel out of your womb. This rodent you are pretending is a heart.

"Liar," she screamed as she stumbled to her feet, her thoughts fixed on the man. She grabbed a mounted fox, then a wolverine, a condor; whatever came into her reach she held up to her ears; she moved their mouths, she pounded on their voice boxes, but no sounds came out. "Maybe if I take all the pieces," Rose considered, "and throw them into the water, cook them up, and eat them myself, or feed them to each other until they themselves get confused as to who is who, maybe then they would talk to me, talk to me because if I do not have some word soon I will go mad." She took a cleaver from his worktable. Madly she chopped them up like onions: the animal bones and flesh.

But instead of words or even aimless noise, the only sound she heard was her own deliberate knife. Hacking them up, she found to her despair that inside every one of the creatures there was hardly any real animal left. Their bodies were filled with cotton and sawdust, held together with wire, gum, and glue. Why had she never noticed before, what the man was really doing to the dead in the taxidermy shed?

She wept over all the animals she had killed, who were not saved from death by her killing. She realized that everything she had believed most important in life—the ways in which to save and nurture life—were not true. She felt such a sorry homesickness that no destination, no remedy of place or person, could soothe. She knew now that whether she was girl or bird, she would live with this feeling for the rest of her life. She had no way to escape the tragedy of her acts; the senseless killing, the childish suspension of disbelief in service to what she had been convinced was a profound truth rather than a comforting lie. She hates him. Hates herself.

What was she to do? Where to go, as her home, the Hotel, was being dismantled bit by bit until now only the thirteen front pillars were left standing? And whom to cleave to, as her mother had no desire for anything but selling off their legacy and her sister had fallen into a hapless, lovesick madness? What was the sense of any of it, for bird or girl? She hated the worlds of man and nature. It was a lie that one could fuse them to any benefit or promise. The blood was thick as paint upon her hands as the last animal she had stuffed lay in pieces below her. And she realized then that the one to whom she was trying to give eternal life was herself; that she had been the object of all her desires for a better life; that life meant her life, that wilderness meant her bit of wilderness; her wild life. She knew then she had been the same as Trapper: grandiose and self-in-love but without his honesty to admit it.

Rose destroyed all the trophies they had made. She never returned to Trapper's shed. She left home forever that day. She had no faith anymore in the story told to her by the man. Now she believed solely in what her senses told, what she saw. She had no reason for faith, any faith at all.

She knew she belonged to the glass house.

THE BODY SHE CUTS UP

In the glass house, an idea occurs, an island of sense, of direction in her wandering. She hurls herself against its glass panes over and over again until her body is a topography of shredded skin and flowing blood. "Here is a map I can remember on," thinks the girl, entranced by the bleeding arms. She puts her hands through the walls of windows, forces her arms back and forth like saws through the broken glass. And her hands pull in fist after fist of blood. "Now I shall cut a trail through the wilderness," cries the girl in triumph as she admires her skin. "Here is the only real eternal life: a landscape to be cultivated for the recording of memory."

Each day now, she goes out beyond the glass house to the city of shapes, locus of miserable ghosts. Her veins are as open as blooming flowers, her flesh ruffled and shirred as feathers. As she walks through the city, its events and memories sink into her gutted pores, sear pictures into her skin, make imprints in her bones. Before, in the city of shapes, she could remember nothing. Now her body remembers it all.

Each time she returns to the glass house, she puzzles over the new mutilations the city has carved upon her and goes to work to make them more defined, unforgettable. In the glass house she takes up the tools she had once used in taxidermy and expands and embellishes and clarifies the scars upon her flesh. And when cuts and gashes are no longer enough, she takes blue, black, and green inks and injects them into her skin through the spun-glass needle until her body is a mass of impermeable tattoos. Her body becomes home to the delineation of roadways, landmarks, forks in the road, crosses in the air, indications of mountains to be climbed and rivers forded. Upon her forearms graze crudely etched animals while cryptic sayings bejewel her neck and behind her knees children weep. Half-human lunar creatures she tattoos into her pink freckled chest and everywhere inscriptions of all the languages of the earth weave in and out of the pictures like lines connecting the stars of the constellations.

Sometimes, along with needles, ink, razors, and knives, she uses her own clawed feet to scratch her body so deeply that it surpasses bleeding into a bone-deep brand of a map that would leave its bearer no excuse for lostness. As she journeys through the city of shapes and its inhabitants commit more invisible atrocities upon each other, the girl makes more indelible marks on her body, until there is no more space on her skin for one more map. The colors and the lines, the arrows and their directions are squeezed so tightly together that Rose's skin turns blue and black, until it doesn't look like skin at all, but the bruised, molting feathers of a scavenger bird. Illegible to all but herself, she is, head to foot, an illustrated atlas and almanac. A living book of all imaginable maps.

In her sleep, Trapper tried to woo her back. How he tried! She dreamed he threw up little fortune cookies into the sky that burst open and birds flew out and chattered all the secrets of taxidermy in her ear. But Rose shook her head no, and the birds scattered and crumbled like charred confetti. She would never again believe that embalming creatures would give them the gift of eternal life.

"Let them be dead," she cried, her body ready to swoop and fall for the shining.

"Let them be dead."

PART FOUR: WINTER

Maps of Misery

And he shall take to cleanse the house two birds alive and clean, and cedar wood, scarlet, and hyssop. And he shall kill one of the birds in an earthen vessel over running water. As for the living bird, he shall take it, and cedar wood, and the scarlet, and the hyssop, and dip them and the living bird in the blood of the bird that was killed over the running water. And he shall cleanse the house with it dipped in the blood of the dead one, and with running water and cedar wood, and the scarlet, and the hyssop. But he shall let go the living bird out of the city into the open fields and make atonement for the house and the house will be clean.

Leviticus 14:4-7

To make a map of misery you must mark the house of poverty and the long road of despair that leads from it into the wilderness until, finally, there is a clearing, a place to set another house, a happier one; but soon you realize that fertile valley is misery, too, and all your hopes are hopeless. This map of misery I color green for all the life and plenty it is missing.

Poverty, whether of body or of soul, is the starting line and finish of misery. I decided to make a road map of poverty so that all could know exactly where it lies and where it leads from and to; in this way to know how to avoid it so that the map itself would one day be obsolete like the cures for illnesses that no longer exist. Poverty's abode: A cramped house with no windows, covering all directions with its broken corners and its lies that you will only be there for a short time that is not forever. This house is the only thing of size that the starving have. Man may chisel and whittle away at it, but only an act of God, of cataclysm can truly destroy this house — earthquake, tornado, flood, famine, and the like — only by these is misery wiped off the map.

Misery is the slum at the end of despair, an invisible city inside the acknowledged city; where your days are filled with hunger, your children's days are filled with hunger, and the nights you tumble through are dreams of such repetitive boredom and senselessness that you are dying to wake up again and suffer, because that life at least has elements of change and chance to it that may lead to some way out. Misery is the condition of this charted land. Like a river's course, it shapes the shapes around us and becomes the interior of humanity's map.

from *The Book of the Cartographer*, Chapter IV

HER, WITHOUT HIM

When the stranger left, it was dead winter. And it was dead winter again and still he was gone.

He didn't even wait for the ice to break. Some said he flew over the frozen river on a sleigh; others said he didn't live through the first mountain pass. There were rumors he had drowned, the boat sunk by the weight of its cargo of canvas. Other folks said the wolves ate him or the Indians scalped him. Then there were the ones who said that he not only survived, but that he had become famous and had made the river famous too. It was the panorama that did it. Everyone everywhere wanted to see it and nobody could believe it—what it was and how it rolled along on its mighty cylinders as if it really were a river and the audience members were the brave pioneers lining its banks.

Of all the stories floating around about the whereabouts of Benjamin Emerson, Miranda did not know which to believe. She believed them all; she believed nothing. The one thing she did hold to was that the truth would one day be revealed to her on the attic floor. Each night she would take out the willow branch, set herself in the middle of the floor and wait to see what would happen.

The first night she painted an eagle with a snake in its beak, flying furiously over the mountains. As it passed, its wings cut deep shadows into the forest.

The second night she painted his face and the smell of his face.

The third night she painted his body, running; but his legs were the iron wheels of a train.

The fourth night, she painted a miniature of the panorama. All the details were there, though now each segment was the size of a postage stamp. She even reproduced the minute stitches with which she had sewn their two worlds together. Depicted in their variety was every season and the labors

attached to them; the many kinds of beast and fauna of the
land, how and where they grew; the characters of the people,
native and foreign; the phases of the moon; the fires on the
sun; the rock formations of the earth; the carpet-lush valleys;
the desert vistas; black, deep seas and all the supernatural landscapes and creatures that had scared and haunted her for many
a year on the attic floor. Every bit of it was there, except one
thing was different: In each place where there had been a picture of herself, the image had been scratched out, over and over
again, like some evil eye. She could find herself nowhere in the
panorama, nor could she seem to paint any new likeness of
herself there. Every time she tried, it turned out a black
smudge.

On the fifth night, she painted him again. He was dressed
in astonishing finery, such as she had never seen before on
woman or man.

"Where are you?" she demanded of the figure she made.

"Who are you?" it demanded back.

"You know who I am," she begged, knowing too, what he
would say.

"Benjamin, Benjamin" she implored, "it's me, your Miranda.
Remember? I made a whole lot of this painting."

He turned slowly to look at her, and he looked at her as
though she were mad. He pointed at her; his accusatory arm
was coming through the canvas. The audience that her brush
suddenly painted in the background heaved an uproarious
laugh.

"I made a whole lot of this painting," he mimicked her in
a shrill, tremulous voice.

The audience howled.

"Benjamin, I made . . ."

"Young lady, didn't anyone ever teach you that to lie is to
sin?"

Beside him came a mountain lion.

"I'm not lying."

"This is my panorama," he said, "mine and mine alone."
He stood now next to the jackal.

"You must remember," she implored.

"I can't talk to you anymore. You're a crazy woman." Now
by his side, a starving wolf. A heart without a body rolled by,
then a gypsy juggling golden knives.

"Benjamin!" Miranda cried, but she was painting something else now and he had vanished.

As the nights went by and piled into months, the pictures
she made grew bleaker and bleaker, until there were no gay
audiences, no exotic beasts, no panorama at all, even Benjamin
was gone. She no longer scanned the day trails for sight of him.
She no longer rifled the mail for word of him. And finally she
no longer picked up her brushes, thereby to find him. She just
stared out the attic window, and in her staring, she made a mistake; she leaves a blank spot. This must be where he escaped
her, she thinks.

After she stopped looking for him, she started searching
for the paintings she had made on the attic floor. She wanted
them back, but he had left her none. None, that is, but one.
She found it propped up against an ash tree in the farthest cultivated field. It was the only one she'd made of him. Standing
tall in his coat and vest, with his grandfather's golden chain of
master keys.

The girl held the picture in her arms and laughed falteringly.
"When all I wanted was to get back my own paintings, he leaves
me just one thing—the portrait of their thief."

TIME THAT A YOUNG GIRL SPENDS
BETWEEN EARTH AND SKY

In birds, how is lightness attained?

Their bones are hollow sacraments of air while those of mammals are solid or full of a dense, rich marrow. The lightness of bones is what makes flight possible.

She comes down when they're sleeping to rob the larder. They don't know what's happened to their sister-daughter. In the morning, they find all the bread pecked through and all the eggs sucked out. Inside the empty shells, there are little notes that say things like: *The road goes a long way but it always comes back to the same.* Or *Your mind is a heart. Don't break it.* And: *The indecision of a moment becomes the chaos of a lifetime.*

The words don't appear to be made by pencil or pen at all, but by some other sharp, pointy thing. A beak, perhaps, the beak of a child who has taken wholly to the skies, or claws maybe, the claws of a girl who has given up on walking. A girl on the lam, on the wing, so to speak.

Rose forgot about ever having been a girl. She forgot about everything to do with being a girl, or being part of a family of girls. When she looks down and sees her family in the big Hotel, they are a pack of wolves, with plaster and rubble, carcass and meat hanging out of their mouths.

Sometimes she tries to imagine what it would be like to be human again. Like them. She watches as her mother paces the widow's walk, as her sister roams the empty autumn fields, and she wonders how it would be to go through life on one's feet, the plodding lurch forward of it, the essentially falling nature of it. But she can't imagine it, because flying is such an opposite act. If she did, she'd never fly again.

Sometimes, out of curiosity, she hovers over the house watching the family that isn't hers anymore, doing the daily things of human life that don't mean anything to her anymore. After a while, her family just figures that she's dead, because they never see their Rose again, and as Cora says, "She'd never go off and disappear out of the blue like that." But nevertheless they set out on foot to find her every day. They whistle, they scream, they call her name, "Rose, Rose, Rose," through the cornfields. When in brief, confusing bursts, she does remember her other life, she whistles back, "Mama, I'm here. Sister, it's me. I'm coming." But all they hear as they search is the damn "caw, caw, caw" of the ravens eating up their crops. No girl-sound comes out of her, no girl-look comes from her charred and tattooed body, so who will believe that she is a girl, least of all she who can barely remember? She goes back to the fields, to the scavenging the dead, of whom she, the unrecognizable girl Rose, is one. She goes back to raiding the pantry, thieving the garden in raucous voice until the air is empty of currents to carry, until the larder is vacant of crumbs to feed, after every living being stops listening. To her family, she is as good as dead. They finally stop looking.

But it was not lost upon the mother, that when her daughter vanished, many of the Hotel's valuables started to disappear too.

MIRANDA IN THE FIELDS

They sent her like a scarecrow to stand in the fields and frighten off the scavenger birds.

Miranda in the fields. After the end of him. She stands in the fields after the end of him, and she wishes the field were the sea. Then she could swim to him on the other side of the world, where she is sure he is wandering. She looks north, she looks south, looks west and east, north south west east. She makes a cross, a navigational crucifixion, with her staring. Point to point she gazes, looking for Benjamin.

Her tears have made an ocean in her throat that she can't get over, poor scarecrow girl trembling under the ravens she's been sent to scare away.

"Benjamin," she screams as one of the ravens' feet graze her head.

"You have such sweet tears," she remembers him saying when something he did made her weep.

"Sweet tears. What does that mean? Why must my tears be sweet," the girl cries, "my distress a jewel to be mined?"

The whole of her life lay open, empty harvested as the field she stands in, while time passed and passed. Still she is nowhere as the black birds swoop.

"My God," she cries as a bird pecks and a welt of blood rises on her scalp. "My God," as it dives for her again.

She raises her arms to protect herself, lifts them up as if she might pull out the whole carpet of growth: the profuse vegetation of sky, the crop and the weed, the fruit and the pestilence. And when it all was torn away, she'd find in its place an endless sea of tears. She would float her face there as the centuries turned over their suffocating pages and her face would be the sweetest salt brine. She'd float her arms there, on the heavy surface, outside the fleeing, noxious eons, and the arms would billow out above her like angel wings. Her arms would be flying to save the face that looks for him under the sea, the face that believes it is water she must breathe. But nothing can stop her face from drowning, except perhaps to lift it up into the world to be set upon by the beaks of birds.

STEALING

A bird is a natural thief, robbing the air of its weight in order to ascend. It flies by stealing currents of wind, its wings making up for the lack of hands. Many birds steal the most with their feet, which have a powerful ability to cling. They would rather starve than to let go of a tree. The feet of some birds look exactly like leaves.

She would swoop down in the middle of the night, through a crack in a window, a rift in the roof, and rummage around the vast house to see what she could loot. While her mother emptied the cracker barrel that was their forsaken home, the bird-daughter built up her own stolen treasury.

Little by little, day after day, the Hotel emptied out of its belongings, like a huge balloon with a tiny hole pricked in it. As Cora auctioned off everything in sight and piles of money replaced all their possessions, Rose the raven began to venture home in the middle of the night and sneak around. She went there to see what she could salvage, what she might steal before her mother sold everything.

For ravens only survive two ways: by scavenging the dead or thieving from the living. Shiny things, things that remind them of the sun—the closest thing to the divine in their bird's-eye view of life. There were many glittering treasures left in the Hotel that the bird-daughter coveted, that she could imagine dripping out of her ravenous mouth, clutched beneath her protective wing, stowed under her beady eye: a golden locket engraved with two hands clasped in friendship; silver candlesticks from a church in St. Petersburg that smelled of centuries of incense; a set of superbly faceted jet buttons. She even tore the gold tooth off her sleeping sister's breast, leaving its chain dangling and twisted around Miranda's neck.

So it came to pass that Rose, whether girl or bird, was united in her split self by the common talent of stealing. The best part of her now lived to commit robbery, to save the Hotel's objects from being traded in for money; to rescue from anonymous dispersal the things she believed were her family's legacy, her personal history, which the green paper bills strewn all over the vacant house were fast replacing.

In the branches of the oak tree that grew in the river, she built a birdhouse made of all the things she stole from her family's Hotel. The illuminated manuscripts from the library became the roof of her house; its walls were the bronze sheaves from the attic cupola, her parents' gems became its drawing room furniture. Her father's double-cased gold pocket watch became her favorite leisure chair, her mother's silver and ruby earrings she wore on her clawed feet as ice skates to glide upon the frozen river that ran through the giant tree. For a time, Rose the raven was happy here in this, her first home of her own.

MIRANDA DREAMS HIM TRAVELING

*"Tomorrow I will go away," says the gypsy heart to her every day. The
gypsy tooth sparkling on her chest bites into her like a ripe apple.*

The pigments froze and faded, the brushes collected dust, the
floorboards dried and cracked, and Miranda, in her attic,
would fall into deathlike slumbers lasting for days on end, even
weeks, nothing but sleep, where she would meet him again and
again; and this time he was traveling. She would follow his
journeys in these dreams, behind his back, casting so large a
dark reflection that sometimes he imagined that the shadows
that had once chased him West had come East to claim him.
He never thought they were the girl's dreams disturbing him;
in fact, now that he had taken and absorbed her body of work,
he never thought of her at all.

She dreams him traveling; north, south, east, west. She
sees every place he goes, everything he does, how he presents
their panorama, how he talks of his adventures, which in his
retelling she never shared. The rooms are full of his followers,
and they are many: captains of commerce, men of trade, aris-
tocrats, philosophers, intellectuals, artists, a whole galaxy of
sycophants; and as they court him, lavish gifts on him, as much
as it hurts her, she can't help but marvel at his ability to make
them feel they are the finest, brightest, most beautiful souls in
the universe. And because she is invisible, a see-through girl in
this journey of his that she dreams, Miranda puts herself in the
place of the women who pursue him. She calls his name, she
pounds his chest, she laughs, she weeps, she waits at door after
door, but she's gone from his memory and he falls through her
shadow into other flesh. Nothing she does can bring him back
to her. The worst thing about her dreams is that she is forced
to hope the dream will change. That they will be together

again. When she awakes, which is never for long, she's crushed by this hope that has no reference point, no truth in the gray frozen land to which she has come.

She follows him all over the world in her dreaming, and only later when the news came would she discover how accurate her dreams had been. Everywhere he went, the people flocked to see his panorama and hear him talk of the river. And then they would dream of the river too, and some would even lay their coin aside, pack their bags, and go there, forsaking all—job, family, comfort, love—to go to the places he and she had painted. The ones who came, they all knew him; he was their inspiration. But to them she was nothing. It was so convincing, so complete an obliteration, that she, too, would have believed herself nonexistent but for her suffering, which would not go away. The people that came because of him, these pioneers that Benjamin had made, seldom visited the Hotel, because it didn't appear in his famous panorama. In the end, the Hotel didn't fit his picture of the wilderness, so he had cut its image out.

Sometimes, by pure coincidence, his followers would come upon the Hotel in their pilgrimage. They would watch Cora's Sunday auctions curiously and laugh as the artifacts of the old country, things they had done their best to escape, went up on the block and drew such extravagant bids. The legends that these newcomers told about Benjamin did nothing to help Miranda believe him gone from her forever, a thief and a traitor. For in them, he was as kind and adventurous, gallant and brave as any man could be. But one day, a traveler happened down to the auction and left a foreign newspaper absent-mindedly on his seat. There on the front page, she saw an illustration of him, just his head in profile, and by its side a reproduction of a portion of the panorama, one she had made of a willow tree with the hanging silver babies. The caption read: "Don't miss Benjamin Emerson's superb paintings of the Wild West, the rage of the continent."

Underneath the article, he had taken out a half-page ad:

Famous artist/explorer Benjamin Emerson will be showing
his three-mile-long amazing panorama of the biggest river
on Earth all this week. See the pioneers of North America
battle for their lives and country against massacring Indians.
See the strange natural wonders of a thrilling new land and
the awesome beasts that roam it. You are guaranteed to feel
as if you yourself were there or your money back.
Three shows daily and five on weekends. Children half-
price when accompanied by adult.

And then in smaller print was a list of the panorama's
prominent scenes. Eagerly she scanned the page for her name.
But she could not find it there.

Her nonexistence in this newspaper was what finally made
her realize that he was never coming back, that he had never
planned to come back, or for that matter, never dreamed of
taking her with him in the first place. It was at this time in the
journey of her grief that Miranda forgot how to sleep. Her
body, continually awake, was in unendurable pain, as if every
excruciating emotion she had inhabited her muscles and
bones. Walking, she appeared almost hunch backed as she tried
to move forward under the weight of betrayal, one shoulder
lurched forward and leading like a defeated boxer bent still on
punching.

She: curled-up on the floorboards. Animal. Edging slight
increments at a time across the attic, her nostrils working hard
as bellows as she tries to smell out refuge and rest. When she
would find a certain position where she was not in agony, she
would freeze there, no matter how awkward or uncomfortable.
If she moved the slightest degree to the left or right, up or
down, she would lose this merciful place and the shooting
pains, the suffocation, the tears would break her open again.
When she could not find her pose of sanctuary, she would hunt
up and down the house and grounds all night without rest,
because moving with this anguish seemed better than taking it

passively. Those nights, there was no peace for the girl, only the eruption of memories over the absence of life that her life had become.

Each night and day she suffered her love of him, crushed and bottled up, disfigured and deformed in heartbreak. That the life between them was dead while they lived on, was what she could not resolve. There was no completion, no memorial for it, only unacknowledged abandonment. And as there was no official closing to their love, her wounds remained open, and they festered. But no pain was worse than when she believed he might come back for her.

SAVING

"You can really rest on money," Cora mused to herself on the day she sold off all their luxurious carpets and rugs. "Why, it's soft as grass, a prettier green, and it doesn't ever die in winter."

Cora, curled up in a ball on the counting-room floor, protecting all the money she can make or trade or find; the place expansively empty but for the green, green bills. She would never take payment in gold or silver or any metal coin —how she had come to hate those things, how they reminded her of the years in the mine in the South with her absent husband and her loneliness; but the dollar bills were so clean and *light, my dears, light and pure as angels' wings* . . .

"Money," she would say to anyone who would listen, "money is the only thing that can make money, which is what we need to save our home, our traditions, indeed our way of life. We must go after money or die."

That was the way her hunger for dollars had started. Her desire to save all their exquisite things had come to this airy vacuity.

"Oh Emmanuel," she would exclaim in a pitched, distracted voice as she held up the stacks of bonds to nail into the wall that once held his portrait.

"This one is worth ten thousand and in five years will be good for fifty thousand when properly invested," she announced, just the way in earlier days she had said: "And with this we'll repair the roof; with this we'll buy lawn furniture; with this we'll build an addition in the Byzantine style, which we do not as yet represent in our architectural diversity."

But now the "going once, going twice," the hand waving "yea," the affirmative slam "sold" meant only money, until nearly all the furnishings of the Hotel were replaced by rolls and rolls of greenbacks. Cora became a creature of paper money—that is of abstraction—a substitute for the gold staked behind it, which nobody wanted anymore; it was too heavy. She was safe in the dollars' crisp folds, protected from the wilderness she survived in, from the civilized objects that she held responsible for her isolation here. An isolation and a confusion that had started from the moment her father sent her out to collect curiosities for his museum and deepened as she became her husband's accomplice in building.

But he never came back, never came back. She had tried to bear up under the Hotel after he left; at first by identifying it with him and later, when that proved useless, by identifying it with herself. But how could it ever really be hers, having come to it while wandering in his dreams? She was not an irresponsible woman; she tried to save the Hotel from deteriorating, even after she knew it was hopeless. That was how she came upon the solution of money, until the making of money became for her much more than anything else. The paper bills were her true light and joy, as she watched night after night from the edge of the widow's walk for Emmanuel's return, her hands overflowing with sweet cash. She called out:

And this stack will buy 1,000 shares of preferred stocks.
And this one will buy the same in numbered bonds.
And this one will be put away for six months to treble itself.
And this one will rest in the bank for one hundred years.

Talking to the sky, to the husband who is never there. Cora.

The bird-daughter perched on a limb of the tree in the river looked down and saw her desperate mother, so determined to make sale after sale of their beautiful belongings. The daughter vowed to keep on stealing.

MIRANDA PAINTS EARTH AND SKY

"Help me," she cries, "kill me, help me, kill me." The brush in her hand, the barren floor, him gone, the stick in her throat. "Hang on" is an expression she's heard too much to believe it has an end. She's a girl who hates an injury to any living being. So what can Miranda make of her own suffering? What can she make?

It would come over her suddenly, clear and clean as rain. Like a vision it would strike her, illuminating her lack of faith in her destiny with him, all the while knowing that her hope was a curse, her trust a delusion. Then she would want to be gone from the earth because it seemed to her a crumbling, rotting ball that she alone inhabited. She realized now that all her gypsy heart had ever wanted was to outrun the vicious, punishing sphere upon which she was trapped, to run faster and faster in hopes of saving herself from the sinking implosion it promised.

Eventually, she forgot she was looking for a man as eventually, too, she forgot that the floor she sat upon was once painted by herself. She just stared out at the river, the one safe place, the one action secure against the incoherent disputations of her angry heart and tortured soul. She stared into the water until she stared it dry. And the water of the river became tears in her eyes. This was the beginning of the time when Miranda, who could no longer paint nor sleep, began to cry continuously.

She wept so much that a raw, eroded trail carved gullies from her eyes to her chin. She would remember, laughing, as the tears poured out of her eyes, how her father had promised her that all good girls must breathe water if they were to breathe at all. Then, as in a deluge, her thinking swept away and she'd find herself staring vacantly through this sea of tears onto the dark attic floor that seemed more menacing now in its immaculate barrenness than it ever was in the bright days of the nightmares she had once painted there. At the time Miranda started to cry, the heavens began to pour. Days and months go by, she wants to die, but all she can do is weep. All she can do, knowing he's never coming back to her, is be the cipher of atmospheric upheaval—snow, ice, hail, rain, sleet, all come pouring over the Hotel through her bloodshot eyes. People from miles around hear tell of a girl who paints the sky and controls the weather. A sad, grieving girl with her heart on the outside of her body. Half-wolf, half-gypsy. So the legend goes.

Miranda paints the sky today, paints it gray and the clouds begin to gather. The faces of all the people in the valley are dyed gray by the girl crying out the sky. When they come to her and implore her to choose another color, that they cannot live ashen, cold, and damp forever, all she can offer is buckets of hail and mud. Now the people are covered in mud and they slide around their houses like rooting pigs. The whole valley begins to run out of umbrellas and galoshes, which start to cost as much as prime workhorses. Women pawn their furs and jewels to purchase tarpaulins. Husbands forsake their weekend gambling to mend leaky roofs. No one wants to buy anything that is not water-and mud-proof and "How many beautiful things are that?" moans Cora, as her auction business falls off badly. She begs her daughter to stop, stop, stop her grieving.

"Everyone for miles around is suffering, not just you," she reprimands the girl.

"I don't know how to stop, Mama," she sobs, her face a blistering sore. "Teach me to stop," she pleads as the river runs down her cheeks. Miranda is painting the sky today; the sky is gray. Instead of hot in summer, now it's freezing ice. Instead of light, now it's dark. The harvest corn lies blanched on its stalk, the black soil is petrified, and the Hotel is covered with a frozen patina so that it begins to look like a palace carved from ice. No heat, no fire seems to be able to warm the cold and wet of Miranda's heavenly paintings. The people in the valley are all turning blue, as if their skin were a massive network of veins with no red blood running through them. But one day the unbearable cold she has made begins to affect even the numbed Miranda. Her tears freeze in her eyes so she can no longer cry, which stops the skies from sleeting and the fog from hunkering down. Then the sun comes out, the land begins to bloom, people's complexions return to pink, and they begin to laugh again, and live. Bonfires are lit all over the land and the whole valley melts. Only the girl with the gypsy heart is frozen stiff in the eyes, her grief permanently paralyzed. People ignore her now. It's easy because she's truly become a see-through girl, a shadow of her former self, practically disappeared by the hungry heart and hermit lips that have starved her body to a willow stick.

In the middle of the night the people in the territory jerk awake. Their faces are red and burning, the walls of their rooms are bleeding, and such pain is in their hearts that they think they must be dying. But they don't die, they just suffer the heart and soul of red. Who would have thought such people would ever yearn for gray again? But they did.

Miranda is painting the sky today. The sky is red. She wants her stolen pictures back; yearns after them as they float down the river, as they cross the seas, as they amuse the crowds, as Benjamin points and explains, as he rearranges their order and history, as the white-coated apprentices roll up her paintings in their traveling shrouds. But as he journeys farther and farther into the Old World, Miranda's violet eyes can no longer see him, can no longer paint the skies in the sinking hues of her loss and grief. Now the people of the valley, like the traveler Benjamin, are free, and the weather is released from the vagaries of emotion to follow its own unpredictable nature. Now, her room alone wallows in red and her heart alone has shriveled to a small blackened seed. She goes down to the river to escape her bloody room. She's gone down to the river to wave goodbye to the empty waters, to taunt the deaf air with her hollow eyes.

THE HULK OF THE HOTEL

After the raven, having stolen all it could, flew away, and before the
woman got up to sell what little was left. . . .

In the hour of sunrise, with its muffled light and retreating
shadows, the Hotel looked like one of those desolate phantom
pirate ships presumed by all sea-worthy sailors to be maraud-
ing the waters in search of the fearful alive.

It appeared gutted by earthquake or flood or some other
natural disaster, for it seemed impossible that human hands
could create so much damage. But the hulk of the Hotel was
not the work of nature, only the result of its keeper's urge to
sell its goods away. Its windows were as vacant as the eyes of an
abandoned idol, for Cora had sold off all their glass panes. The
door frames, too, were empty of their fine wooden doors and
stood gaping like so many mouths of missing teeth. The whole
magnificent structure was leaning precariously west for she had
even sold off most of the thirteen Corinthian pillars that held
the building up. Now, with only two crumbling columns
remaining, the Hotel had become prehistoric in its aspect, and
one stood before it like a child in awe of the giant carcass of
what once had been.

Every time Cora looked at what was left of their home, her
eyes were the eyes of a vulture searching for one more morsel
she might tear out without the whole edifice caving in.

> *Going once,*
> *going twice.*
> *O! ladies and gents*
> *do I hear*
> *is that all?*
> *Going once,*

twice,
thrice,
half-price, then,
Sold!

Even her tortoiseshell combs she put on the block, her hair then falling in a luxurious sweep down her narrow, nervous back, now bared, for all her garments but her underclothes she put up for sale too. She fed on the buyer's fantasy of refuge in the thing bought, as if they, by the power of purchasing, could withdraw into another universe, one without the violence and boredom of their workaday lives, a heavenly dreamworld of materiality.

There she stood, night after night, the lady auctioneer in her threadbare slip. She looked like a child, a beggar waif, except for her luxuriant gray hair. It meant nothing to her now, the relinquishing of things, as it had meant nothing once to Emmanuel to give up his precious gold mine in exchange for objects of man-made beauty. But meanwhile there were still a few things more left to sell.

She told herself, in the dreaded moments when she feared he might come back, that all this selling was a noble sacrifice, a way to save some increment of the grand Hotel. To hold onto the core of it, she reasoned, she must auction off in their entirity its two great wings. They were bought for salvage by the Railroad to use in the new hotel it was building.

Cora stands in her auction house, the ballroom of what is left of the grand Hotel, and she waits for the buyers to come. She stands in the middle of this room, huge and hollow as the mounted skeletons of whales in her father's museum. What a repulsive, mesmerizing monster it seems to her now, this Hotel, insatiable in its emptiness, in its gargantuan, hollow bulk. She watches her customers roaming through its gaping spaces, between the blanched bones that once held the magnificent structure up, picking their way through the ruins for a bargain. Oh! The sacrifices she had made here! All she had given up. Just to save it. She looks at her audience piteously. But secretly, she was happy; soon she would have no home.

AND A WILLOW SWING . . .

She prayed on her knees for one last chance to have him steal
from her. She told herself it was better to be robbed blind than
to live trapped in a place where she'd never be heard, never
seen. The gypsy heart that once lived for adventure won't let
her go after him. It tells her it's a cripple now; it's no longer
made for traveling. How she has changed in winter, this snow-
drift prisoner of an ailing heart! Its red walls are beating her
down, the blue veins are squeezing her in. Miranda looks at her
hands, searching for the remnants of her soul. All she finds
there is a massacred field. How can you fight with your own
hands, she wonders? Her heart, her hands—the same tied in
knots and brutalized, the same unrelenting choking—these
two twin moons of her being.

She searches and searches but can't find one reason to agree
to the torture of living. She climbs out the window, down to the
willow tree. Vaguely she remembers the joy of swinging, the form
in space, the body neither here nor there. But the old swing is
broken, the wooden seat rotted through and hanging by a single,
frayed rope. How will she swing now? she wonders. How will she
hold herself afloat in the merciless air? Where will she put her
mutilated hands, her runaway heart?

Hanging by her weary arms, her legs pump her up. She's one
big hope and she knows there's no hope. She can breathe in this
suspension, she discovers, in this place between thoughts. It keeps
her pumping, the knees working back and forth as she flies past
the Hotel, the river, the forest. From this height, she can see the
continent's two oceans. The stars are out in the sky now: a dizzy
string of pearls, broken apart, at the instant before they fall. She's
only looking for the right moment to jump.

How she loves her neck! She smiles as she wraps the rope
around it. Arched over her body like the bough of a weeping
willow tree; beautiful and slender as a swan's, this neck. Upon
it, the glittering chain that had once held the gypsy tooth, now

lost or stolen, the naked loop of gold hanging around her throat. She can do this one thing, in agreement, at last, the heart and soul of her; she can swing. In the swinging, the heart and soul of her meet—pendulum and hour hand, flight and stasis. Upon the dangling rope, with the chain around her neck, she's swinging out as far as she can go.

The final leap free over the frozen river.

Her feet hit the highest point the swing can reach. Then the frigid air: hard as a brick wall it slams her, the gravity of the land sending her down. As she falls, she sees, perhaps for the first time since Benjamin had come, exactly what's beneath her. She sees the riverbank, the snappers, the leeches, the pine stead, the topiary gardens, the Hotel itself, which, having melted much in the period of her weeping, stands in a body of its own water, like a deserted island. She sees the swamp and what's beneath the swamp, the riverbed and what's underneath the riverbed—the snails, the fish, the worms, the microbes breeding there—and she can breathe and breathe in the water until she hits bottom and with it, the dense suffocation of river mud. She wants to know so badly what's beneath this mud. She is certain therein lies another atmosphere of water in which, killed of earth, she can breathe. She swims down and down, under the bottom of the river. She opens a hatch door in the river floor that leads to the sea.

All this time, she marvels, *all along, the place of forever-breath, the respite from a life of drowning, right under this muddy riverbed, right here, beneath my feet . . . the sea.* She's walking now under the water. Deeper and deeper into the sea; and the deeper she goes, the easier it is to breathe. Just like her father promised. And this time it's not a dream.

A SISTER'S LAMENT

Time passed, and one day, as she stood outside her birdhouse and looked in, the bird-girl saw that it wasn't a home at all but a junkyard. There it was, all the beautiful booty, piled up in monstrous heaps with neither order nor foundation nor meaning. This was no place like home, Rose thought. She had no home, she realized, as she began to hurl all the stolen things off the treetops into the winter river. Beauty's not pretty at all, wept the girl, it's ugly.

A black sun, a red moon.
The sky is pouring.
This is not a gentle day.
Miranda, shut the window, dear,
The rain, it's coming in.

But her black-haired twin is out there swinging.
The starched white dress, the golden chain
Around her neck, the broken rope of the willow swing.
Her head snapping back and forth, as if attached by a puppet string.
Miranda, shut the window, dear,
The rain, it's coming in.

But the black-haired girl can't hear her sister.
She's swinging out from her willow tree, over the sky,
Into the river, where her sister is hurling all the lovely things.
Miranda, shut the window, dear,
The rain, it's coming in.

Birds aren't light, Rose thinks in envy and in grief. As she watches her dead sister swing. We still carry the souls of our ancestors, the dinosaurs, inside. And so it hurts us to fly. There's no joy in it, no matter what it looks like from earth. It hurt to be a bird, just as much as it hurt to be a girl.

DREAM OF A MAN HUNTING

He dreamed he was shooting for eagles that day, but all he was bringing down were ravens. There were owls, there were jays, there were starlings in the sky, but everything his finger to the trigger made fall down was raven. All the ravens in the world falling dead from the air, tearing out his eyes as they hit the earth and died.

Trapper could not claw his way out of the cave. Time and again he tried, but the paintings of the animals held him back in mute revenge. Sometimes the only way for a man to escape is to turn into somebody else entirely—to go back to being a thin, wiry boy who can crawl through the smallest space—a mine-monkey they'd called him: Emmanuel.

Trapper, dreaming himself out of the cave, a man come back out of the wilderness, dreaming to bring order out of the fur and flesh and fangs of the wild as a law cannot or a city cannot or the collection and preservation of precious antiques cannot or works of art or the raising of a family cannot. "To hell with beauty," he laughs, shaking his head like a wet hound. A bringing of order to human society, that's the thing to aspire to now and to this end, he wants to stuff the human body, to bring some lasting form, some eternal sense to it, without abandoning the wilderness, without forsaking the fecund chaos, without forgetting what has passed.

Man comes up in the middle of the river, his mouth full of mud and river. He has no air left when he finally surfaces, his breath having been spent in watery struggle between painted cave and river's end. He has no strength left to swim, he realizes as he reckons the distance to shore. With the prospect of drowning all around him, *why*, he thinks, *why did I even look for a way out? Why didn't I go to sleep down there like a bear in hibernation, but forever and ever?* He wants to sink back under but his body keeps struggling up despite him. His eyes see something moving in front of him; a fallen tree, perhaps, floating downstream. It looks so luminous, he thinks it must be hammered out of pure gold. *Eldorado*, he weeps, *Eldorado*, his mountain made of gold. His hands reach out against his memory to grab hold. He floats to shore on the shining dead thing that cradles in her limbs a willow stick from a weeping willow tree.

IN WHICH A PROPERTY
IS SOLD AND BOUGHT

*Her powers of theft had left her. Even for the shiniest things she had no
hunger. Seeing the body of the girl by the bank, she dreamed it back to
where it belonged, to the top of the house, the attic overlooking everything.
Then the raven flew down from the tree to see him, the final bidder.*

The last customers held their breath for the bidding to begin.
After a long silence, Cora's voice:

"Going once, going twice."

Her cry rang out like a huge cracked bell.

"Going once, going twice."

Her arms stretched out in such a way that they seemed
to be trying to grab everything while trying to throw it all
away.

"Going once, going twice," she cried.

Silence and more than silence, an echo of silence feathered
down over the crowd.

"Ladies and gentlemen, the bid!"

The crowd began to stir, from row to row, a viperous hiss.

A thousand cigars glowed in the dusk-dark room.

A thousand knitting needles furiously clicked.

"Going once, going twice," she cried, but she could not for
the life of her say "gone."

Suddenly, a man's shadow in the back of the room. A creature made of leather and beard, and dripping with mud. He
stepped forward and said quietly: "I bid fifty thousand," and
fixed his gaze to the ceiling where a spider was furiously weaving.

Cora's eyes followed those eyes, as burning as his voice was
sweet. But for the rest of him, he was a man you could not see,
as if obscured by the weight of his own enraged shadow.

Cora said: "I beg your pardon, sir, I seem to have misheard
you."

"Pardon, ma'am, no pardon's due." He laughed, his eyes never moving away from the progress of that spider along its rich and varied web.

The crowd in the room started humming, like wind tearing across a parched prairie. Cora put her hand across her forehead, squinting hard to see this stranger's face.

"I said, sir," she continued, "I must have misheard your bid."

"Mishear away, good lady, mishear away. I'll say it again as clear as day: fifty thousand for the Hotel and all the contents therein."

He spit out a toothpick from between his widely spaced front teeth and started rummaging under his waistcoat for some things that he pulled out, the way a magician conjures a roll of endless handkerchiefs.

It was money, Cora realized through the dust of the distance that settled between them in the long room. Money. Fat, new greenback bills, so many that when he took them all out from under his clothes, he lost his girth and turned into a slender man.

Even with the bald spot and the pearly hair, even with the slump of age on a proud man's shoulders, she knew him, Emmanuel, her husband, come back after all these years. There he stood before her with a great pile of cash in his hands. He turned to the people gawking in their seats and roared, "You go home now, auction's over. We've got nothing left to sell. Come back when we reopen"—he glared at his auctioneer wife—"under new management."

Cora, left alone in the empty hall with her long-gone husband, his hands full to overflowing, hers empty but for the gavel. Every moment of her life she knew he would return, that he was waiting for her to commit this final sale. She always knew he must come back to them, his family, his blood, to put his mark again upon their post and door.

ROSE TELLING

Through the doorway, I saw them, my parents, sitting together at the auction block as if they had been doing so forever. His eyes were off the ceiling now, the spider discarded from his thoughts; he looked my mother in the eye. It was then that I saw his face. It was Emmanuel, my father, but with Trapper's face. Trapper come back as sure as living day. He was laughing.

"Fifteen years, Cora. Didn't even recognize me living in your own backyard. What kind of love is that? This is my Hotel, always was, always will be. Get out of here and don't you ever come back."

He chased my mother out from the Hotel, down to the river with a thousand footsteps heavy as boulders, a thousand laughs louder than thunder; Trapper and Emmanuel and a million devils in between. Farther and farther away he chased her until she was just a speck on the horizon. I never saw my mother again.

The man was yelling: "Miranda, where are you, your papa's here to stay."

"Dear Miranda," he coaxed, "come here, come here, come here!"

This is not my papa, thinks Rose, *this cannot be my papa. My papa's in the city with white clean hands.*

From room to room the man searched the empty house for the eldest twin.

All this time.

The first floor, the second . . .

To see as I have seen.

The third the fourth . . .

Trapper and Emmanuel. Emmanuel and Trapper.

Finally, at the attic door, banging.

To have done what I have done . . .

"Miranda, Miranda, your father's home!"

He knocked on the door for his beautiful daughter.

This is not my papa, weeps Rose the raven. *This cannot be
my papa. My papa's at the bottom of the earth saving us all,
breathing dirt.*

But the door was locked tight. He had no time for soft
words, his need was urgent.

"Miranda, let me in!"

He kicked down the door. The attic opened up was a
painted cavern, the walls, ceiling, floor, every inch covered
with pictures—the primitive stick figures of the hunt. A window lay open; there the willow tree in its winter straw swayed
slightly in the damp wind. There, the long, swinging cord of
hair, black as night, a blackness you could never fill, and the
gold around the throat; then the delicate feet swinging like a
child's who cannot reach the ground from the chair at the dinner table; and finally, the hemp rope around her neck.

"Why didn't you wait for me, child?" he cries, reeling the
body in, "I could have saved you; could have taught you how
to live this life."

Oh Father, Rose thought, gazing at the corpse, her sister's
body a cold northern sea. *Father, you taught your daughters far
too much.*

The next thing I remember I was helping him take her apart.

He made a slit down the middle, from forehead to pubic
bone. She's bleeding a lot, a river of blood as he cuts, the red covering up her naked body like a tight silk robe. She knew that if
he had not believed before, he believed so now: that to save the
child of his, he must stuff her. Rose saw, as her father sealed the
frail body with chemical fluids, as he sewed it neatly back up, as
he painted her cheeks pink, her lips red, as he brushed out the
fine black hair one thousand strokes, that he did love her so.

I never wanted to hurt my father, but when I saw him
lying on top of my sister's body, moving slowly in and out, like
a weary breath, I dropped my knife and grew wings. I ascend-
ed in flight only to swoop down again. I tore out his throat in

one stroke, for a raven's beak is sharper, surer than any taxider-mist's implement. Now for him, there was no air. No ability to speak.

How he had gone on, she thought, licking the blood, naming the names. How he had gone on as if his knowledge, his reflection, his his his his his, was everything a body need ever know to go on. But when she saw him lying on her still twin's bones she knew that to go on meant to kill. How she would miss him, hunter, father, liar; she is weeping like a lost child. Why, she wonders, is that always the way, to know too late? Why is time everything to the tale, with the sequence rather than the events defining the journey? She leaves him there in the attic, leaves him for dead, for the ravens to pick clean his bones, for the ravens to pluck out his sparkling eyes and carry them up as trophies to their treetop nests.

He looked real good dead, my father, thought Rose returned to her girl-form, his bits of self scattered all over the attic floor like wedding confetti. But could any amount of dis-membering keep him from returning, from hurting them? She lit a candle and held it over the pieces of his body, his hands and arms as far from one another as she could throw them. She looked at the fragments of the man and tried to imagine them all of a piece. It was as if she had never seen him before. This was not Trapper or Emmanuel; not her father at all, just some luckless stranger out to make his bid.

This man I killed.

I have to go now, thought the girl, nothing for me here, no home . . . I'm not sure I will ever know what the word "home" means again. She saw in her head the man's severed arm around the empty girl's slender waist; a pair of torn-off lips quivering against the stillness in the moment before ashes, and the heart's blood upon her young hands. Now that was her only image of home. She had to go.

But for Miranda. She was my sister, my twin, I couldn't leave her to disappear in the rot of wilderness that was coming to claim back our place, to grow over with weeds, with spring flood, with winter ice; the walls eaten up by termites, the floors a sea of worms, the windows a feast of spider webs, the whole of her decomposing into moisture and dirt.

Rose grabbed the man's knife off the attic floor with her two trembling hands. She stood before her sister's body, the cavity gutted but the skin as fresh and warm and white as when she had been alive. Her eyes came to rest on Miranda's hands. How beautiful they seemed to her now, even the gouges and tears upon them looked like delicate patterns of tree trunk and coral. Rose held the blade high above her head like a shining crown and slammed it down upon her sister's hands. She hacked them off at the wrists.

She placed one hand under each of her arms, and stretched out those arms until they grew into wings. She flew away to the tree in the river, where she hid the hands in a hollow, that she guarded day and night. She watched the earth below and waited for it to catch up with her.

The fields grew up over the last remnants of the Hotel. Birds nested in the rafters, rats scurried from stair to broken stair, goldenrod broke through the foundation rock, fungi invaded its walls.

And this is all there is for many a year while Rose the raven soars up and up with the last of her stolen treasure, this pair of her sister's severed hands.

PART V: THE BOOK OF THE CARTOGRAPHER

Maps of a New World

She saw things opposite the way a cartographer should.
She saw the thing rather than the outline of the thing.
The points of destiny she made flesh
when they should have remained articles of faith.

from *The Book of the Cartographer*, Chapter V

THE FUTURE OF ROSE THE RAVEN

Her powers of theft had left her, even for the shiniest things she had no hunger. Her wings shriveled to stubs. Her feathers grew back like girl hair and her body turned back into a girl's body, only she wasn't the girl in the hotel anymore. There was no hotel no mother grandmother no sister father trapper no stuffed animals. Not anymore. Just this glass house.

—I want to know where I am, she asked when she arrived in the glass house she had been in for a long, long time.
—This is the future, they told her. Welcome.
—How do I know this is the future?
—Look, have you ever seen anything like it before?
—Many times, I've been in this glass house many times and now it looks exactly the same.
—That proves what we've said, they said, and shut the door and locked it behind them.
—There is one difference, she muttered to herself, the door's different. It doesn't open up.

They called her Cartographer.
"Cartographer" here is your lunch.
"Cartographer" here is your candle.
"Cartographer" your bath is drawn.
"Cartographer" here is your empty chart. Hurry up!

And so it came to pass that Rose the raven wrote

The Book of the Cartographer

in absolute secret, to escape the maps she was forced to shape.

THE BOOK OF THE CARTOGRAPHER
CHAPTER I. INTRODUCTION

I gave them the measurements they wanted. Then, I got me down to my real work.

This is my new world and it is made of maps. In it I have put all the measurements of the universe, not only the distances between material things but those of conditions, thoughts, feelings. A map of poverty drawn by no chance; map of misery drawn by no hope; map of rage drawn by choked aspiration; map of the disappeared drawn by their killers; map of mountains drawn by the sea; map of seas drawn by the moon; map of memory drawn by forgetting; map of family drawn by the history of hate and loving; map of homelessness drawn by the greed of ownership; map of a life drawn by the age lines on its bearer's face.

A map, I make a map of the heart; the coordinates of its circumference; the natural boundaries that cordon off its chambers; the rivers that comprise its bloodstream; the colors we use to describe its weight; the lines we draw to contain its longitude and latitude; the distance, as the bird flies between this heart and the soul, which is known as homesickness; and then a detail of the heart's rooms—a worm's-eye view of its chambers told in the pulse of the earth. The time between beats is the distance of travel.

Trace the marbleized edges of veins upon each of the heart map's skin-thin pages, the tightening ropes of the arteries where reason must sit in the bowl of blood passion, from which the heart attacks its prison-home, the insensate mountain of flesh and bone. This one is a map of my sister's heart. Follow the clean red lines of blood in her veins, her river in her veins. North is not a constant here, but a variable of emotional climate. The only thing you can actually map of her, that is—depend upon for stability, is her hands. They go up and we are in the land of praise; they touch her lips and we are in the valley of fear, they reach out and we are in wonderment's worship. This is where the body hurts, the hands tell the map maker and this is where it heals. And this is the road of yearning and the range of hoping and the trail of tears. And this, this round spot, is the faith of children. And this indention is also the faith of children, but in specific, those children who have nothing, who are nothing, who will neither be heard nor saved.

Map. I make a map. Map of the mind. First: How far is it, this mind, from the heart, and is that distance the same reversed? No, I'm sure its closer from the heart to the head even though the journey's uphill. And what does it do there, the brain, at the pinnacle, in the terrible altitude that is thinking? How does the brain love while it is planning, scheming, dreaming? And is that love as rich a lode as the love in the chambers of the heart? How do we go from the one to the other? On our feet, on our hands and knees, on wings, on spit? Map, map of the mind; how we do go on.

This is an empty atlas, its innumerable pages as blank and thin as the skin of an onion. Here we trace the routes of trade across the world's feelings. See the line I am drawing that connects envy to adoration. See the circumpherence of need and desperation, and the metropolis of rage that is built up and imprisoned by the engorgement of so much feeling. Inside the nerve center of such a city, there is another city. Call it what you will, this unearthly city; call it, if you can, the ghetto of spirit—the invisible patter of the soul determining that love and hate, deceit and trust, violence and quiet are, none of them, enough; that what matters is how they mix—where they intersect and where they miss; where they disappear into the longest rivers, the deepest oceans, the highest mountains; where they leap into feeling, and smother feeling to regain love. This is a map that will cause you to dream and make you resent until you find yourself walking both the physical and the invisible together. Then your sense of balance might return to you—a whole picture and its close-up; the extent of a universe and each molecule its own universe.

This is where you go, where you put your hand to the sextant and the ruler, your eye to the compass and the astrolabe. This is what your hands are for: to gather in the cosmos. To chart the metaphysical map of the soul.

HOW IT WAS THAT SHE
BECAME A CARTOGRAPHER
CHAPTER II. A BRIEF HISTORY

She mapped the world before the world knew its size. With the palm of her hand stretched out to the night sky, she figured out the shape of things. She blamed it on the place she lived as a child: a glass house high up, with a glass roof and a glass floor. So that the air was really her earth and the ground below seemed as distant as heaven.

She walked the sky with her sister's hands, but only at night when she could be guided by the hunters and the lions, the fish and the half horse-men that traversed it in the forms of constellations. At night when she was sleeping, the hands would leave her and travel around the world in search of navigable routes. During the day, when the sun blinded her from the signposts of travel, she drew what the hands had seen in the dark. She held them up to the rising light and read in their flesh, bones, and veins the routes of their journeys.

All over the glass windows, ceiling, and floor, she laid out rows and rows of the finest onion skin, upon which she traced the longitudes and latitudes of a world delivered in her dead sister's hands. She discovered that it was much larger than the one presumed. Not one hemisphere, but two; not four continents but seven; and so the size of the world doubled, secretly, in the girl's glass house. Now, when the sun hit its walls, all the colored places on the map lit up like a stained-glass window. And the girl learned not to fear the far-away earth, for it was stretched out like a body in her glass house.

She couldn't remember who her real family was. She knew she was in her teens when she left them. But the difference in the life before and the one since was so extraordinary, it was if that first child died and a new one lived. The people who took her in, who locked her up and gave her the instruments of cartography, thought she did her work by some weird intuition or miracle that precluded science. They couldn't conceive that she measured the world by empirical knowledge, through the arduous journeys of a pair of severed hands. At first, the girl would take from the hands only that information which would enable the people who kept her to get where they wanted to go: some physical place on a relief map. She ignored the other destinations of the hands—the colors and the tastes, the emotions and thoughts, the hopes and disappointments that had also been their points of travel.

At noontime, when her guards appeared, she would point wordlessly to the new maps she'd made, which they would then take away, replacing them with fresh blank ones. "Good girl" they said, leaving her food to eat and locking the door behind them.

She wonders what will happen to her after she finishes mapping the world and she knows it will end as certainly as she knows that the world has its limits. But *how limited*, she worries, because she knows that as soon as her job is over they will kill her to seal the portals of this knowledge. And of all the things she has learned to fear, death is the greatest. *Maybe*, she thinks, *if I can keep making the map of the world bigger, they'll let me live a little longer.*

So she begins to pay attention to the other information the hands carry—the invisible worlds of spirit and feeling that are marked upon the ivory skin and the translucent veins. She decides to map the other things that the hands bring her: the heart, the soul, the hope of the planet, and the planets outside this planet, and the universe and the universes outside of the one she knows. And since this should take a very long time, she hopes to extend the time until she must die. But this only makes her keepers angrier.

"We don't want these things," they tell her. "They make
it too hard to see the roads. You must not make this map,"
they say to her, their noses pushed against the glass, their
eyes bulging, their fingers wagging. You must not!
— Why not? the girl asks desperately.
— Because there is no room. The earth is very crowded.
There's a finite amount of space, and if you trace the routes
of anger and the seas of jealousy, the forests of hope and
the rivers of passion, the mountains of aspiration and the
stones of love, there will be no place for the maps that
mean.
— Mean what?
— What's important.
— What *is* important?
She was fingering the arteries that wove like spider
stains back and across her forbidden map.
— What's important is the promise of expansion.
— I'm making expansion here. Look.
— You're making the irrelevant. There's no room for
them now — emotions and mysticism. The earth is too
jammed as it is.
"But," the girl argued, "what you want is exactly what
I'm making; for what better way 'to make space' than to
discover another dimension? The emotions are a vast
country, so vast we can never know the limits of its
boundaries."
"Why do you punish me, thus?" she implored them.
"Twisting and turning orderly charts into a labyrinth, a
mockery of journeying, when I am only doing what you
asked for — clearing some sense out of this chaos. For
those who are lost, who have no sense of direction and little memory of the past, these maps are a life-line. If the
world were not so broken, we wouldn't need them, we'd
get around by intuition. But in this time and place there's
too much confusion to trust to that."

"Oh," sighed the map making girl to her keepers, "I have seen the shape of wilderness and it scares me. This shadowy rotundity in a black and starless emptiness sky, lumbering blind through space with its viper green prisoner stripes around its head and tail, and a veil of fog across its middle. Therein lies my family. Their bones are the latitudinal lines of my shape in the wilderness they came to inhabit. They are my roadways forth and back and to and from. They make my understanding the way a trail is cleared, hacked out from the brush."

It was then that her keepers decided to take away her dead sister's hands; for although they did not believe that such macabre mutilations really did the wretched mapping, they weren't taking any chances. But when they came for them, the hands had mysteriously vanished. The girl said they had wandered out the night before and never returned. In truth, she had hidden Miranda's hands under the glass floor of the glass house, where they became just another detail of the map girl's maps.

Then they held her body down and forced her hands through the glass windows. They made her rip out the stars from the sky, and now her hands are shredded with cuts from broken glass and bleeding from broken stars. And the sky is all darkness without its stolen suns to light it.

"You won't do this anymore," they scolded, and left her.

She begs them to send her home, to her family.

They say, "Home? You have no home, no family. Look . . ."

And she stared through the broken windows of the glass house and saw that they were right: Nothing was there of the land she had loved, neither its valleys nor its mountains nor its rivers. A gaping hole was all that remained.

"See," they said: And still she begged to go back.

On her knees now, she tells them they're torturing her
with their demands: "Map girl, decide the length of this,
avoid the width of that. Map girl, that far? this close?" She
can't remember anymore what it is she's supposed to forget, what to know and tell. She tells them that she wants
to go home, she must go home, but where that could possibly be she doesn't know. She thinks it was probably too
many years ago to get back there. Now. At the end of
everything. Just where could she presume to go back to?
To stare at the gutted hotel in the wilderness? To weep at
the grave of her sister under the willow? To search for her
mother who had disappeared across the river? To spit on
the bones of her father in the cave of pictures? To journey
after the boy with the stolen panorama? Just where was
she to go back to?

She couldn't stay where she was. They wanted her dead,
her customers of maps, the keepers of the glass house in
the future where she'd come to be trapped, making maps
when she thought she had finally gone free. This place she
had fled to for sanctuary was now the place of imminent
death, and she wondered if there was a future beyond this
future where she could venture. And if so, how would she
end, ascending future past future until she found a place
where cartographers were not forced to disappear for
practicing the extent of their craft.

They began to destroy the maps of hers that they considered wicked, until almost everything she had created was
gone. In order to save them, she took the memory of her
maps and tattooed them into her already-crowded skin.
There they could be preserved as a record, a testament. For
as long as she might live. She carved in her flesh a universe
of sound and story, image and feeling, of discarded and
future knowledge. Sometimes, instead of needles and
knives, she used the finger nails of her sister's hands to do
this work. Retrieving them from under the glass floor, she

would hold the hands in her hand and make them scratch her body so deeply that no blood was let at all. But when her keepers came to observe her, they never saw a girl made of maps. They only saw a tattooed freak.

She knew that they would kill her. It was only a matter of time until they believed they'd gotten everything they wanted of her. She knew now that the maps they demanded she make were never intended to promote discovery, or encourage exploration, or reward inspiration. Such maps were only used to confirm their flat, tiny world; to help them steal the riches of the new worlds she found and make those worlds disappear into the old one they knew, the one they cherished, the one that ate them up, that kept them small, pinched, dead, hidden, self deceived, cruel, enriched, but ultimately unchanged from the predator-beast. She vowed that if she ever escaped, no other girl would ever be forced to take her place, to do the work of lies and coveting, in the name of the-good-of-mankind and in the guise of human progress.

The map girl decided she must set the glass house on fire, for only fire could make it disappear into nothing. She put together her cartographer's pigments, inks, and charcoal. She crushed them under her feet, mixed them into the linseed oil, turpentine, and kerosene used to carry out her charting. She poured the liquid in wide sweeps across the transparent floor. Then she took out Miranda's hands from beneath the glass. She held them high above her head, then she touched them to her mouth, and like a fire eater, she swallowed them down. They swam their way down her throat to make a home in the cage of her ribs. There the hands floated, like two pale, iridescent fish underneath the girl's soft pink lungs. Then she struck a tiny wooden red-tipped match. She held it out in front of her and waited until the bluish sparks caught on the putrid air. For tinder she used the only paper she had, The Book of the Cartographer that she was writing. She held it to her breast, in the glass room, as the flames came up like grass all around her. She held it tighter and closer as the pages caught fire, and the book burned itself into her flesh and fell to ashes upon her skin, and became the skin of her skin forever. The blue flames turned to orange flames, which reflected themselves across the house of windows until they looked like a thousand rising suns to the girl who was surrounded. She stayed until she was sure there would be nothing left. She stayed until she could see nothing outside the house and her vision was nothing but smoke. She stayed until she was sure that the glass itself would melt into tiny grains of sand and blow away into nothing that could ever be recreated.

The day she escaped the glass house, she crashed through the exploding windows, a burning ball of flames, blazing in the air, unquenchable. She turned pitch-black except for the maps imprisoned in her skin, which were the only part of her pink in her body's blackness. She tumbled through the air, pursued by the shattered glass that followed her like shadow demons. In her falling, she remembered the principles of flight. She had invisible wings now; no bird but more than angel. In her tumbling, she saw herself, and it begged to become something free of the agonizing weight of earth. But gravity pulled her out of the deep-blue nothing and fulfilled its essential objective: to bring all floating bodies down. Down she tumbled, until she fell upon the earth that had once held the Hotel.

As soon as she felt the land in her mouth, she knew that she was home. It was as if her years in the glass house, in the cartography prison, had never taken place. But they must have, she struggled to reason, *they must have.*

Or the future I have lived could never have become.

PART VI:
THE FIFTH SEASON

Coastline river route mountain road island sea monster enshrouded in sea weed palm tree with polar cap the names of fabled cities inscribed in gold desert with a school of whales conquerors flag green valleybody. This is where the people lived and this is where they were taken over by invaders and killed and enslaved by them and this is where they fled and laid waste to others in the misplaced fury and the righteous hunger for space on earth and this is where they died of starvation in the midst of plenty because it was not their plenty. This point that direction point direction. Look I'm marking it all out for you — a journey map for each inhabitant of earth. I use the finest inks and there are no better craftsmen than the hands I employ, no more honesty than the brain that conceives them and the heart that guides them or is it the heart that conceives and brain that guides — no matter — they are in an agreement when it comes to charting these routes through the provinces of truth, that land comprised of what has happened and what might have been.

from *The Book of the Cartographer*, Chapter VI

HOMING

Time traveled in a bucket and every time it passed, her hand was a dipper.

"Come drink me," she said. But it was her thirst.

So she went home.

The last cold snap ended. There was the first of green on the trees. And the river started rushing again. She kept to the outer banks, crossing over to the row of pine trees. The path, once a tender bed of needles, now was overgrown with nettles and weeds. It may have been hours, it seemed days, before she emerged from that pine stead, her bare legs scratched and bleeding. *How I wish I had a pair of wings to fly over this bitter wild,* thought the girl. *Like before.*

Finally she reached the clearing. She saw before her a gargantuan wooden frame that seemed to have grown out of the charcoal earth. It looked more like the skeleton of a prehistoric creature than the gutted body of an enormous house, abandoned, immured in unidentifiable debris. Walking through the ruins, she came upon the remains of a ballroom, its walls (that is, what was left of them) covered with graffiti, its floor a jungle of animal excrement. An auction block stood upended on its side, and an elegant flourish of windows hung glassless on their rusty, broken hinges, their rotted frames warped and battered by a hundred years wind and rain.

In the destroyed earth she found, intact, the foundation stone of the Hotel. She took it up in her hands, and for the first time in her life, she walked the railroad tracks to town. The people in the town, whom in the past she had only seen from a distance, viewed her like a curiosity. They pointed and jeered, "look at that poor black homeless thing. She must be mad as a hatter."

Am I mad? Rose wondered to herself, while she wandered the streets of this town that had flourished while her parents' dreams had failed. I would gladly be crazy, for then there would exist cause for my pain and therefore a sense of justice at the end of madness. But it doesn't change anything, and therefore I will not be mad. I will go on asking questions until the configuration of questions makes a house I can live in. And she spit on the town that gave her no shelter.

She set up house by the river. Black woman, charred girl, raven. From there she could watch the people scurrying back and forth to work in the town, and she could gaze across the waters at the remains of her family's hotel. She built a simple house, a house of rock with no windows; for she believed that to really see anything she would have to enter right into it, with no barriers of glass in between. Where she was living now, time kept running forth and back as if the river was a churning panorama of moving pictures in which she could see with utmost clarity all her ancestors in the north and south of her past, and the effects of her smallest actions on what was to come, out beyond her reach.

Across the river she could see them rebuilding the Hotel, scraps of rusted iron and steel joined the marble and wooden ruins. Young strangers with much enthusiasm. The garden of topiary monsters gone wild and to seed was being trimmed, and the bears, the tigers, even the dinosaurs started to take on a domesticated, docile appearance. Fragments of the mosaic floor that had once guarded the veranda were now being combined with bed springs, car parts, and plastic cups to make a new path down to the river. The stony faces of Roman gods and their mutilated torsos were scattered about the property like wandering minstrels. Although it had seemed that Cora sold everything off, it wasn't true from the vantage point of this new era, itself a barren, stripped age where a single brass door knob was an extraordinary find, a work of art that might focus a room like a master painting did in days of old, when Rose had been a child in her family's Hotel. Now she was the one that was old. She, Rose.

Most of the townspeople were frightened of her and they stayed out of her way. But the miserable, the defeated, the without-hope, without-recourse, beyond-choice—they got over the hurdle of fear and prejudice built up from superstition and habit and came to seek her advice. Always they were desperate (or they never would have come), and she would calmly show them, on her body, black and gouged as ebony wood, the maps of her skin. "Here is where you can go, she'd say, left or right. If you take the former road, you must expect these trials of landscape, these vagaries of weather; if you take the latter one, be prepared for a weakness in the soil and a fluctuating climate, which will make the journey both easier and harder. You choose, but it seems to me . . ." and indicating a bone-deep tattoo on the crossroads of her belly, she would point to the route she thought they should take to escape whatever had sent them running to her in the first place.

As time went on and passed by the last future that the Rose the raven had escaped, more and more people from town would come by her house, and fewer and fewer of them were afraid of her. Boys would hold dares of courage there, and lovers would vow love there, and fanciful folk would pray for their dreams there. They'd all ask her questions and hardly a one was heard that she hadn't asked herself. Many times in the course of their lives they would follow her advice, for she was wise; having lived a very long time and under much travail for the most of her life.

For some who came, she would turn her body a certain way in the light, and they could see two slender hands shining like transparent gold inside her. Upon them was written another kind of map, invisible but for the dots that made up its emptiness. "Here is another way to go," said Rose, pointing to the hands that stretched up inside her, two tablets of prayer beneath a tabernacle of breath. "And between these two, universes."

Then one day, quite suddenly, the old woman became sick and no amount of healing could help her. "Homesick," she laughed. "How can I be homesick when I'm already home?" she asked, searching her body. In its grooves and mutilations, human-made and nature-made and time-nourished, she could trace Miranda's voice: "Don't be afraid, Rose. Home is not forever the same place. It changes, Rose, changes like a body grows."

Like the flight of angels, its all perception, she thinks, ascending, *there's no progress at all but this perceiving.* She thinks she's falling, down, into the past, before man, before the bitter concept of time; but really she is flying past everything that ever was, and into what has not yet become. She looks for her family. They are gone. She looks for the Hotel. It isn't there anymore. She knows that she, herself, the girl Rose, is long dead and even those who could have been her children and her children's children would now be dead. She is no longer alive but still she is seeing, like a star that gives off light though it is a million years destroyed of light.

It began to pour, torrents of rain turning the earth to perpetual mud, the land to endless flooding. Only the oak tree upon which she's perched, grown in the water, reaching to the rain, remains steady; inextricably rooted to liquid, to motion out of time. She hears the ravens in the sky calling out to her from the invisible distance.

Now go, comes the cry of the ravens.

Now you can go.

COLOPHON

This book was set in Garamond, Cochin, and Castellar MT type faces with Zaph dingbats. It was smyth sewn for durability and reading comfort.